THE CIRCLE OF KIRKE

MATT LARKIN

The Circle of Kirke
Tapestry of Fate Book 8
MATT LARKIN
Editors: Sarah Chorn, Regina Dowling
Cover: Felix Ortiz, Shawn T. King
Map: Francesca Baerald

Incandescent Phoenix Books
mattlarkinbooks.com

TITAN ERA
OKEANUS
THULE
HYPERBOREA
HNITBJORG
KELTIA
ILLYRIS
SALON
RASSENIA
MNEMOSYNIA
OLMECATL
THRINAKIA
TARTESSOS
KARKHEDON
KARTH
KEMET
MEMPHIS
TIWANAKU
TIWANAKU
INUMIDEN
OSIRION
THE GREAT VELDT
KUSH
HY-BRASIL
KONGO JUNGLE
KGALAGADI DESERT
AZANIA

KER-YS
NYXLANDS
ISSEDONIA
XIRONG
WAKOKU
ARIMASPIA
FLAMING MOUNTAINS
YAM
HYLEAN WOODS
JINYANG
YINDAI
YAMATO
KIMMERIA
XIANYANG
YING
XIAO
PHLEGRA
THEMISKYRA
GEBI DESERT
XIANG
BO
WANGGEOM
OLYMPIAN MOUNTAINS
KOLCHIS
KOLCHIS
DANGUN
AXEINOS SEA
IOLKOS
PHRYGIA
UNIUN MOUNTAINS
ELLADOS
ILIUM
ARAD MOUNTAINS
BYBLOS
YUESHANG
PHAEAKIA
DELPHI
THEBES
CLESVOS
PHOEBA
VYADHAPURA
ITHAKA
ARGOS
KORINTH
SKYROS
PHOENIKIA
KROKYLEA
KRONION
NUSANTARA ISLES
MERITUM
NAXOS
RHIOS
LYDIA
AEOLIA
HELION
HAWAIKI
ATLANTIS
KNOSOS
OGYA
ATLANTIS
THALASSA
NUSANTARA
UGART
NESHIA
MUGEDANG
BADIAN STEPPES
NINEVEH
DREAMING DESERT
ASUR
EMPTY DESERT
BABILIM
BABILIM
DREAMING LANDS
BULU
KISSATU
RAPA
DURANKI MOUNTAINS
MU
NYSA
SUMERU MOUNTAINS
SHALMALI
HURSAG MOUNTAINS
BARBARIKON
TAKHKHASILA
PATALIPUTRA
HINDUSH
DHANYAKATAKA
KUMARI KANDAM

THE WHISPER

It starts with a whisper, a haunting intimation of a World askew. That we are, in the end, caught in a death spiral, time nearly played out, whilst entropy tugs ever harder upon the Wheel of Fate.

Looking now into the dying embers, we at last apprehend Truth, and in it the revelation that the vaunted tales of old were not what we thought ... And neither, in fact, were we.

For if we have lived before, might not all we've dreamt be but our souls' memories of Worlds become dust ...

A QUICK NOTE

For full colour, higher-res maps, character lists, location overviews, and glossaries, check out the bonus resources here:
https://tinyurl.com/hw52dzss

And if you liked this book, be sure to check out my offer for a free novella at the end.

PROLOGUE

A deluge of war and blood swept across the World, and Aodh found himself no longer able to doubt the time had come for a second Eschaton. Though his gambit had allowed Man to persist for thousands of years beyond his otherwise allotted time, still, the thought of the price come due churned Aodh's gut.

Would bearing such—the knowledge that this manifold death fell at his feet—grow easier with each revolution or yet more unbearable as eons of guilt choked him?

Oh, when Man had risen against the cities of Dark Faerie and the druids had created therianthropic bloodlines, he had thought perhaps the Eschaton upon them then. But they had broken Falias and the other cities, and the Earth had endured a time more.

Aodh no longer knew who was right and if there was even such a thing as *right* anymore.

So he walked this lush green island, trying without much avail to revel in sylvan expanses that must teem with faeries. If the Children of Danu took note of his presence, they gave no sign, and Aodh made his way deeper into the woodland, wending between oak and ash until, at last, he came unto the grove. At its heart poked through a gnarled, massive root of the Tree of Life. From its power, the druids would work the Art and change the World.

And Aodh would let them, despite himself, for he could not gauge if weal or woe would come from all this.

Latsatian—Donn, now—seeming far too comfortable in his druid's robes, turned at Aodh's approach, though Aodh would have sworn he made no sound moving through the forest. Certainly none that could be heard over the ruckus of a nearby cataract pitching down onto the rocks and joining the burbling brook that ran just outside the grove.

The druids had erected stone monoliths to demarcate a circle of power, turning faerie tactics against them. Aodh had always considered sorcery the last resort of the desperate. It was, in the end, drawn from the forces that formed a tainted World and thus drew back to foulness, perpetuating a sick circle of corruption. Khaos was the fire that became its own fuel.

Other druids continued their preparations for the ritual they intended to enact this night.

Donn paused to clap a warrior—Camulus they were calling him now, though this Destroyer seemed to have gone through almost as many names as Aodh himself—upon the shoulder. Camulus, too, looked to Aodh with haunted eyes and, perhaps, a hint of accusation at all that had passed and what he must now endure.

It was ... Aodh's fault, of course. The Destroyer must suffer once more. So many times more.

Donn flowed through the glade as if a part of it, taking Aodh's wrist to lead him away, out of earshot from those he guided—or deluded—until they stood before the brook, watching the last rays of sunlight glint off the waters.

"I was not sure if you would come," Donn said, when the moment stretched on longer than either of them could bear. "Sequana told me of the things you showed her. Confirmed for her."

Aodh inclined his head, hardly knowing what to say to that. In a moment of passion, pain, and desperation, he had allowed her to see some fragmentary glimpse of the Ontos. He had gifted her—*damned* her —with the knowledge, while she dared to hope that Gnosis would prove salvation for Mankind. As if they could see it. As if they could fathom it. But whatever he gave them, he could not help but fear they would twist it to fit their views rather than take the harder route of altering their conceptions to fit the knowledge they gained.

"She drew you into her quest for Gnosis, then."

Donn nodded. "Kratu first, of course. But she told me, and I believed." He raised his empty hand, showing the lack of orichalcum ring binding him to the Archons.

Why was it not more relief to see his erstwhile brethren freeing themselves from their chains? Perhaps because they still could not see the more unbreakable fetters that bound them. Even if loosed from direct bonds to the Archons, they remained fettered by the far stronger chains of Fate. By the Wheel of Fate that was, itself, formed from the Wheel of Life and the loathsome Wheel of History, that one which Aodh himself had helped set spinning. Which he now kept spinning.

They were all damned, and he kept deluding himself that they could be saved.

"If you enact your plan," Aodh said, "you will pay a price for it."

Donn huffed. "Your visions told you that?"

Aodh said naught because it didn't matter. That he had seen Donn do this meant the fallen Watcher *would* do it and would suffer for it as Aodh had foreseen. His attempts to dissuade the man now were doomed to failure. They were, he knew, petty attempts to assuage his own conscience at letting anyone suffer such an end as lay before Donn. And being petty, they failed to achieve either aim. Aodh did not know why he had bothered coming here at all; he was powerless to help anyone here.

Donn grabbed him and spun him around to look him in the eye. "What would you have me do, Matarśivan? Shall I stand by and let Danu's brood ravage Mankind from now until the end of time? Especially knowing that hint of the Ontos, how can I? These beings *serve* the very parasitic Elder Gods you taught us to abhor. Whether they know it or not, whether they will it or not, they are tied to the putrid essences of the Archons."

"True," Aodh admitted. The faeries carried forth Archon agendas with Archon-infused power.

"Falias is in ruins, but still these abominations remain. I will break their grasp upon this world and thus better the whole of the World.

When I am a done, a Veil will encircle the Mortal Realm, and these faeries shan't be able to touch us again. No one will further step between Realms and drag the children of Men into the night, screaming for lost mothers. Otherwordly dangers shall no longer stalk dark woods. What if I could end the very Wild Hunt?" He huffed again, steadying himself. "If I refuse the price to myself, is that not mere self-interest?"

Oh, Aodh knew quite a great deal about taking up an unbearable burden for the betterment of Man.

"You won't stop me," Donn said.

"No, old friend." No, this was more the farewell, for Donn—as he was —could not survive his plan. Nor did Aodh mention the thousand Men whom Donn must sacrifice to enact the most awesome sorcery ever wrought.

Men like poor Camulus.

All died now, perhaps, because of Aodh. Because he had judged the cycle of Eschatons the only alternative to the worse end he had foreseen. Even if it but delayed the inevitable.

Unable to bear to watch, Aodh waded through the brook, away from the glade. His pyromantic visions had told him well enough what would unfold. This place would become a charnel house, and those he cared for would die to buy the World another Era.

But this one had proven worse than its predecessor, and Aodh could not shake the fear the next would prove more dire still. Was that then the course he had set the Earth upon, to spiral ever downward into greater Darkness until, by the end of it all, the distinction between life and the horror he sought to avert became one of precarious semantics?

If he tried to explain, would they listen? Mostlike not, nor could he afford to allow them to falter in their course. This was the gambit. Even should he somehow spoil Donn's plans, should he save him and perhaps this world, the end result would be the wakening of the Hidden God and the consumption of all the cosmos.

The death of one world to buy the next and forestall the final end.

So, wracked with guilt that twisted his chest into vicious knots, he knelt amid roots of the forest and prepared himself. And if he beat impotent fists against the roots, there were none there to see his self-recriminations nor witness the tears that welled in his Fate-touched eyes.

With those eyes shut, he felt it as the sun set. As the night drew on.

He was far enough away not to hear the Supernal cants, and considered himself blessed for that, though the anticipation was almost too much—

A rush of pressure washed over him, forcing him to look. The World shuddered. The air trembled. His ears popped.

And a cascade of ripples inundated him, suffocating him, dimming his vision at the edges. Drowning him in arcane import that would have ripped Donn apart and transformed him into a new kind of horror, one consumed by bloodthirst.

And the Earth itself shook and quivered, threatening to crack asunder as it was torn from its rotation, thrown askew by forces the druids had not comprehended.

It was done ... The World was forever changed.

And he had let it happen. Again.

PART I

For stories pieced together by those rare intrepid souls who—driven by wanderlust or thirst for adventure—dare trek beyond lands known, we can infer four great continents comprise Gaia. Our lands lie within the central ranges of the vast span of Kêr-Ys. Across the sea, one finds our closest neighbour, Kumari Kandam, a land of steppes and deserts and dark, trackless jungles. There is distant Hy-Brasil, known for strange shores and stranger still customs. And farthest of all lies mysterious Mu, of which we know only from the Nusantara sailors that sometimes voyage to Phoenikia.

 — Kleio, Analects of the Muses

1

PANDORA

384 Dark Age

A nebulous path of flowing smoke and grasping shadows spread out before Pandora, funnelling her toward a cliff. Though she could see the lights of distant torches, their glows seemed muted, unreachable. The sea smashed over the cliff, again and again, as if intent to shatter stone with its relentless anger. Behind her, the smoke formed up into a barrier, one ever encroaching upon her, forcing her toward the precipice. There was naught for it save to stride toward her ending. She knew, if the smoke engulfed her, it would devour her, body and soul. If she fell from the cliff, she would break upon the rocks or drown in the churning deeps.

And still, onward she pressed, bound for her doom. Always, always toward her doom.

The walls of smoke flickered on one side, and from it strode an inchoate image of a man, his form hazy but crackling with energies.

"Morpheus ..." Pandora rasped, her words choked out as smoke strove to find a way into her lungs. He had found her, but in the turbulent hold of dreams, her mind could not parse the circumstances of the how.

"I warned you to desist in your pointless defiance of Fate." Slivers of stone

rose like earthen worms and coiled about her legs and abdomen, holding her in place.

Still, despite her powerlessness here in the dream, Pandora found the strength to laugh at him. "Were it so futile as you claim, it would not so vex you or force you to strive so hard against me. Your very efforts only reinforce my convictions. You and the Anunnaki, the Unseen Order, Mithra, the Moirai. All of you are so desperate to stop me from interfering. And yet you would have me believe I have no chance of success?"

"You fall prey to the Gnostic sin, it seems."

Oh, Pandora had little love for the Gnostics who had so long held her imprisoned. Still, had they come to her under other circumstances, had they striven to become her allies rather than her captors, she might have found common cause with them. She might, if Ananke had proved kinder than it ever seemed to, have even liked Kronos and his ilk. "Get your tortures over with, oneiromancer. I cannot imagine they will prove as tedious as another debate with one so doggedly entrenched in his ideas."

Morpheus strode closer, his form turning solid, taking on his usual aspect. "Are you any less devoted to your own ideals? Do you not worship upon the fool's idol of free will, as if such an ephemeral illusion might have aught to offer you save perpetual disappointments? Surrender to Fate, Pandora, and embrace the freedom of the soul that comes with acknowledging your will is not, has never been, your own. You cannot even control your own thoughts, born as they are from causes beyond yourself."

She wheezed out a weary sigh. Despite her taunts, she dreaded whatever agonies he would visit upon her. Even experienced but a single time, his tortures had left her ravaged and haunted for months afterward. Now, two years since, still sometimes she awoke in a fright and in dread of him. Perhaps, even, her fears had been what alerted him to her presence now, centuries after he had last found her.

"I've no wish to visit harm upon you," Morpheus said. "You have but to submit to the will of the Moirai, and all is forgiven."

"No." He called it defiance, and she supposed it was. She had tried appeals of logic, of hope, and of humanity, but none had reached this man. In the end, it came down to choice. Perhaps his words held truth, and even that choice of hers was spawned in the events that had shaped her. But that, to Pandora's mind, did not mean she was, in fact, any less her.

"Oh, sweet girl." Morpheus ran fingers along her cheek in an almost affec-

tionate gesture. She might have expected such a tactic to be laced with some predatory lasciviousness, for men so oft turned to such threats against women they could not otherwise cow. But the way he touched her didn't feel sexual so much as conciliatory. "I tried to spare you, Pandora. But you have their attention now, and they will not be so gentle as I have been."

She groaned. "One more attempt to get me to fear you and yours." Though he seemed in earnest.

He shook his head. "If you chance to dream again, perhaps we might try this conversation once more. Mayhap I can still spare you."

Abruptly, the binding earth fell away from her, and Pandora was tumbling, the whole cliff giving way. For an agonising instant, she was free-falling, plummeting toward the sea.

SHE AWOKE WITH A START, then hit the ground hard, landing on her left shoulder. Were it not for the Phoenix Pneuma coursing through her body, she'd probably have dislocated it on impact. She had, whilst falling in the dream, tumbled out of the tree branch on which she'd slept. For a moment, she lay there, groaning, taking in the burning light of dawn as it broke over the plains and spilled onto the Hursag Mountains.

After a moment more, she pushed herself up on her arms, gentle with her left one. "Dammit, Morpheus."

For nigh two years she'd lived in Mugedang with Prometheus. With her *husband*. That thought brought a smile even through the grimace of pain as she rose. They had their home, a comfortable house of bent wood they had constructed together not long after the wedding. They built it away from the city, upon a hill by the sea. Most days, her husband went to Mugedang and embroiled himself in the politics of the Queens of Mu, whilst Pandora busied herself researching the Unseen Order.

At least as much as she could do so on Mu. They had agents here, of that she was certain, but she they seemed strongest on Kumari Kandam. Still, her studies had uncovered a connection between the Anunnaki and the Hursag Mountains. At some point or other, the bloodline had built a stronghold amid these peaks. It was a place feared by the locals of the Dreaming Lands, she had heard, though few in Mugedang had ever heard of it or knew much about these southern peaks. Lilinoe had been here, though, had climbed these mountains, and though she had not visited the Anunnaki stronghold, she had seen it on a far slope. The queen had warned Pandora it was a place best avoided, claiming it haunted by ghosts of old, but Pandora needed every piece of knowledge available to her.

So she'd travelled a long way to reach the mountains, hoping for a lead. As far as she could, she'd skirted the coast in a tiny outrigger—Prometheus had taught her to sail one in their first year living here and she had taken to racing Pokoharau on occasion—and when she could bring the boat no further, she beached it and began the climb.

Higher, she could see where the peaks were encircled in rings of white. Up there, the trees vanished, and she would have little shelter. Knowing that, she'd thought it best to manage a full night's sleep and start the climb fresh, hopefully reaching the Anunnaki redoubt before nightfall. She had not counted upon a visit from the oneiromancer, nor on it sending her spilling out of her resting place.

She worked her sore shoulder in slow rotations, staring at the slope she'd need to climb this day. It ran steep, and rugged, almost sheer in places. And that was before she crossed the snow line and would have to deal with years of packed ice and loose powder making things even more treacherous. Still, delaying would not bring the summit any closer. She paused long enough to relieve herself, to gnaw on some dried pork she'd packed from Mugedang, and to wash her face in a mountain stream.

Then it was for the climb.

HAND OVER HAND, ever upward, she worked her way along the cliff. Despite the chill, sweat dribbled over her brow, oft running into her eyes and stinging them. When she reached a shelf above, Pandora heaved herself onto it, rolling to one side and panting. At some point, this had all seemed like a good idea. She was certain it had seemed prudent before she started.

She could have burnt through Pneuma to manifest fiery wings and launch herself skyward, but if she encountered trouble, she might want that Pneuma to defend herself. Besides which, she didn't necessarily want to confront the Anunnaki, if any remained, having burnt off her kebaya and left herself clad in naught save a sarong skirt. And all that was assuming her wild flights even carried her to a safe landing. No, it was climbing for her. A little further, and she'd reach the snow line.

"A bit more," she told herself. As if the frozen peaks would be the easy part.

THE ANUNNAKI REDOUBT LOOKED, to Pandora's eyes, more like some ancient temple than a fortress. It was framed by vast, snow-covered stone gates. The sides of the gates were free standing, not joined in the middle, each one a multi-tiered carving, though the rime obscured the details.

Beyond, the temple was chiseled right into the mountainside. An overhang created a roofed portico, with domes rising from that roof. From most of the domes jutted an almost oblong point that narrowed at the top. Perhaps they had all featured such, but some had broken away with time. A hundred feet or so past the gates, a steep, ice-crusted ramp ran up to a landing where the cave entrance was. Below the ramp, the rock was cut away in terraces, an effect that reminded her somewhat of the ziggurats of Babilim, though these seemed older. Timeless, in fact.

Careful of her footing on the ice-slicked ramp, she managed to pick her way toward the entrance. Faint, flickering firelight glinted within, making plain that, outward appearances aside, this place was not quite abandoned. Last Pandora checked, ghosts did not tend to light lamps or braziers.

On the landing, her breath frosted the air, her panting seeming to echo off the cavernous hall beyond the doorway. It was vast, indeed, supported by circular columns graven with fading pictographs. The only source of light came from a wide fire pit, its dwindling flame failing to adumbrate much of the vestibule she found herself within. A short wall, a hair wider than her arm span, acted as a room divider. It too was carved, the geometric symbols perhaps astrological in nature. Beyond the wall rose a tremendous statue of a bearded man, his palms spread open.

Pandora had not wanted to give herself away too soon, but she needed to see this place for what it was, so she snapped her fingers, sparking a candle flame into her palm. The fire she held closer to the wall carvings, tracing a finger of her other hand along the crumbling grooves. Years of dust and grime came away at her prodding, making the design somewhat clearer, though she no doubt knocked away some of the base stone as well.

With the dust cleared, she could see the arcs formed two intersecting circles within the scope of a greater circle. Lines radiated out of each, connecting everything in a vast, complex web.

This was not just an astrological observation. This was a pictorial representation of the Wheel of Fate. At the sound of footfalls on stone, she jerked away, blazing her flame into a full torch. The man who came into view was no Muian. Rather, he had a Kandamian aspect to him, dark haired and with a thick, oiled beard. He bore a strange cap topped by numerous horns that might have come from oxen. By his height, he was clearly of Titan blood.

"In dreams," the Titan said, "he said you would come to us. Thus forewarned are we, about you who would side with the misguided Gnostics." At the fringes, she saw two more Titans stalk closer, one with a naked akinakes in hand. The other bore an iron-studded club, though neither man yet hefted their weapons.

"I come but to talk," Pandora said, raising her hands to show they were empty. The gesture was, perhaps, somewhat weakened by the flame still blazing in her left palm. "I am Pandora."

"Nunamnir," the man said, a hand to his chest, "though perhaps you have heard of me by the name given me in Nineveh: Enlil." Pandora had to stop herself from drawing a sharp breath. She stood in the presence of one of the very patriarchs of the Anunnaki bloodline. Which meant, she thought, she might have overshot her information gathering mission here by a hair or so. "My son, Suen," Nunamnir said, indicating the man with the sword. "And this is Tishpak," he said, when the club-wielder edged in too close for her comfort.

Nunamnir made no further threatening move, though he need not, considering Tishpak seemed intent to convey all the threats for him, in posture and in visage. "So," Nunamnir said. "You come to talk."

Pandora swallowed and nodded, grateful no one had attacked her as yet. She might be able to overcome one or two of them. She misliked her odds against all three, especially given Nunamnir himself had plainly survived many millennia of life. "Which ties bind you to the

Unseen Order? What connection holds betwixt them and the Anunnaki?"

The Titan snorted. "Why? You hope to sever that thread?" He shook his head in genuine, or perhaps mimed, dismay. "The fate of all worlds was carved into stone at the dawn of Eras, laid down immutable by the hand of your own beloved, in the Tablet of Destiny. With the past and future laid out plain before us, what fools must we be to deny our eyes? You would come here, planning to hack through a thread, but instead you find chains of adamant bind us together, we who embrace Destiny as necessity. Is that not the very meaning of your word, Ananke?"

"So you serve Mithra, do you?" And he claimed Prometheus had carved the Tablet of Destiny?

Nunamnir laughed with vicious mirth. "Or perhaps he serves us all. Suffice to say, we work toward common ends."

"So the Anunnaki have been in bed with the Unseen Order from your first days."

The Titan lord extended a palm toward his son. "Did not I wed my son to the daughter of Enki, before the bitch betrayed all we hold sacred?" Suen winced, turning his head away, as if ashamed of his wife's actions.

Pandora sneered at Nunamnir for that. "You underestimate the bond betwixt mother and child if you thought she would bide meekly as two of her children were dragged down into the Underworld and you stood there proclaiming the glories of Ananke. What comfort lies in Fate to replace an empty room or a silent hearth?" Pandora knew that pain better than most, and she would have ripped apart worlds—or time itself —to reunite with Pyrrha. Small wonder Ningal had turned on these fanatics.

Suen steadied himself on a column, as if even hearing this came as a shock. As if he had never accepted—or shared?—his wife's unbearable agonies.

"Oh, she betrayed us even before the death of Inanna, we think," Nunamnir responded. "And you, Pandora, ought to have taken what solace you might from having fulfilled what role Ananke found needful for you. Now you force us to drive you to it, or down to oblivion, if that please you better."

Behind her back, Pandora began setting the Box. She had come woefully unprepared into this situation. Had she been wiser, she'd have set a destination to jump to before walking through the door. Now she was faced with the choice either to try to engage all three at once or time-walk from here and confront the Order on her own terms. The latter option seemed more palatable.

She could deal with when or where the Box sent her as soon as she figured that out.

"Wait," she said, buying a moment more to ensure the device was ready to activate. "Surely we can come to some compromise."

Nunamnir frowned as if he might want to consider it but found it impossible. "Sometimes, the chasm separating two sides runs so stark no middle ground exists, save for both to plummet into the ravine betwixt them. There can be no partial adherence to Fate." Pandora wondered what he would say were she to reveal that was, so far as she could tell, *exactly* what Prometheus intended. "You serve willingly or we force you to serve. In any case, the Wheel turns, and the World persists, with time-walkers such as you but as grease upon its axle."

"Well then ..." She popped the top to activate the Box. "Do slip on grease."

The bubble of light engulfed her even as Suen and Tishpak rushed in, weapons raised. If she'd had a moment more before the collapsing bubble swallowed the light around her, Pandora would have flipped them a rude gesture. As it was, she contented herself with a sly smile.

THE BOX DEPOSITED Pandora in the sand, at night, and before she even knew what was happening, a chill wave crashed over her. In surprise, she shrieked and rose, hugging herself against the cold. Only a moment later did she realise the wave had seized the Box, and the device was being swept out by the tide. With a wail, she flung herself at it, snatched it, and came up sputtering, spitting seawater from her mouth in the process.

She heard a whoosh even as she began to turn, a dart flying at her. The Phoenix flared within her—heat, fury, and the Pneuma to enhance her reflexes—and she caught the javelin. The firebird's wrath surged in her breast and she spun, hurling the weapon back at her attacker. The man, who'd thrown it at her from on horseback, toppled from his mount and tumbled down onto the beach.

Bedraggled, dripping wet, and no little aghast that the Phoenix had driven her to kill so quickly, Pandora hurried along the beach toward her fallen accostor. When she reached him, she dropped down in the sand and found the weapon had pierced his side. He lay there, grasping at it with feeble fingers, powerless to dislodge it. Just as well, for had he succeeded, the wound would have bled more freely.

Who was he? Someone from the Unseen Order come to stop her? An assassin like Nemesis?

"N-Nike?" the man gasped, eyes alighting on her face and looking at her as though she had betrayed him.

Jolted by the call, Pandora leant closer, one hand upon his chest, the other on the javelin. He knew her, but she had never seen him before. Dark-haired and blue-eyed, she judged him a Tethid. "Who are you? Why did you attack me?"

"We've ... had raiders ... off the sea. I saw you in the waters ... at night ... thought you ... pirate. You ... why ... this ... twenty years to the day ... you saved me from ... the Laestrygonians ... at Telepylus." He sputtered in some private mirth.

Pandora grimaced. She'd seen Kala push Phoenix Pneuma into Mundilfari to heal him, but Pandora had never managed such a feat. She had to try though. "I-I'm sorry. I didn't mean to ..." But, of course, she had meant it.

Burn, burn, burn.

The Phoenix's eternal refrain echoed through her soul, ever and anon driving her to consume all around her in conflagration. All it had taken was a simple, momentary threat to her person to drive her into a killing wrath. Gods! She was just like Herakles in that, wasn't she? A Destroyer herself, and this time, destroyer of a man who thought himself defending his home against raiders.

"I have to take it out." Already, his eyelids had begun to flutter. His gaze had turned unfocused. "Come on." With a single, Potency-infused heave, she yanked the dart from his chest and tossed it aside. Blood burbled in a dark fountain, almost black in the moonlight. The man gurgled and lolled to one side, senseless with pain and blood loss. Pandora pressed both hands upon the wound. "Come on!"

She willed her Pneuma to flow into her victim. Flooding it to her limbs had become second nature. She could direct it to her own wounds to speed healing or alleviate pain. She could give herself strength and reflexes far beyond the limits of Man. She could summon heat from within herself and release it as flame to scorch her foes. So why in Nyx's dark expanse could she not drive that energy into another living being? Why wouldn't it obey her in this one thing? "Work, damn you!" she shrieked. "Work!"

The man's ragged, wet breaths ceased. The flow of his blood from the wound slowed to a trickle, now no more than seeping out of its shell.

Pandora toppled over onto her arse. "Fuck." She raised her trembling fingers up before her face, staring at her dark-stained palms, refusing to permit herself the release of weeping over what she'd done. She had killed before, yes, but not like this. Thickening blood oozed between her fingers and slithered along her wrists, dribbling toward the crooks of her elbows.

She had killed an innocent man. A twinge pinched in her chest, above her heart. No, no, no. He had *attacked* her. Surely that abrogated some portion of her culpability for responding in kind? But no. His actions might have triggered the Phoenix, but she could have chosen to exert her will first. To demand her attacker identify himself. It had not crossed her mind to do so. All she had then was the scorching heat of her rage, tinging her vision red. Still shaking, she let her hands drop into the sand, scraping them over the grains in a vain attempt to cleanse blood that forever remain within the creases.

Or maybe it was the price that came with a warrior's strength. All things had a cost, and the ability to kill must surely bear with it an instinct to do so. Either way, it came back to her. In her failing, in her loss of control, she had slain a man.

And he had known her. Had claimed that twenty years prior, on this very day, she had saved him from a place called Telepylus, from whoever or whatever those Laestrygonians were. Her drenched hair hung limp and sticky across her face. With her forearm, she tried to mop it away from her brow, no doubt smearing blood in the process.

If she spurned the time loop, if she denied this particular twist of the ouroboros, her victim would remain dead, and she would in the process deny him the last twenty years of his life. Surely, then, she owed it to him to carry forth the inverse prophecy he had given her and travel back, saving him as he had proclaimed. She could not restore his life now, but from the grey in his beard, he had lived a long life afore now. One Pandora hoped had had its joys. All lives ended with death, sooner or later. The meaning had to come from the moments along that road toward that end.

So, then. She must lengthen his road. She must give him what aid she could, meagre though it would prove in his final moments.

TELEPYLUS, Pandora learnt, was an island off Neshia, one avoided by all sailors, for it was peopled by Gigantes. When she arrived, sailing close on a small skiff, she saw three great ships moored across the bay. But the man had not claimed to be in danger there, but on Telepylus itself.

Pandora tapped a finger on her lip before sailing round the island, seeking a hidden place to anchor. When at last she found one, she leapt to the shore. She would need to stalk the island—hopefully without attracting the attention of the Gigantes—until she found Men in danger. Challenging Titans, especially Gigantes, did not much appeal, but she owed at least this much the man she'd slain.

Somewhere, on this island, a sailor was in danger.

And she was going to save him.

PANDORA STOOD upon the deck of Odysseus's ship, watching the man with her eyes, feeling the guilt roil in her gut. Here he stood, alive and vivacious, much younger than the man she'd seen hours ago, dying upon the beach. Alive—until she had killed him. Even now, all she could picture was his blood seeping between her fingers. Her failure to heal him paraded through her mind in endless repetitions and, in her fancies, she had not failed, and he had gasped, saved and vibrant once more. But ever and again, the daydreams would crumble to dust, and she would look back and see the younger Odysseus there, studying her with his bright blue eyes, ignorant of her crime against him.

There was perilous cunning in this one, she knew, though never in his wildest dreams could he have guessed the truth of how she came to Telepylus or of her desire to save him. Still, it was, perhaps, best not to give him overmuch chance to dwell upon events and question her. "How came you to face Gigantes?" she asked to keep him busy. "And in such a remote isle as that?"

"Oh, that tale is a winding one which would be long in the telling." From the way he spoke, she suspected he fair burst with desire to enthral her with such a story. The man overflowed with self-confidence, perhaps even arrogance, and he expected everyone to bow before his charms. Though Pandora owed him a debt she could not repay, still his attitude chafed her nerves. When she folded her arms over her chest in answer, he deflated a hair. "Yes, well, but the short of it is, I begin to think a curse lies upon this ship and her crew, one that ensures our every effort to return home ends with us cast further astray."

"A curse?" Pandora unfolded her arms, frowning. Who had these people vexed that someone should lay a curse upon them? In her guilt over his death, had she, in fact, aided men who might not have deserved it? No. No, she would not indulge in such a line of thought. Whoever these people were, whatever they had done, they could not have deserved to be eaten by Gigantes. For the rest ... While she could not spare Odysseus from his eventual fate, she could, she supposed, help him reach home and make the most of his next twenty years. "There is a sorceress I know, on an island not so far from here, known as Aiaíā." And, of course, Pandora had long intended to visit her granddaughter there. "If some curse does prevent you from reaching friendly shores, she might identify it and tell you how to be free of it. Either way, it does not seem like you make it far from here."

"Aye, that's the sad truth," Odysseus agreed, worry creasing his brow. "Though I can't say I'd place much trust in witches or sorceresses." Maybe he'd have said more, maybe objected to the course she plotted, were it not for his desperation. The driving need to push through, no matter the cost, had him, and it was a feeling Pandora knew all too well.

2

ARTEMIS

800 Bronze Age

efore Artemis, the walls of Troy lay scattered and blown apart, as though some great foot had kicked over a construction of clay. Cyclopean blocks were strewn across miles of beach. As she watched, cracks rived those blocks as well, pieces of once unassailable defences flitting away in showers of dust. She turned, gawping at the etiolated ruin of a city many thought eternal. Now, the broken shells of homes and shops stretched out like skeletal remains upon an ancient battlefield. Where the acropolis ought to have stood instead opened a gaping maw of burbling shadows.

The sky was streaked with grey, the land locked in twilight. Everything was still, save for the void where Priam's palace should have lain and the currents of dust billowing in a chill breeze.

"What happened here?" she asked herself. She reached for the dagger at her waist, but its sheath was empty and Artemis was left unarmed.

"This is but a construction of your mind," a voice answered.

Artemis spun to behold Morpheus, the dark-haired oneiromancer having seemingly stepped out of thin air behind her. The man had always had an ill cast to his features, visage fixed in a sneer as though he knew worlds of things beyond the ken of others. Now, though, that aspect of him seemed softened. Or perhaps she imagined the hint of sympathy in his eyes. It was hard to tell, for the shadows of dusk loomed over him like a shroud. He was too comfortable in the dark of this space, that was for certain.

"I dream," Artemis said and, saying it, knew it for truth. With that truth came a sigh of relief, for the profane state of this place was not real. Her grief and fears and the strain upon her body and mind had conjured up a nightmare vision of a ruined city.

Which was not to say Ilium would not fall. Perhaps it was inevitable.

"Did Zeus send you to haunt me, oneiromancer?" Artemis asked. Morpheus had known better than to violate her mind whilst she served on Olympus, but perhaps the tyrant king now forced his hand.

A shake of his head was her answer, his movement sending the shadows around his face skittering like a colony of ants. "Like yourself, I have severed ties with the hateful mountain and its corrupted king."

Artemis did not dare allow any hint of hope to bloom in her chest at his words. Morpheus was a more powerful oneiromancer than Kirke, or so she understood. If he could be recruited to her cause, then perhaps ... No. She could not afford to let herself think him a friend. "Then what do you wish with me?" she asked instead.

"I am but a messenger, bid to tell you that, if you weary of your lonely struggle against Zeus, you can find allies in Babilim." He strode closer until she could at last see his visage plain and the dark that clung to him was pushed to the fringes.

"You serve ... Mithra?"

"Yes ..." He edged forward until he could reach two fingers toward her temple. Artemis recoiled, but before she could twist aside, he tapped her head. "Wake. Before flames take you."

༂

AS MORPHEUS HAD WARNED, the city was ablaze. She smelt the smoke and heard the crackle of flame amid the screams. It ought to have alarmed her. Yet Artemis continued to sit, wrists upon her knees, legs tucked up almost against her chest. She had holed up in some desolate larder of the palace, hidden away, unable to face the empty condolences of well-wishers. Every word of pity had become a razor flensing away another piece of her withered soul. More so, for she had mumbled a thousand such impotent laments over the past decade, and to many of the same people who would now feign sharing her grief.

Weary as she was, she must have dozed, but now Morpheus had forced her out of that reprieve. In waking, a thought rumbled up time and again, no matter how oft with what fury she beat it away, cursing her mind for such treachery. Had she and Apollon deserved such an end for their callous use of the people of Ilium in their war against Zeus? They had known countless Men would die through their machinations and had named it a fair price to pay for the overthrowing of Olympus. So how could they then balk when the same price was asked of them?

Some bitter muddle of laughter and weeping spilled from her now. The scent of smoke grew stronger. So they had breached the walls, at last. Athene herself would come for Artemis, no doubt. Perhaps she blamed Artemis and her fallen twin that her brother, too, had died in the war, though it had been Athene's own champion who'd slain Ares. Perhaps she was still leashed by loyalty to her tyrannical father, unable to shuck the chains about her throat.

Either way, a reckoning between the two of them must follow. Athene had taken Apollon from her, and the woman had to know there could be no forgiveness for that. Not for that. Besides, no one who had ever sat upon a throne in Olympus deserved forgiveness for aught. They were, all of them, Artemis and her brother included, corrupted, tainted by power and immortality.

Yes, Artemis had dismissed the lives of Men as less important than those of Titans. Even now, in this war. Especially now.

Slowly, she rose, dagger in hand, though she had no recollection of having drawn it. As she strode down the corridor, a quiver ran through her chest, the tremor building into a wound-like pain that had her bracing against the wall, gasping for breath. A moment, she stood there, panting, one hand over her heart. Could an immortal Titan even have a heart attack? Could she die of a broken heart? Stories spoke of the latter, but she'd called them idle fancies.

She was fooling herself, she knew, if she thought she could best Athene in such condition. With Ares dead, with so many champions dead, the two of them were the finest masters of weapons yet living, so far as she knew. And Artemis, at present, found it hard to put one foot in front of the next.

Still, she trudged the halls, ducking aside from a flaming tapestry and keeping low when the billowing smoke ahead grew too thick to breathe. Waves of heat washed over her, scorching her exposed skin. She could have used Pneuma for Tolerance but lacked the will to bother. Maybe some part of her welcomed the pain.

She broke out into the balcony rimming the courtyard, and Helen ploughed into Artemis, shrieking and wild, the demigod almost impaling herself on the dagger still in Artemis's hand. Artemis caught the woman and held her at arm's length. Artemis's brother—so many people—had fallen because of Zeus's bastard daughter. Because of Artemis's insane plan to use this woman to start a war and thus give vent to her wrath against Zeus.

And now the Elládosi had broken the walls of Ilium and would soon rescue the girl—though Helen no doubt dreaded reunion with her husband—and return to her homeland. All of it for naught, wasn't it? They had not broken Olympus but instead lost Ares and Apollon, allies *against* Zeus.

So how could Artemis allow it? How could she, after all this, abide the invaders achieving victory and taking home the prize they had come for? She could throw Helen over her shoulder and run, perhaps eluding pursuit. At least for a time. But, rather, she knew, she would not be able to stop herself from going after Athene if she saw the woman.

Artemis raised a hand to her lips. "Shh."

Helen looked to her, face stricken with terror. Eyes as pale blue as her blighted father's. There were no prizes to be had this day. Only pain. Only loss.

With a Potency-fuelled shove, Artemis sent Helen reeling. The girl collided with the balustrade, flailed, and pitched over the side with a brief shriek. When Artemis followed to peer over the edge, she saw the girl, her skull shattered upon the cobbles below.

No prizes for anyone.

THE THROES OF UTTER DESPERATION, Artemis found, made one amenable to bedfellows one would otherwise not have countenanced. She had fled the blazing ruin of Ilium and hunted for Phaethusa but, in the chaos, found no sign of her sister. Artemis had dared not linger there for the final sacking of her home. Athene would hunt for her, as well, and her hydromantic abilities would give her the advantage. Thus, Artemis took one of the fleeing ships and made her way to Phoenikia, ever in mind of the message she had received from Morpheus about allies in Babilim.

What choice had she now, anyway? If she went to Helion and Zeus learnt her father sheltered her, she risked the Titan King's wrath coming upon her kin. The same was true of her holdings in Phoeba. Her city's only chance lay in distancing itself from her. Nor could she go to Kirke and expose her involvement in all that had transpired. So Artemis sailed for Neshia on Kumari Kandam, watching the Phoenikian bireme thread through azure waters, and glancing skyward, fearing the shadow of Olympian pegasi.

They would come for her, she knew. Athene might not realise Kirke or Phaethusa had joined Artemis and Apollon's rebellion, which, Artemis prayed to Thoth, might allow her sisters to escape notice. For herself, glancing back and forth between sea and sky, all she could think on was the incessant wondering of how they had gotten Kassandra's prophecy so very wrong. How, when the woman had foretold the doom of Olympus would begin with that war, did Olympus yet stand whilst its foes had crumbled, reduced to dust along with the Ilian walls?

She had no tears to shed for her slain twin, though oft enough she wished for the release weeping might have provided. Instead, every-where she turned, be it in the shape of clouds or the glint of the bright morning sun upon the waves, she saw his face or his golden eyes. Always, they asked the question: how had she let such an end befall him? How had she so failed him, that she should live whilst he had fallen?

For that matter, she did not know for certain that Phaethusa had escaped the carnage that followed the city's breaching. She had written to her father of her concerns, but Helios had no way to respond, even if he knew more of his daughter's whereabouts. So, sullen and morose, Artemis would spend hour upon hour watching the leagues slip by her, the ship carrying her away from all she had hoped for, all she had striven for. All those she had once loved.

In the port of Ugart, now a part of the Babilimian Empire, she found two Magi awaiting her. They had set themselves up in one of the dockside inns, and though she had not seen him in person in years, Artemis recognised Morpheus as one of them. After taking a breath to scan the tavern for any sign of threat or hidden danger, Artemis made her way to the hearth by which the sorcerer-priests sat, sipping beers and whispering in conspiratorial tones, heads bowed toward one another.

Morpheus looked up at her approach, eyes widening as if he almost had not expected her to answer his invitation, then rose.

"So," she said, "this is where you disappeared off to? Joined the religion of foreign lands?" She had heard some tale the Magi worshipped fire. Rumours claimed they offered sacrifices to the flames in the name of their god of light. Then again, she had also heard tale that Mithra, first of their order, had proclaimed himself a god-king and taken the throne. It was hard to keep straight the details of the gossip brought in by boisterous sailors, but Artemis had made some few inquiries before making for this continent.

Morpheus frowned, not missing the hint of accusation in her words. They had all, Morpheus included, allowed Zeus to cast Titans as gods, and many of their own kind had even grown to believe it truth. Now Mithra—was he a Titan too?—had taken a similar tack here in the far south, and Artemis was uncertain she cared for it. What would poor Kirke, so desperate to remove the Titan heel from the throats of Men, have thought about Artemis siding with yet another self-proclaimed god? "Good thoughts, good words, and good deeds. I dedicate myself to Truth, wherever I find it, and thus it is never foreign to me. This, to say naught of the fact that I hail from these lands." The Magus motioned to a bench across from himself and his companion, and Artemis sat.

"You serve Mithra, then? He's one of us?"

Morpheus apprehended her meaning at once, a grin spreading across his face. "The god-king is more than any Titan, but yes, he is among the Anunnaki, the Titans of Kumari Kandam. I know you have spoken with him, in years past."

"When he came for Kassandra's hand, yes." Artemis hesitated. "I know Kurus II died some years back. What became of Kassandra?"

Morpheus's smile washed away like a sandcastle smashed by a sudden wave. "Dead." If the oneiromancer knew Artemis had cared for Kassandra, he made no effort to soften the blow. "She was unable to bear the loss of her husband and her son, may they rest in Light."

Given she had not heard of the woman in years, Artemis could not say she was surprised, though still it hurt. Had she more left within her breast to spare, she'd have grieved for the princess of Ilium. Events, however, had left her bereft of aught more to give. She moved through life now a ghost, trapped in meaningless motion, unable to mourn herself, much less anyone else. "So now you will take me to Babilim?"

Morpheus nodded, face solemn. "You have made powerful foes in Elládos, but not even the Olympians will dare to seek you out in the heart of the Babilimian Empire."

"Why shelter me at all?"

"Is it not enough that Babilim called Ilium friend and thus names those who sacked her foe?"

No, Artemis rather didn't think that enough. But perhaps Mithra sought to recruit her, thinking to use her knowledge of Olympus against Elládos. If that was his plan, Artemis supposed it was better than any she had for the future.

3

___

KIRKE

1 Dark Age

Five decades of waiting proved, to Kirke's surprise, worse than five decades bereft of hope. Artemis came a few times, once even bringing stolen Ambrosia to help fortify Kirke's Pneuma for the struggles to come. Mostly, though, her sister remained too busy with her plotting against Olympus, stopping by only for advice. Phaethusa made more visits to Aiaíā over the years, when she could manage it. She would come with news of the happenings of the world, which Kirke appreciated more even than the wines her sister imported from Phrygia.

Through her sister, Kirke heard about the disastrous battle Phaethusa named Seven Against Thebes, and together they mused over whether it presented an opportunity to take advantage of. Certainly, having the poleis of Elládos fractious and at one another's throats would destabilise Zeus's rule, but Kirke misliked the thought of Mankind used as fodder.

Too, she heard how Atreus, the successor to Eurystheus, had slain Hyllus, the son of Herakles. Such news evoked a twinge of sadness on

Athene's behalf, though as it turned out, it had all unfolded years before she heard about it. The tale came up later, when Phaethusa explained how Artemis planned to spark a war over Zeus's bastard daughter, Helen. The demigod had been married off to one of Atreus's sons, a curmudgeon named Menelaus. Then, of course, Artemis had—with a bit of help from one of Kirke's lust potions and some oneiromantic manipulation—prompted Paris, Prince of Ilium, to seduce Helen and run away with her.

Yeah, so they had their great war and more innocent Men died. Kirke hadn't expected it to go on for ten years and, worse, for word sent from Artemis and Phaethusa to abruptly cut off. In the village, folk claimed the war had ended with the fall of Ilium—decidedly not the outcome Kirke's alliance had hoped for in inciting all this.

When at last she could stand it no more, she reached out to Artemis in dreams and found the fallen Olympian's mind closed to her. If she lived, Kirke could not imagine how Artemis could have shielded her dreams, which left a hollow ache of dread rumbling in her gut, one which no amount of wine could fill. Next, she tried Phaethusa. Her mind, Kirke found, was a broken, desolate place.

A BOLT OF LIGHTNING, searing white, streaked across a half-formed sky. In a moment drawn out into an eternity, the blast struck a flying pegasus, sending steed and rider plummeting toward Gaia.

Behind Kirke, Phaethusa hissed. Kirke turned and found the other woman sitting on decaying grass, arms wrapt around her knees, rocking like a distraught babe. Kirke did not bother commenting on Phaethusa watching herself get struck down by Zeus. Dreams had a logic all their own, and it was hardly the first time she'd seen a dreamer in two places at once.

Rather, she crouched in front of Phaethusa. With one hand she grasped her sister's elbow. With the other, she snapped her fingers before the woman's face. "Come on." Mother had been so much better at this. The problem with visiting someone in their dreams was their conscious mind didn't control what was going on. Sometimes it didn't seem to realise what unfolded around it, and oft the dreamer wouldn't remember conversations had thus. Unless the oneiro-

mancer could pull consciousness into the dream—without waking the sleeper —and turn it lucid, any attempted exchange of information was mostlike to prove limited, if not futile. "Phaethusa." Another snap of her fingers.

The other Heliad's golden eyes focused on Kirke's face now. "W-what are you doing here?"

"It's not real," Kirke said while stroking Phaethusa's elbow. She didn't want the woman jolting into wakefulness and breaking their connection. "It's a dream, but you need to stay in it, yeah? Just focus on my voice, on my face, and we can talk."

Phaethusa nodded, eyes once more going glazed. Such a delicate balance between letting the subconscious rule and letting the mind fully awaken.

"Where are you now?" Kirke asked.

Phaethusa looked around, as if trying to piece together her location from the ever-shifting surreal landscape of her dream.

"No, not here," Kirke said. "This place is an amalgam of memory and imagination and fear." She pointed into the distance. "That's Evenor Mountain on Atlantis. That wasn't where Zeus hit you with lightning, was it? And those hills are from Father's palace on Thrinakia, nowhere near to Evenor. I need to know where you are in the real world."

Phaethusa stared at the hills, bitterness creeping over her face. "There."

"Back on Thrinakia?"

"When the walls of Ilium fell, Father sent me back, afraid Zeus would learn of my involvement with Artemis and all this."

So Zeus had won, at least through Elládos. Artemis had hoped, when Priam defeated the kings of Elládos, Helios and Phoebe would step in to unite Phrygia and Lydia against the insane tyrant of Olympus. Now their great plan had failed, it would seem. "What happened? Is Artemis ..."

Phaethusa sighed. "I don't know. Last I saw her, she lived, but things were chaos. Athene slew Apollon." Apollon! Such seemed impossible. Her brother was this invincible force ... And killed by Athene? "Ares is dead too," Phaethusa said after a moment. While Kirke would little grieve Athene's sadistic brother, his recruitment to their cause had been a boon, and Kirke grimaced on that account.

They needed to focus. There would be time for grief later. "How were the walls breached?"

"A trick. The Elládosi seemed to be in retreat after the death of their cham-

pion. They left an offering, a wooden horse. The Ilians brought it within the walls as a prize. Only, come nightfall, warriors hidden within snuck forth and opened the gates. Then ... So many dead. So much carnage, slaughter."

And hope was lost. Just as Kirke had once striven to elevate Man against Titan with Nectar only to make things worse, so too had their great plan failed. She withdrew her hand from Phaethusa.

"Kirke ..." the other woman said, her voice slurred with sleep.

But there was naught left to be said now.

All that remained was ash.

❧

DESOLATE AND ALONE, Kirke wandered her island prison.

These days, little held her interest. Ever and anon she began a weaving and abandoned it after a few hours of work. She took up scrolls and realised, after struggling for half an evening poring over them, she had no idea what she'd read. Preoccupied with the war and his rebellious son, Zeus had not returned in long years. Now Ares was dead and the war had ended, so perhaps he would come again, demanding more Nectar. Still, she had little desire to tinker with her brews.

So she walked. She roamed the circuit of her island again and again until she could have found every nook and cranny blindfolded. She climbed the mountain ranges that framed the island. She walked along the light-dappled forest floor hunting herbs and mushrooms she knew she would never bother turning into brews. In the denser southern forests, she trod along wolf runs, musing over the idea of breeding a new pack.

But why? So Zeus could murder more of her pets when he finally came demanding something else from her? She swam in the Pithkias River and imagined never coming up for air, as if she might simply pass the Ages beneath nestled in the silt and wedged between the smooth-worn stones.

Sometimes, she thought of leaping from a mountain peak or taking a knife to her veins. But she knew, even then, in the depths of her heart, she was not the sort to escape her woes thus.

So she climbed along the rocky edges of Aiaíā's shore, letting the waves lap her heels and soak her sandals. The wind whipped her hair, threatening to tug strands loose of her braid, mocking her with its freedom. She imagined, as she had considered in days past, swimming the wide channel between the island and the Phoenikian coast. It was an impossible swim, though, and she could no more bring herself to attempt so suicidal an endeavour than she could slit her wrists. Thus wandering did she spy the ship drawing nigh, battered and worn, with kohl-lined eyes painted along the bow.

No pirates had dared defile her shores in decades. So who would come here, and not toward the small town, but off the rocks, as if they did not know where to moor? Whoever it was, they had lowered a small boat and begun to row toward her, perhaps having spotted her watching them from the rocks.

Well, then. Perhaps she needed to stop by her manse and dig up a transformation potion, just in case.

MANY POSSIBILITIES HAD CROSSED Kirke's mind on her way back to her manse. She had considered, perhaps, that Artemis had come at last. Or Phaethusa had fled from Thrinakia and sought her out. Or worse, that Zeus had come, for some reason by ship rather than pegasus. Then, of course, perhaps the new generation of pirates had forgotten the lessons of their forebears and would need a fresh taste of her dark alchemy. Even, she mused, the ship could have come from Father, intent to end her banishment. Of all the explanations that crossed her mind, never once did she imagine the person who would first emerge from the boat would be her grandmother.

And yet there Pandora was, leading a Tethid man. Other sailors vaulted the edge of the boat and pulled it ashore but did not follow Pandora and her guest as they made their way up to the ledge where Kirke awaited them. Kirke tucked the phial of Nectar into the recesses of her peplos, certain she would not need it now, though she had no idea why Pandora had come here after all this time.

When Pandora drew nigh, the Heliad woman reached an arm toward Kirke, and Kirke clasped it. Part of her wanted to ask how much time had passed for Pandora since they had last seen one another, back in

Themiskyra. More than seventy years had slipped by for Kirke, but given the Box, it could have been less or more than that for her grandmother.

"My friend and his crew seek refuge and a place to repair their ship," Pandora said, still holding Kirke's arm.

"My aunt has a village, nestled betwixt the northern and southern mountain ranges. It's the only place for a large ship to moor safely, and I imagine, if they can pay, they can find food and supplies." Kirke gave Pandora a firm squeeze, as much to reassure herself the woman was really here as for Pandora's sake, before releasing her arm. "As for you, you must come with me to my manse. Yeah, I imagine we've got at least a thousand things to talk on. More, maybe, if we've had enough wine."

"The right vintage does tend to render even the most prosaic of topics compelling," Pandora's companion said.

Pandora looked to him. "This is Odysseus, King of Ithaka, come of late from the siege of Ilium."

Ithaka was, if Kirke remembered correctly, an Ionian Island, which meant this man probably fought *against* Ilium and thus had helped thwart Kirke's hopes for the future. Still, she could hardly blame a Man for her own failure to unseat the Titan King. "You come, as well, then. I'd love more of the tale of the city's fall, if you'd be willing to share."

"Oh ..." He chuckled. "The telling of tales is something of a favoured pastime for me, an art handed down from my grandfather, in fact. Have you the wine, I can at least provide for you the evening's entertainment."

It was, Kirke supposed, a better offer than any she'd had recently.

OVER THE COURSE of more than one evening, in fact, Odysseus told his tale. How he had been compelled to fight for Menelaus and Agamemnon, though he had not much wished to go. How the war had dragged on when they found they could never breach the walls of Ilium. How great Achilles had slain Hektor and Ares, only to fall to Artemis's wrath. Too, Odysseus told of his travails after the sack of the city. His ship had drifted from disaster to disaster as though cursed, meeting with such misfortune Kirke began to suspect some spirit or other tested the man.

"I thought these Laestrygonians would prove the end of us,"

Odysseus said at last, words slurring a hair from the drink on the third night. "Who would have thought Nike would come to our rescue!"

Kirke glanced at her grandmother, who had said very little these past days and nights, ever lost in the moil of her thoughts. It was possible Pandora had showed up in time to save Odysseus by pure chance, but Kirke thought that less likely than the odds of a pride of lions appearing in her manse, holding a symposium, and debating the finer points of ethics. Based on the cunning she'd seen in Odysseus, despite his attempts to conceal it, she imagined he too had his doubts. Of course, unless he knew about the Box and timewalking, Odysseus could never have guessed the truth.

"Well," the Ithakan said, "so then the goddess guided our ship here, saying we could be safe here and she knew a sorceress who might help us find our way home." Like most Tethids, Odysseus had eyes deep as the sea, bright as cobalt. There was a vibrance there, Kirke had to admit. Despite the unspoken plea in his words, he did not supplicate himself before her, nor beg, nor even ask for her help. Did he think she would volunteer to work the Art for him?

"Take your rest, King of Ithaka," Kirke said after a moment. "I'm sure you must be weary from these ordeals." Yeah, and Kirke needed time to think over the nature of his unspoken request, and whether she ought to acquiesce to it at all. It was the rarest of occasions when good came from the Art, she had found.

Odysseus took his dismissal with a nod and retired to the chambers Kirke had granted him. Given the manse had a dozen rooms, she had figured she could spare a couple for Pandora and her captain friend. When the Ithakan had departed, Kirke moved to sit beside Pandora, who crouched before the hearth like some pyromancer, though Kirke didn't think she had the gift.

"He will come to a bad end one day," the woman said without warning.

Wait, what? *Was* Pandora a pyromancer? Her grandmother picked up new talents like a buxom wench picked up admirers whilst strolling drunk and half-naked through a tavern. Or was it rather that Pandora, timewalking, had seen the future in non-Oracular means?

"And you want me to help him find his way home before that, yeah? What about the implication of so doing? Have you considered the smallest shift might change the course of his life and thus preserve it?"

Pandora sighed. "Yes. Considered it, mulled it over, massaging all the sharp angles of the issue as if it could be shaped into something palatable. You imagine that, were Odysseus to fail to return home, perhaps he would not meet whatever dire fate I have beheld for him. But if he had not met that fate, I would not have known the need to save him from the Laestrygonians, and he'd have died twenty years sooner than the Moirai have decreed for him. Most oft, even a dying beast, one suffering grievous pain, will fight for but one more breath." Now Pandora looked to Kirke. "Should I deny him twenty years of life for the chance to say I spat in Ananke's eye?"

Kirke groaned. "And when you put it like that, I'm not left with much choice about whether to help him or not. I mean, I could choose to be a selfish bitch, and yeah, maybe I've made that choice once or twice in days gone, but that's the only choice."

The other woman shrugged, perhaps in sympathy or perhaps in mutual resignation to the whirls of Fate.

It took several nights of oneiromantic wanderings to find the answer Kirke sought on behalf of the Ithakan, and in the days between he entertained her with his stories, feats of archery, or quick wit. Pandora had taken to wandering the woods beyond the manse, morose and lost in her thoughts in a way unlike the woman Kirke had gotten to know in Themiskyra. But then, time wore on them both, playing its ruthless games, until it left them chafed and sullen at such abuses. Maybe all who walked through time found themselves ill-used by Ananke.

If so, Kirke asked herself, were the foul twists of fortune a punishment from the Moirai for meddling in their Tapestry? Or would anyone who saw past the curtain of time tremble from what they beheld just as mediums paled upon first gazing into the Penumbra?

With Odysseus, lounging in the bright sunlight, Kirke could pretend she had not learnt things no mortal ought to learn. She could cast aside the burdens of unwanted knowledge and strive, for a moment, to exist in neither past nor future, but only in the fleeting breeze of the *now*.

It almost made her sad to reveal what she had seen and thus send him on his way. Did his wife pine for him after ten years had passed? Such was an achingly long time for mortals, and according to Odysseus, he and Penelope had not been together more than half a year when he was called to service with Agamemnon. Given the choice, Kirke would have idled more time here with him, though she knew it selfish to deny him a home to balm her own lonely soul. Too much so, she supposed.

"I dreamt for you," she said when the sun had set and the first stars began to twinkle in the firmament. He had been searching for familiar constellations, though he was far from home.

"Sounds more or less a fancy way of saying you dreamt about me," he teased.

Kirke looked away. His jest may have struck closer to the mark than he suspected. Oneiromancy, like all aspects of the Art, was no science and tended to seize upon the wild currents of her fears and desires and paint them upon the canvas of dreams like a frenzied artist driven mad by his obsessions. It had, after all, been long since last she'd felt a tender touch. She was not, however, quite certain she wished to admit it to this man.

She knew his type well enough, she thought, and he'd have lied or flattered or tried most any tack to draw a woman to his bed, all whilst claiming his love for his wife remained true. Perhaps he would even believe in his own faithfulness. Though Kirke couldn't quite say she minded his flirting and those glances that lingered overlong upon the exposed flesh of her shoulder or neckline of her peplos, nor did she fool herself into thinking the Ithakan would not have tried the same with any other woman he met. Huh. Well, to be fair, though, she supposed he *had* spent ten years at war and probably not enjoyed those tender touches as oft as he might have wished.

After a moment, she turned back to him. "I'm an oneiromancer. That is to say, an Oracle of dreams. Into those mists I looked on your behalf, and it's where you'd have to go to learn how you can return home."

"Then there is some force keeping my ship lost at sea."

"There is. The siren, Thetis, holds you to account for the death of her son, Achilles. Her magic haunts you."

The man groaned, clearly aware enough of why Thetis might bear such a grudge.

"Do you know of the sage Tiresias?" Her words came out slow, and not just because she did not want him to leave but because it was bitter to deliver foul news to someone. Well, unless it was someone who earned one's ire, she supposed. Yeah, giving bad news to a foe, that was more like biting into a honey cake and revelling in the saccharine explosion it induced.

"I know he died sometime around when the Epigoni sacked Thebes." From what little Kirke had heard, the Epigoni were sons of the ill-fated Seven Against Thebes who completed the failed missions of their fathers. "Are you saying the ghost of a dead Oracle haunts me?"

"No." Were he haunted by a mere ghost, she might be able to turn to sorcery to drive the ghost off. "No, rather, my dream revealed that Tiresias alone holds the answers to the route you must take to return home."

"Uh ... all right. Guess I'll just ask him."

"You must," she agreed.

"I think, perhaps, 'dead' means something else where you hail from."

Kirke glanced back up at the stars, mind whirring at how best to say the next part. "I am most known as a witch for my alchemical experiments."

"Yeah, me too."

She rolled her eyes at that. "I can brew a draught that would allow you to pass into the Underworld, as a kind of temporary shade. You could then question the fallen seer."

"I rather mislike any plan that involves visiting the Underworld," Odysseus deadpanned. He was no longer looking at her or even at the night sky but at something unseen in the middle distance.

Kirke knew that far-away feeling all too well. It was the slow rising dread one felt when realising just how cruel the Moirai could be in their weavings. "I would need a season or so to grow the necessary herbs before I could brew it." If she omitted that it was *possible* she might be able to send someone to buy what she needed from Phoenikia and have the brew ready in just over a fortnight rather than months, well it was a small omission.

An omission of that truth in favour of the greater truth. Kirke *did* want someone to warm her bed. She wanted to feel alive, to feel aught save the gaping void of dread that forever threatened to open inside her chest. Her timewalking had revealed the twisted horror of history to her.

Her attempts to overthrow Zeus had failed *again*. Her life amounted to darkness, death, and failure. So why should she not seize a few moments of bliss for herself before she found herself once more abandoned, exiled on this desolate island, and left to her pointless, solitary pursuits?

So she let her hand alight on his and squeezed. "I have never made such a brew myself, nor such a sojourn, but my mother has. I think I can coach you through how to survive it."

4

———

ENODIA

730 Bronze Age

 ncounted miles of catacombs wound their way beneath the necropolis of Kek like worm-eaten burrows carved out of ancient bones. Ossified protuberances seemed to reach for those passing through those halls, intimating misshapen limbs, as though an entire city's worth of skeletons were welled up within those hateful walls. The maze served as a haven, of a sort, for the necropolis's disaffected shades, those hiding from Hades's wraith enforcers. And yet, Enodia knew well enough that other, darker predators stalked these tunnels. Those who ventured into the sepulchral depths oft vanished without trace. Even Hades's elite hesitated to chance the catacombs.

This, of course, meant they served as perfect locales for the clandestine meetings she held in her striving to overthrow Hades's court. Upon a shelf of bone, Persephone reclined, dour and grim faced. Enodia did not miss the sporadic glances the other ghost cast down the tunnels, fearing her husband's ever-vigilant servants might have followed her here, despite Enodia's protective wards. "I begin to doubt our success," Persephone admitted. "Even could we challenge Hades, I've seen Kerberos tear a dozen shades apart before they scarce knew the beast among them." Ever, Hades's wife remained terrified of the fell beast, and Enodia suspected the ghost king had perhaps threatened her with the creature in days gone.

In truth, usurping Hades's throne had not proved the simple process Enodia had once hoped. Her opponent had soon learnt of Hekate's death and had apprehended the danger she represented. Then the hunt had been on, and Enodia had been forced to move in secret, ever evading his ghost armies, whilst struggling to keep concealed the ghul army she'd raised in Vulgeth. She was not ready for open war between her own wraiths and Hades's, for if she took that path and failed, she would most-like have no second chance.

So instead, she'd plucked at his power base from the shadows, siphoning his strength like so many leeches. She'd conquered the necropolis of Irkalla, though its queen, Ereshkigal, had proved almost too much for Enodia to bring low. But once she had destroyed the vampire queen, Irkalla's army had joined with Enodia's own, and she had used the remnants of those forces to harry Kek and keep Hades busy, all whilst gnawing away at the foundations of Hades's support. But Persephone was right, the centuries had drawn long, and Hades's regime was far from crumbling out beneath him.

Enodia leant against the wall of bones, shifting as a protruding joint dug into the small of her back. "Patience ... Already my agents in Xibalba have begun recruiting those loyal to us." The Xibalbans had no love for either Kek or Hades, of course. Whether they would remain loyal allies after overthrowing Hades, that was another question entirely.

"Patience," Persephone rasped. "Always patience, patience, patience. For hundreds of years I have dwindled beneath the cruelty of the husband who abducted me. Who condemned me to lifeless existence dwelling forever in this gloom-shrouded city. I grow weary of the refrain of *patience*. Such is an easy cry for those not locked in the throes of desperate straits."

Enodia didn't justify that with an answer. If Persephone thought Enodia had not suffered in the intervening centuries—of which far more had passed for her than the other woman—she had sorely misjudged Enodia's circumstances.

"What of our emissary to Youdu?" she asked instead.

Persephone huffed, a wispy, breathless sound. "Orpheus says they will not throw in with us unless we demonstrate our strength." Orpheus was a recently dead bard, one recruited by Persephone for his particular loathing of Hades. He'd proved a surprisingly adept agent thus far.

"Meaning," Melinoë said, "the bastards will side only with whoever comes out on top."

Persephone shrugged. "Their dynasty has endured ages for a reason. They wear caution like a familiar cloak, thinking it can shield them from every storm."

And yet, there were dangers in hedging bets. Whoever triumphed would remember that Youdu refused to aid them in their darker hours. Such knowledge did not make for easy alliances. "Take heed," Enodia said. "I warned you I would get you out from beneath Hades's grasp, and I shall, though it may take centuries more yet. I will never abandon you, Persephone." Pushing off the wall, Enodia moved to where the other woman sat and laid a hand upon her chill cheek. Enodia had failed to stop Hades from claiming Persephone ages back. She would not fail now.

IN PERHAPS THE lowest depths of the catacombs, places where light had never stained the eternal darkness, Enodia had gathered her generals. Her Hel-wraiths, she called the seven of them, for the barbarian name for the Underworld had struck a resonant chord with Enodia, and she had never forgotten it. It was that first, blighted journey into the Nyxlands that had brought her to the Box and thus ensured the continuation of her circular destiny. Thus, in perverse honour, she had dubbed her seven great wraiths the Lords of Hel.

She did not know who had built the osseous chamber, with its vaulted ceiling and its chipped columns of bone from which jutted harsh spurs, but on stumbling upon this place, she knew what she had found. For she could not have asked for a better site to hold council with her most valued lieutenants. Each of them sat upon a seat hewn from bone, eyes glinting red beneath their frayed burial shrouds, malice seeping off them in palpable waves. Keuthonymos was the first, the highest of them, if perhaps not the most powerful. That honour probably fell to Nephthys, the one Enodia needed watch ever closest, always tightening the reins of her necromantic bonds. Inanna and Phobetor she had slain the same day as Nephthys, and they were lesser shadows of the Kemetian wraith. Hypnos and Enyo had died other times, and only with extreme effort had Enodia tracked down their ghosts and bent them to her will, collecting the souls of the broken Circle of Goetic Mysteries like trophies.

The Circle had given rise to the sorceress Hekate in a sense. It was they who had possessed the Sefer Raziel that had become the grimoire housing all Enodia's secrets.

Of the seven, Melinoë alone had never studied within the Lodge of Whispers. But like Keuthos, her loyalty was beyond reproach. The only being the wraith loathed more than herself was her father, and Enodia knew well Melinoë would have ripped away the foundations of the cosmos so long as Hades too would have drowned in the ensuing maelstrom of Khaos.

Her Hel-wraiths had arranged their seats in a semicircle around her own and Enodia felt their regard and anticipation crawl across her necrotic flesh like an army of ants. They were hers, yes, but most not by choice.

"We are not enough ..." Keuthos rasped. "The ghuls you raised in Vulgeth are spread thin, enforcing our will across the vast shadowscapes between necropoleis ... Irkalla has not the forces enough to launch a siege upon Kek."

Melinoë hissed, for she had been the one—perhaps at her mother's urging—to push for war now. The ghost punched a fist into the arm of her throne, splintering pieces of bone.

After assuring herself Melinoë was not about to launch herself at Keuthos and sup upon his soul, Enodia ran a thumb along the irritated fringe of skin on her face where it shredded and gave way to bare skull. Her plan had been to gather the power to overthrow the baleful Elder Gods themselves, and here she lingered, thwarted time and again in her attempt to bring down her own creation. She had made Hades, and now he stood as a perennial obstacle before her plans.

"We need more allies ..." Nephthys said. "Those capable of challenging even the wraiths of Hades ..."

Who still outnumbered those belonging to Enodia. Sorcerers proved rare enough that, even among the dead, they seemed hard to come by. Or perhaps the Realms ought to count that a blessing, that wraiths did not flow over the Penumbra in great abundance.

"I'll not hear more of the greater vampires again," Enodia interjected. Reckoning with Ereshkigal had proved disastrous enough, and she would not risk waking the slumbering ancients of Vulgeth's day as things now stood. So long as the vampires left her people alone, Enodia would keep them at a distance as well.

"No ..." Nephthys agreed, and Enodia almost thought a horrified shiver flitted through the ghost. "But there are great powers ... beyond ..."

This again. Inanna, too, had suggested they might venture past the Roil, into the Spirit Realm, and enslave dryads or harpies or lampads, draw them into their war. The Hel-wraiths were, after all, sorcerers and could still work their awful Art upon other eidolons.

And perhaps Enodia could no longer demur to walk that dark path. She had, heretofore, relied upon sorcery but precious little in the Ages since her death. Indeed, she avoided taking any action that might draw Aeshma's eye toward her soul. But sooner or later, if trapped, one had to test every possible avenue of escape. A time came when caution no longer availed, becoming its own invisible prison. Did Enodia think she could bring down the order of the cosmos without risking her soul?

"I will go to the Rimefells, then. I will see about recruiting lampads to our war. Keuthonymos will accompany me and bring a score of his ghuls. Melinoë shall remain here, in command in my absence." She paused a moment. "Hypnos, go to Xibalba and make plain only those who move with us will share in favour henceforth. Inanna, back to Irkalla, and ready the army." Inanna had been, in fact, sister to Ereshkigal. On her death, she had turned to Ereshkigal for succour and found instead scorn and torment. Thus, she leapt at claiming rulership of her sister's necropolis.

Almost as one, the seven Hel-wraiths bowed, obeisance and hatred mingling into a thick miasma Enodia breathed in like the richest of perfumes. Soon, she told herself. Soon, she would sit upon the throne of all the Underworld.

5

___

ATHENE

399 Dark Age

For decades following the end of the Ilian War, Athene scarce left the sanctum of Olympus. She passed the years alone, wandering in the silent moil of her thoughts, brooding ever upon the faces of the Twelve Olympians. A number now much diminished, cut in half, in truth, though Artemis remained out there, somewhere. Father had not found the Phoebid, and Athene refused to look into the Oracle Mirrors to try.

"She lives ..." Hestia had said once, though the pyromancer would say no more. Hestia, as always, was lost in her mind, the workings of which she revealed to no one.

And, of course, Hebe and Poseidon lived off the mountain, leaving only Athene, her father, Hestia, and Hera here now. How empty the slopes seemed these days.

Athene had thought Hera would have taken the loss of her only son badly, but the woman spoke little of Ares, spending time instead with her peacocks and her snakes, and with, to Athene's shock, her husband. Indeed, had Athene not known better, she'd almost have imagined the two of them thought to replace their lost child, they spent so much time behind closed doors.

All Athene's life, Hera had seemed a font of endless vitriol, quick to spew venom like some cobra. Now the Tethid kept actual vipers as pets, but her own poisons seemed to have run dry. She no longer lashed out at Athene with half-concealed barbs or insults, nor had Athene seen her hurl abuses on the servants or courtiers.

Or perhaps her temper had cooled now that her husband had no bastards left alive, save for Athene herself. Even Dionysus and Hermes were long dead. "The Firebringer's prophecy is averted at last," Hera once said, when Athene dared broach the subject whilst they walked along a winding path around the backside of the mountain. "Zeus has no more sons whom he must fear ending his reign. Were he to sire more of the brats, we would again need fear the fulfilment of that awful foretelling."

"Once," Athene said, pausing to look out over the plummeting side of the cliff and imagine how the world below must be changing with her, "I might have thought you would welcome the end of him."

Hera cast her a sharp, appraising look that had Athene fearing she had overstepped. Only now, after so many centuries, did she manage something akin to a civil relationship with her stepmother, and she had little wish to sabotage whatever had begun to develop here.

"Do you know all your father has foreseen in the depths of the Oracle Mirrors?"

Athene started. Zeus oft raved about the things he saw, but not in any way which allowed her to make sense of them. Did he now permit his wife into the chamber as well? Did he share his deepest secrets with her in a confidence he had never before bestowed onto his daughter? "He speaks of souls and death and reincarnation. Of predators beyond the edge of our senses, ready to feast on ... us. He fears something he calls Unseen." He seemed, all too oft, to have crossed the threshold into madness and Athene had no idea how to help him back from that edge. Over the centuries, she had mused, in dark moments, on what her life might have been had she been someone else's daughter—or, rather, had her father been another man. Her greatest goal was to aid Mankind, but not even her desperate need to do so could come before loyalty to her parents.

Hera folded her arms over her chest. "The weight of too much knowledge can bow even the mightiest of shoulders. Behind the shadows of history lurks the Unseen Order. They move kings and nations around like pieces on the draughts board. They shape the course of destiny, ever moving toward hidden ends. What mind would not tremble when forced to vie against such implacable foes?"

Something in her words had Athene shivering beneath the mountain breezes, and she rubbed her arms. Though Hera seemed in earnest, such claims seemed the products of unhinged minds. The idea of a vast conspiracy stretching across continents, across millennia, defied logic. Who could orchestrate such gambits? Who, even among immortals, would have the patience and foresight to enact schemes that might take generations to come to fruition? Only once, in all her life, had she met anyone who might dare think on the scale of eons.

Was it possible, then, that her grandfather, Prometheus, was involved with this Unseen Order that so terrified her father and stepmother? He was, after all, the one who had first spoken the prophecy that Zeus's child would slay him. Athene had not seen her grandfather in long years now. Where had he hidden himself away?

But ... no. She had no doubt Prometheus played games with destiny, but she did not wish to believe him involved in the machinations of this Unseen Order. The question, really, was whether Hera bought into her father's claims because he convinced her or because there lay truth in them.

It was a weight on her soul, but she would need to tread with great care if she was to investigate this Order. If there was any chance of truth behind this tale, if men could lurk in the shadows and pretend to be the Moirai, weaving Fate, she did not want their eyes upon her. Yes, she would look, and if the Unseen Order existed, she would uncover its webs, one silken skein at a time.

PRESCIENT VISIONS of old had warned Athene that, sooner or later, the day would come when Babilim would prove her undoing. What had once been an all but unknown minor polis on a far-off continent had grown into the centre of the greatest empire the world had known, and

Athene watched its calamitous rise with unshakeable foreboding. To see its relentless expansion was like gazing into the heavens and beholding an eclipse; she knew not the sum of its portent, but even a fool could not miss that an ill omen rose.

Babilim took, so far as anyone in Elládos knew, the whole of Kumari Kandam. They said that its Magi, sorcerer priests, turned to dark powers, offering strange advice to the immortal god-king who sat upon his golden throne. Tales claimed all manner of outlandish abilities for the Magi, and Athene could not credence every rumour that passed by Olympus. Humans, sacrificed into fire pits, and shadowy entities called up from worlds unknown. It strained credulity, she felt.

Owing to the similarity in worship, Father insisted the Magi must relate to the outlawed Fire cults of Prometheus that had, since the Golden Age, cropped up across the Thalassa world. The Olympians had always named the worship of Prometheus as blasphemous, and the more so after Father had bound him in Tartarus, and yet Men thought him their patron and burnt offerings to him. Prometheus had told Athene once that even when he protested, when he told Men in plain words their faith was built on misconceptions, they only grew more obdurate and unwavering in zealotry. Not even the appearance of their vaunted messiah was enough to gainsay the momentum of a religion he had neither wanted nor supported.

For her part, Athene doubted the Fire cults had any connection to the Magi. Never, in all the centuries the Olympians had spent attempting to stomp out the religion, had she heard tale of those people turning to the Art, save for pyromancy. Of sorcerous practices, there had never been the least rumour. For the Magi, sorcery and spellsongs and other mysteries beyond her ken seemed part and parcel, and Men and Titan alike feared them.

Not nigh so much, Athene thought, as they feared the endless thousands upon thousands of warriors all sworn to Babilim. Their ships clogged the Thalassa Sea, and, as the empire spread across Phoenikia, Lydia, and Phrygia, their armies closed in around Elládos until her land became the last bastion of freedom against an empire poised to claim all Gaia.

Such were her thoughts, the day the emissaries arrived in Athenai.

"They ask each polis to offer token tribute and thus be spared," a senator chimed in. The full Senate, all hundred and twenty of them, had gathered at what had once been the royal palace of Athenai. Her city had long since cast out its kings, ending the royal bloodline that had flowed from her, through Pandion, and all the way down to Theseus, the last of the great kings. Before today, Athene had not walked these halls in over a century, and even now, the Senate seemed to tolerate her presence more than welcome it.

By her side, General Themistokles huffed, shaking his head. "A token tribute now, yes. But once we bend the knee, they are free to decide on any *annual* tribute that pleases the god-king. More, we shall no longer rule our own destinies. Are Elládosi boys to answer the calls of Babilimian kings, to fight foreign wars rather than take up arms in defence of their own homes? Are we to surrender, forever, an autonomy we have held since the days of Kronos himself?"

The general was a populist, well loved by the common folk, though the aristoi loathed the man, who laid claim to no genos at all and seemed to care more for the concerns of the public than its rulers. Athenian democracy, Athene had observed since her return, was structured to give a voice to all citizens—but the voices of the poor counted as much as the noise of buzzing insects to be shooed away at leisure. The facsimile of fairness served to keep the populace complacent, unaware they had traded one king for a hundred and remained no better off than they had been before.

Themistokles spoke the truth, and even the self-interested senators could well see it. They loved naught more than their own wealth and power, and if they bowed before a foreign emperor, it would mean surrendering those things.

"You will turn their emissaries away," Athene stated rather than asked, for the mood was plain and she'd needed to do naught at all to convince these people not to cave.

"Goddess," Themistokles said with a respectful incline of his head. "I rather think it best if *you* are the one to spurn their emissary. Let them see the gods of Elládos stand at our sides. Let them know we are cut from altogether different cloths than the weaklings of Phoenikia or Lydia, so quick to bow in fear."

So it was that Athene found herself heading toward the harbour, to meet the emissary, and stilling her face to impassiveness on seeing

Artemis there. In some ways, it was a relief to see the woman again, after centuries apart. But there could be no further love between them now, after the Ilian War.

"Artemis ..." she said and found, despite having envisioned seeing her again so many times over the years, she had no real words to say. No way to reach out with the rivers of ichor and blood that separated them.

Artemis glowered. "Some memories have a taste so bitter they cut through the haze of our unending lives, remaining forever acrid, churning our guts."

Because, of course, Artemis dwelt on the same pains which Athene could not shake. "Apollon fell in war, the same as my brother."

"Yes, but it was your side who slew the both of them, so you can hardly call us even."

Damn her. No one had asked her to betray Olympus! Athene wanted to scream the accusation at Artemis, but then, Father had slain her beloved child. How could Artemis have reacted any other way? "Ares fought for Ilium because you enticed him into your wretched war."

"He fought for Ilium because your deranged father threw him off a mountain for imagined disloyalty! Nyx's dark bosom, Athene! What would it take for you to open your eyes and behold Zeus as the blight on this world he truly is? How can you, for centuries, live alongside a festering cancer and not smell the rot? Are you inured to the stench, having known it all your life?"

Athene glowered. She had known peace would prove impossible here. "You speak as though a self-proclaimed god-king who would rule all the Earth, by the sword if need be, is somehow more worthy. Somehow less a tyrant than the kings of your own homeland."

"I am Lydian," Artemis spat. "And I do not come to treat with you, but rather with the Senate."

But even had Themistokles agreed to come himself, the answer would have remained the same. The general was right, Athene needed to do this, though not for the sake of the Babilimians, but for the Athenians themselves. They needed to know they faced these foes with Titans at their backs. "They appointed me to speak on their behalf and deliver the simplest message, Artemis. Athenians will never bow before the Babilimian Empire. Elládos will not cave. If you would have peace, turn your ships back to Kumari Kandam. Flee across the Thalassa Sea and never think to encroach a single pace further than you have in claiming Kolchis. Fail to heed this warning, and you will face foes more dire than all of those you have fought thus far on behalf of Mithra *combined*."

"You think your cause righteous, but your vaunted father is but a puppet to one who pulls his strings from the shadows."

What? Athene gaped. "What nonsense do you spout now?"

"The Gnostic Cabal has *infected* the Olympian Order, and you do not even realise you are no longer masters of your own actions." The woman paused a moment. "In the end, your father will cast your life aside as a mere token and never once grieve for your death. At best, it will serve as a pretence for venting his petty rage."

She had heard enough. "Return to your ship. You have no welcome here or on any shore of Elládos. And if I see you again—"

"The next time you see me, it shall be with my blade at your throat."

INTERLUDE: ODYSSEUS

1 Dark Age

*I*n the end, the shining city of Ilium was reduced to an empty shell, its walls the decaying bones of a once mighty behemoth. Where ten years of war had failed to crack the polis, trickery had undone them in a single night of bloodshed and pillaging. Ilium's people were slaughtered or enslaved, its citadel left a smouldering ruin, its line, so far as I know, ended to the last man. King Priam was murdered within the illusory sanctuary offered by a temple to the Olympians. His wife, Hekuba, given to me as a slave, I released that she might claim her vengeance against treacherous Polymestor, a Trojan ally who betrayed them to us.

Laden with plunder and slaves, we sailed from the accursed shores that had stolen a decade of our lives, hoping never again to lay eyes upon Phrygia. With three ships under my command, I made for Ithaka, tracking the coast of Phlegra, knowing we raced the coming of winter storms upon the sea. Still, when we came upon the town of Ismarus, my companions and I—flush with bounty and drunk as much on carnage as wine—saw a chance for yet more rapine. We thought we should return home to our otherwise impoverished isle as rich men. I admit, I fancied myself now a king whose name ought to be mentioned among the great of Elládos. I saw, in my fevered daydreams, Ithaka rising to the heights of Athenai or Korinth or Mykenai, and I could not shake such visions from my mind.

Would that we had landed as friends. Would that we had made so many choices differently, unvarnished by the lustre of hubris that blinded our eyes with its brilliant glare.

But alas, we sacked Ismarus, and there, despite my advice, my men set into revels, sating their numerous desires with the town's stores and its women. Intoxicated and thinking themselves invincible—*we* who had brought low impenetrable Troy, after all!—they did not see when the Ismarian men returned with allies from the highlands. My men did not note their presence until the arrows began to rain down amid them. Asleep on my ship, I awakened to the sound of fresh screams, though I'd thought the slaughter over and done. I leapt onto the gangplank and raced through town streets still tinged with an evil reddish gleam from smouldering houses and burnt-out shops.

There, amid that vile place, I saw my men, shafts quivering from their backs. One unhappy fool, a shepherd from the north, had taken an arrow to the crotch. Another man had his head staved in by a gang that had set upon him with clubs. As I watched, aghast, a sailor from the rocky lowlands was caught shoving silver jewellery in a sack and got his hands hacked off for his trouble. I shot his attacker with my bow, but I doubt there was any saving the hapless sailor. I shouted for a frenzied retreat, and I tell you without shame I was the first back upon the ships. It would be a lie to claim I did not, later, lambaste the crew for their arrogance. Not that any of my fervent castigations would restore to us the score of men we'd lost across our ships.

Had we made sail that afternoon, we may have made it to some safe haven, some sheltered bay. Sailing at night, we scarce realised the storm was incoming until it was already tossing us one way and the next. A roil of black clouds obscured the stars, making navigation impossible. Wrapt in darkness, we had no choice save to furl sails already tattered by punishing winds, and to pray, as the waves heaved us about. We prayed to Poseidon that he not capsize us nor fling us onto a coastline we could not make out. So tossed about were we, we no longer knew which way was land.

For days and nights the storms raged as if we had offended Zeus himself or some other fearful deity. I saw war-hardened men whimper and sob in terror. Others I heard claim we had brought some curse upon ourselves. I tried to convince them that, in the face of such furious winds, our survival thus far was a sign of divine favour rather than anger. But as we were hurled further and further from known waters, my words rang hollow.

ಠ

TEN DAYS after leaving the shores of Ilium, we came upon an unknown shore. Though you might think us fools for it, we were so flush with relief at escaping Poseidon's fury we cast ourselves to the sand and rubbed our faces in the dirt, revelling in the luxurious feel of solid ground once more beneath us. If you have never been lost at sea, never wondered if you would ever again look upon the wonder of Gaia's back, you can scarce imagine what it feels like to find reprieve thus.

Had I the oxen, I'd have sacrificed a hecatomb to Zeus or Poseidon or whichever god had seen us to land once more. Or that was how I felt at the time. In hindsight, I'm not certain I'd have offered much praise for whatever mercurial deity cast us upon that isle, of all the myriad land-falls that dot the Thalassa.

Whilst fatigue forced us to linger on the shore for a time, hunger soon roused us, so I sent my men scouting the hills and light woods, hoping for forage or game amid the yew and cypress trees. At that point, not a man among us would have turned down roots or even grubs, should someone have dug them up.

Such thoughts were running through my head as I oversaw the remaining crew's faltering efforts to repair our damaged ships. Our yards had cracked, our sails torn, we'd lost more than one oar between the three ships, and two men had gone overboard, dragged down into the deep. All in all, we looked more like beaten and limping dogs put in our places by the pack leader rather than victors returning home laden with plunder.

So when Eurylochos—my brother-in-law and second-in-command—returned with smiling locals bearing trays of strange fruit, myself and those close by surged over the newcomers with ravenous hunger of starving beasts. Succulent sweetness overlaid a hint of citric bitterness in those amber-coloured fruits, and I cannot even say how many I devoured. I recall tearing away the leafy skin and gnawing at pulpy flesh, the revivifying juices dribbling down my throat, a salvation that brought tears to my eyes.

I am not certain how much time passed. Later, Alkimos, a friend of Eurylochos, claimed we had passed all day, all night, and the next morn doing naught save eating and lounging amid the hills. To this day, I cannot say whether he had jest with us—I thought only a few hours had passed—though others amid the crew confirmed his strange tale. Alkimos was among those who grabbed us and dragged us back to the ship.

Later, the crew claimed we wept like scolded toddlers begging for another taste. That, though in the grips of languorous bliss, we struggled against them when they forced us aboard. One man among us tried to leap the side ... Oh, I shan't name him for fear of his dishonour. Ahem. Yes, but someone sought after the fruit with such desire he thought to test Poseidon's waves if it meant another taste, even though our damaged and bedraggled ships had already gone underway.

I, of course, recovered once given a draught of wine, and guided our ships away from the hateful island that would have stolen our lives ...

I wish I could say we charted the stars and made our way swiftly home, but we knew not where we were, and vessels remained damaged. We needed find safe harbour to make repairs and take on supplies, and we needed it soon. Thus, we weighed anchor at the next island we found, a wooded isle in a bay. There were pine and cypress trees, needful for the repairs, though no oak for patching the outer hull, more was the pity. Still, we found mountain goats with little fear of Man, having—so far as I know—never before laid eyes on hunters. Given that we had three ships of starving men, I imagine, if goats can tell tales, the survivors will spin yarns for generations to come of the fearful savages that came plundering across their shores.

We ate well that night, believe me, and slept even better, as if we had been feasted at some grand symposium. In the morn, I walked the shore and found green meadows and rich soil, such that the isle would have made a prime habitat for any who wished to build a polis. Fresh water tumbled down over the rocks and formed gentle streams through the lowlands. I could not understand why no one had settled yet upon such a rare find. It had me wondering if the storms had thrown us so far from civilised lands that Mankind had never happened upon these shores in the Ages since the Time of Nyx. As I walked the circumference of our little haven, across the bay I spied a larger island we could reach with small boats.

It would take days to make the repairs to our ships, and I was of a mind to explore, having spent more than enough time at sea as it was. Thus I gathered twelve men with me, and we rowed for that far island.

Curiosity, while perhaps a virtue, can carry with it a hefty price.

So we landed upon the opposite isle, which, in days to come, I learnt was named Telepylus, an island nestled betwixt Phoenikia and Neshia. As the currents do not flow there, it has remained blessedly isolated and thus little known among Men. Or perhaps it is rather the case that few Men who walked upon it ever returned to speak of those who dwelt upon the foreign shores.

"This place bursts with greenery," Eurylochos said as our small vessel drew nigh upon the beach. My brother-in-law pointed at the overgrown woodlands, where, inexplicably, grapevines dangled, rich with succulent treasures.

Of course, the men raced to pluck the grapes from the vine, and I admit, I may have popped a handful in my mouth as well, revelling in the explosion of juices in my mouth and the taste of something so fresh. I was no longer starving—not after the bounty of the goats last night— but fresh fruit was rare during our years beneath Ilium's walls, and I rather imagine none who languished there will ever tire of them again.

While thus indulging, I spied an oddity upon the rocky highlands. Standing stones many times the height of a Man were wedged in the earth, creating a frame or fence against a side of the mountain. As I peered, I spotted movement within the fence, though I could not, from the distance, make out the type of beast. "Some manner of livestock," I said, grape juice dribbling down my chin.

"Can't pass that," Alkimos commented. There was a gleam in his eye, no doubt reflected in my own. For a good herd of cattle might be worth as much or more than a pile of jewels or gold. If we sailed from here with stolen livestock, our people would herald us as heroes all the more, and our homes would prosper. Oh, in hindsight, it was as foolish a risk as any we have taken, yes, but then, who were we but desperate fools, seeking a way to change our fortunes?

So we scaled toward the highlands, though the slopes were rugged and blanketed in loose scree, slowing our progress. By the time we crested the rise, the afternoon had waned, it would have been difficult to return to our ship before nightfall. This was a distant worry, however, for within the fence of stone I found a flock of sheep, each beast half again as large as any I'd ever laid eyes upon. Already, my mind was awhirl with the practicalities of getting such creatures down to the shore and ferrying them on our ships. If we could bring them home, with a few rams to breed them, Ithaka could have become famed for our wools, and the life of every farmer in our kingdom could have been filled with plenty.

It was Eurylochos who grabbed my wrist and spun me, forcing me to look upon the mountain that hemmed in the flock. A wide cave mouth opened there, decorated with glossy bay laurels that created a pleasant, welcoming invitation, or so the men chose to take it when they began to venture within. If we found the occupant home, I intended to ply him with Ismarian wine and plunder, and trade for his sheep. If not, well, then, he'd left the animals alone and therefore had no right to complain over what might befall them. Such are the comforting lies we tell ourselves to ensure we feel justified in doing whatever suits us. Men prefer not to think themselves villains or scoundrels, but they cannot escape the basic truth that an abundance of wealth always comes at someone else's expense.

Within the cave, the smell of roasting meat dominated, masking all other scents. Rimming the walls, we found enormous shelves laden with cheeses, salted mutton, and various gathered fruits and vegetables. Too, there were bones cast hither and thither about the cave as though its occupant were a great sloven. Animal skins and furs created makeshift carpets strewn around this strange hall, most gathered around a fire pit. Over the fire pit hung a great bronze cauldron, its contents simmering over a dwindling flame, the source of the strong smells.

Antilochus, one of my companions, dipped the ladle in pot and drew forth a sample, then grunted on tasting it. "Chicken stew, I think."

Which meant we would sup well this eve, I imagined, and thus began to stoke the fire with some wood the owner of this place had gathered.

"Odysseus ..." Eurylochos warned. "Let us be gone from here. Take the cheeses, drive the sheep ahead, and flee while daylight remains."

"We'd have to sleep in the wood," Antilochus protested.

"Besides," I added, eager to earn whoever lived in this place as a trading partner, "if we steal the bounty, it behooves us but once." On first seeing the penned animals, I thought to flee with as many of them as I could manage. But somehow, entering the owner's home had me imagining coming again and again to these shores and growing ever richer in the process. "Imagine Ithakans as the only sailors in the Thalassa who know of this place and its riches."

So the men sat, they nibbled at a block of cheese or helped themselves to the stew, and we waited.

At least until, around dusk, we heard a tremendous crash outside the cave as if a score of trees had toppled over all at once. My stomach dropped out from under me, a sudden fierce dread arising, as I realised I might have made a severe mistake in lingering here. Ever did my dreams of wealth for my island lead me astray. The crash had my men up and scrambling for cover, hiding in the fringes of the cave, crouching behind shelves or amid piles of bones, and I raced to join them.

Not a moment too soon, either, for the owner of this place tromped in, and it was no Man, but rather a Gígas, some ten feet tall. The crash outside, I could see now, had come from him dropping a bundle of kindling big enough to feed his fire for a good many days. As the creature entered, I saw it had but a single, overlarge eye in the middle of its head, marking it as a monster out of legend: a Cyclops. From the way its brow drew together, something had vexed the creature, and I suspected it knew intruders had violated its home.

From my hiding place, I watched as the brute rolled a boulder in front of the entrance to its cave, trapping us all inside. The last rays of light from the setting sun seeped in over the rock's recesses, taunting us with the escape we all knew we ought to have made long afore now.

With a huff, the Cyclops dropped to one knee and began scanning the depths of the cave. That frightful gaze passed over me once, then returned fixing on the place where I crouched in the shadows with several others. I felt it as the others pressed their backs against the cavern wall as if they could melt through the stone and disappear altogether. I knew what they were doing, for had they not been between myself and the wall, I imagine I'd have done the same.

"Who are you?" the Cyclops bellowed in Phoenikian, his deep voice resounding like an echoing gong through his home. "Have you come to Telepylus to pillage?"

His accusation was not far from the mark, I fear. Nevertheless, I was hardly going to admit as much to him, least of all whilst trapped behind the boulder. "We are sailors out of Ionia, lost on our way returning from the war against Ilium. We seek your friendship and trade, only!"

A dark chortle escaped the Cyclops. I shall never forget the malice inside that hateful sound. "Elládosi!" The creature spat the name as though an insult, slowly rising as he did so. "Think you we have forgotten the betrayal of your gods?" He had begun to speak our language now. The Cyclops thumped his chest. "My ancestors fought for Zeus in his war among Titans, and our service was rewarded with scorn and exile! Now they name us Laestrygonians, and we live here removed from your hateful politics. And still you come, defile our refuge."

"We meant no—" I began.

The Cyclops snarled, surging to his feet and pointing to the cauldron. "These hapless Sea People I granted a merciful end. But *you*, followers of Zeus, I shall enjoy slaying." It took me a moment to apprehend his meaning and why he had addressed us first in Phoenikian. Pirates from that land, the Sea People, they must have come here on occasion. And the Cyclops had slain, cooked, and *eaten* them. It was not chicken left simmering in the cauldron. My own sailors, some of them had ... tasted the flesh of Man.

"If you would be spared, earn my favour," the creature demanded. "Where have you moored your ship?"

I swallowed, striving—and failing—to keep from trembling. "Smashed to pieces upon the rocks," I lied, knowing he would send others of his kind to slay every sailor who'd had the misfortune of accompanying me. "Only these men and I survive the whims of Poseidon."

The monster made no answer save to lunge forward. With enormous hands he seized the ankles of two men, jerked them aloft, and slammed them into one another with such force as to shatter bone. Blood and brain splattered the cavern, droplets raining over my sandals. My hand went to my sword, but how was I to fight this thing? Cyclopes were, so far as I knew, of the same stuff as gods themselves—Titans.

One of my men, emboldened by grief or driven mad by terror, raced in with a spear. With a single backhanded slap, the Cyclops crushed his head. He once more took up the fallen men at the ankles and, after dragging them over, tossed the both of them into the cauldron.

My stomach lurched. Someone behind me retched. The Cyclops chuckled. "Perhaps I ought to thank you Elládosi for stocking my larder. What, a dozen of you? Eh ... that much bounty needs be shared among my kin, I suppose." He licked his lips but stalked over to where the boulder blocked our means of egress. He was going to open it. He was going out to find others of his blighted kind.

I knew I needed to rush him, needed to chance it now, for if he sealed us in once more, we could never move such a rock. Not with all of us combined could we so much as nudge the thing. Terror, stark and white and bowel loosening, threatened to freeze my feet in place. Not in all the years of war had I ever felt so helpless, so horrified as I did that night. I cannot say how I managed to draw my blade, but it was in my hand, and I was running for the Gígas.

Alkimos got there before me, his war cry ringing out as he lunged. The Cyclops's foot caught him in the chest with a sickening crunch, and his body hurtled into mine, sending me flying backward. Next I knew, Eurylochos was weeping over his friend's corpse, and I was lying on my back. The only light now came from the cook fire. I should say the fire by which my companions were being cooked.

"We are trapped," Antilochus explained, in case the boulder blocking the entrance had not made it plain enough. There is, I have found, always one among any group who feels the need to sum up the situation for anyone else who happened to have the brains of a tadpole.

I strained to sit, my whole body a mass of pain. I suppose I was lucky

I had broken no bones—or my damn neck—in the impact, but at that moment, I hardly felt favoured by the Moirai. Someone in some corner was weeping. No one ever confessed to it, so I never learnt who; someone, perhaps, with the courage to admit the despair that had seized us all.

"A shout went up outside," Antilochus said then, this information slightly more useful than his previous statement. "Mostlike, these Laestrygonians rally to search for our ships."

I rubbed my bruised sternum and shook my head. "We've no way to warn our friends unless one of you manages to get free of this cave." Rather than dwell on the situation, I forced myself to gain my—unsteady —feet. "Try to move the rock."

It was futile, of course. There were nine of us left, and even by our combined strength, I knew we had as much chance of moving the boulder as we did of pushing over the mountain itself. Still, to try and fail was better than to sit and wait for the Cyclops to return and devour us.

As we set to it, before even I gave the command to shove, the rock creaked, straining in position.

The brute had returned already! We scrambled back, hands to our weapons, resolved by tacit accord to die as men with such valour as we could still muster in these straits. It is not much, but sometimes futile defiance is all a man has left.

"Odysseus?" a woman called, her voice carried in through the crack above the boulder.

My heart surged at the welcome sound. Had Athene heard our prayers? Had she come to rescue us? "In here, Goddess!" I cried, my voice breaking with hope.

"Then gather all among you and push with all you have!" the woman cried, and now, listening closer, I was no longer certain that matched Athene's voice. I had spent countless hours in her company outside Ilium, and she had enthralled us time and again with tales of old, though many seemed to pain her to tell, as if she bore secret grief for every demigod and hero who was now gone.

Regardless, I followed the woman's orders, and my men and I set to, heaving for our freedom. The goddess pushed from outside, and slowly, the boulder creaked aside until a gap opened wide enough for a woman to slip through. I was first out of the breach, but cautious, hand upon the hilt of my xiphos, for I knew not who had come to our rescue. It was a raven-haired Heliad I had not before laid eyes upon.

"That's not Athene," Antilochus observed as he emerged, once more serving to clear things up for the imbeciles among us. Which may have only included Antilochus himself.

"I'm Nike," the Heliad said. "And we must hurry. The Laestrygonians hurl boulders upon your ships even as we speak."

We needed no further prodding to quit that awful place, and we followed Nike down the slope as she skilfully led us along a path we could descend behind the Laestrygonian village. We kept silent, though I doubt the Cyclopes would have heard us over the clamour they created. I could not see well in the dark, but well enough to tell they indeed assailed our friends across the bay.

I did not know why the Goddess of Victory had come to us. Had Athene sent her? Had she her own reasons to save our unhappy lot? Either way, she guided us not to the boat we had come on but to a smaller vessel she must have sailed here. We had to skirt Telepylus to reach the one my crew had moored at.

By the time we reached the ships, two were breached and sinking, and one had taken a hit to its already battered hull before it drew far enough out to sea to avoid the hurled missiles. We rejoined our comrades, sombre and speechless, as we rowed from there, having lost two thirds of our number in the process.

For the first time, I think every man still among us began to doubt whether we would ever again reach home.

IT WAS NOT until morn broke—though I'd not even tried to sleep that night, distraught as I was—that I spoke with Nike. Our mast remained damaged and though we'd put Telepylus behind us, we could not make it so far on oars alone. "I begin to think us all cursed by some vengeful god," I said when she joined me on the deck. "In the space of days we have encountered freak storms, strange natives trying to entrance us with magic fruit, and cannibal giants out of legends of old."

Nike had a far-off look upon her face, but I did not know her well enough to judge what might so weigh upon the Titan. She pursed her lips a moment before she answered. "There is a sorceress I know, on an island not so far from here, known as Aiaíā. If some curse does prevent you from reaching friendly shores, she might identify it and tell you how to be free of it. Either way, it does not seem like you make it far from here."

So, to Aiaíā we made sail.

PART II

Of the denizens of the Spirit Realm, we can know somewhat more. These beings freely enter the Spectral Realm and from there enact subtle but undeniable influence upon our Mortal Realm. Moreover, these are those that we most often evoke or bind for sorcery. They are known, and from discourse and interaction, we may surmise some few things. Firstly, that they hold no love for mortals, least of all sorcerers who try to enforce their will upon eidolons. Secondly, that—and perhaps as a corollary to the first—many or even most of these spirits appear to have been mortal at some point. Does their resentment thus emerge from anguish over what they have lost?

— First Chronicle of the Circle of Goetic Mysteries

6

ATHENE

399 Dark Age

The leaders of the free cities of Elládos gathered in a camp outside Athenai, arguing over troop placements and the intel provided by scouts who had chanced the enemy in Phlegra. "If they pass the Olympian mountains," Leonidas, king of Sparta, said, "they spill into the mainland, and we can never hope to contain them. Not in such numbers as the Babilimians are said to field against us. They will trample every polis like marauding chimeras, and we shall spend the next generation hunting for them."

"And your plan," Demophilus, an exiled king of Phlegra interjected, "is suicide."

Leonidas snorted, shaking his head. "We do not fear death." Indeed, and Athene had heard that when the emissaries demanded the Spartans lay down their arms, Leonidas had answered, "Come and get them." Now the king smirked. "Besides, it is not my plan but that of the vaunted Athenian general. Surely you don't imply Themistokles would send Spartan men to needless deaths."

A few men chuckled at that, but Themistokles glowered. "Considering the failure of either front may mean the loss of all Elládos, I fail to see the least humour in the situation."

Leonidas winked. "A common Athenian failing. Hardly the greatest of them."

Athene frowned. The plan had required the people to evacuate Athenai and the Athenians had misliked it, some of the aristoi going so far as to refuse to leave their manses. Whether they remained determined to die for their homes or imagined Themistokles so invincible he would save them even after the general had admitted they had not the forces for it, Athene did not know. Themistokles believed the key to stopping the Babilimian advance lay in jamming up their army at Thermopylae and holding them until the snows, whilst as the same time blocking the advance of the enemy navy along the Straits of Korinth. To that end, Themistokles himself would lead the Athenian navy from the island of Salamis, whilst Leonidas would take charge of the overland defence of the coastal plain of Thermopylae.

It was a good plan, Athene thought, having consulted with Themistokles about it in private before he informed the others. It was, she imagined, the best they could hope for given the overwhelming numbers of foes they faced. As the kings broke from their council, Athene slipped out of the tent and strolled the grounds. Many of the men she passed would be dead in a matter of days, she knew. But what alternative lay before them? Surrender before the might of Babilim? Even if she turned her back on them, still the proud Elládosi would choose death over servitude.

A shadow passed before the clouds, and Athene squinted, raising a hand to her brow against the sun. A pegasus flew there, closing in on their camp. Had Father come after all? Zeus had claimed he could not risk himself, that such was just what the Unseen Order would have wanted. He had sent word for Poseidon to aid the navy, but who knew if Athene's uncle would receive the message, much less answer. Pontus had their own troubles beneath the waves. Hebe remained on Atlantis, guarding the source of the Ambrosia, and Athene found herself with few Titan allies left.

Though she had resisted, Zeus had commanded Hestia to join the fight, and thus the woman had agreed to go with Leonidas, whilst Athene accompanied the navy to Salamis. Athene found herself wondering just how powerful Hestia's Art of Fire would truly prove. Could it help the Spartan king hold the line against the impossible odds arrayed before him? For hold he must, or all would be lost.

The pegasus landed beyond the camp, and as Athene drew nigh, she realised it was not her father who had ridden to meet her but her stepmother. Before even reaching Hera, already a frown was creasing Athene's brow, her thoughts churning. Only once in Athene's entire life had Hera come to a battlefront, and only because the battlefront of the Gigantomachy had been her very doorstep. The woman, so far as Athene knew, had no martial skills to speak of. Though Hera's Titan prowess meant she might well overpower a single mortal, perhaps even a few mortals at once, raw strength did not substitute for training. Which meant the woman would prove more hindrance than boon on the front lines.

"What are you doing here?" Athene demanded. Propriety compelled her to show her stepmother more respect, but Athene had neither the time nor the patience at the moment. Any time now, the call would come to board the ships and sail for Salamis. They needed to be in position before the Babilimian navy arrived if they were to maximise their odds of success. Hera's voice had risen alongside Father's own in claiming Zeus could not join the fray. Never mind that his lightning might annihilate whole phalanxes of enemies in a heartbeat or send smouldering wrecks of ships down to Poseidon. Neither king nor queen had wanted to hear her reminders that Zeus had changed the course of the Titanomachy and the Gigantomachy with his power. No, Father would not fight his own war, not now. As with Ilium, he would watch, from the safety of Olympus, through the distant medium of the Seeing Pools.

Was Hera's sudden concern for her husband's safety because she believed he could and must save them all from the Unseen Order?

"There is no substitute for firsthand knowledge of the plans." She meant, Athene assumed, Father wanted more details than he could glean from the Oracle Mirrors. "Battle will soon be joined."

"It will," Athene agreed. "And I cannot guarantee your safety should you remain here. The Babilimians have numerous fleets, and we cannot stop every single ship from making landfall. This place may become a battleground in a matter of hours."

Hera hesitated, though it didn't seem fear for her own life that stalled her, so far as Athene could gauge. "The Unseen Order has a most perilous assassin at their disposal. Eyes gleaming with cerulean luminousness, face concealed beneath a helm of aureate plates, she comes to their aid. They call her Nemesis."

Athene glanced over her shoulder. Already, Themistokles was waving her toward him, beckoning for her to join the ships. "Fine. If I see a golden-armoured woman, I shall be wary."

"You must kill her!" Hera blurted. "She is Enki's greatest weapon! Deprive the Order of their high assassin, and they have only their lesser shadows to use against us."

"Who? What?" Athene raised a hand to forestall Themistokles. "Who is Enki and what has he or she to do with any of this? Stepmother, I've no time for these things. If I see this Nemesis, yes, I'll slay her. But my mission this day is not hunting single foes but stopping the invasion of our home."

Hera's face quivered, limned with fear. For a blink, the woman seemed to be someone else. Fatigue and anticipation of the coming battle must have strained Athene. "Mark my words, Child," Hera snapped. "Underestimate the influence of Nemesis at your own peril. We have never uncovered her identity, but we do know her as the greatest weapon of the Order and of the Moirai themselves."

"Fine," Athene said, waving the claim away. "Fine."

She had no time, and if she delayed even a moment more, she risked the ships leaving without her. Not sparing her stepmother another thought, Athene broke into a run, racing for the shore, hoping she would not be too late.

7

———

ENODIA

730 Bronze Age

A gibbering mass of pustules and toothy maws formed the walls of the maze through which Enodia and Keuthos wandered. Sporadic, seemingly bottomless pits dropped out through the floor, the sounds of mastication and groans of agony carried up on foul-smelling winds. The ghuls trailing in the wake of the two wraiths had become subdued, drawn into themselves after witnessing the profane sarcous expanse through which they all passed whilst searching out a route to the Spirit Realm. The Roil, outside the bastions tethered to necropoleis and held together by the wills of godlike ghost kings, represented the purest manifestation of Khaos in all the cosmos.

This place that Man called the Underworld unfolded in infinite, untrammelled horror, the merest glimpse of which might unravel the mind of priest or common man alike. And shrouded, careful to steer clear of grasping appendages protruding from fleshy walls, Enodia had no choice save to pass this way. This Realm, this Khaos, *was* the Dark into which Enodia had so long peered for answers to the deep questions.

And now, dead and damned, she at last grasped more than paltry threads of those answers.

All the cosmos, she felt, must have spawned from this Dark, and to the Dark it would return unless she found a way to stave off the future. Such was what her father had beheld in ancient days and, having borne witness to the abhorrent final fate, he had crafted his bitter cycle to forestall it. But Enodia would do more than delay the inevitable. If Man emerged from the Dark, then it was the Dark she would master and let the demons come to kneel before *her* throne.

"You are lost ..." Keuthos rasped. "Wallowing in musings deep as the pits riving this place ..."

Enodia hissed in agreement, for Keuthos knew her all too well. He knew her better than all others, and still, she did not confide in him the sum of all plans. For to voice them felt akin to revealing them to the hateful overlords of the World, these Archons, as the Elder Gods named themselves. Better, for now, that she pass unnoticed beneath their gazes than draw their ire.

"There are depths that weigh upon me," she admitted. "Dread vaster even than what this place ignites." She cast a glance at the shambling legion of ghuls trailing them. Always, Enodia had possessed a necromantic affinity for the dead, but now they were her people, more than ever. Of a sudden, several of the revenants lifted their heads, exposing gleaming red eyes. At first she thought they noticed her regard, but no ... No, something had distressed them. There was a susurration running through the air, beyond the lamentations of the damned that rose from the pits. "Be on guard ..."

Keuthos nodded and pushed out ahead, scouting the way. They came to an aperture within the fleshy walls, one that opened and constricted in rhythmic pulses, offering egress into what appeared a field of obsidian shards. Across those fields echoed the sounds of distant, repeated crashes, as of a battle fought far away. Enodia and Keuthos exchanged a glance, then Keuthos slipped through the opening and out into the field. Enodia followed, taking in the plain before her. She might have described it as rolling hills, save the hills bore jagged edges of razor-sharp obsidian, like a fractalised nightmare, glinting beneath iridescent lightning that flashed in the stormy sky.

Assuming they had come the right way, there should be some means of crossing from the Roil into the Rimefells not far from here. Oh ... that crashing sound might well be the blades in the river Gjöll, surging beneath the churning waters that separated this Realm from the Spirit Realm. "Follow the clamour ..." she commanded her ghuls, who had begun to filter through the aperture with some reluctance.

She did not begrudge them their dread here. This was deeper into the Roil than most ghosts dared wander, and fear was the perennial companion of all the dead, regardless. Predators worse than revenants—worse even than wraiths—might well lurk in these unexplored shadows. Entities ready to feast upon souls could dwell in the tumultuous sky or slumber beneath the obsidian shards, waiting for something to wake them. These hollow places were not as empty as one might wish.

"There's a bridge, somewhere," she said.

By tacit accord, her party fanned out, scrambling over the obsidian crystals to gain higher vantage points and seek for the way forward. Keuthos, too, drifted from her side in search of the bridge of which spirits had spoken. Sometimes, she had heard, the dead were called here, summoned by the lampads to their Winter Court. Enodia need but find the route they took.

She scaled a crystal-like hill, peering around, then faltered as a tremendous burst of thunder ripped through the storm. Slowly, dreading what she would behold, Enodia craned her neck skyward. There, within the roiling clouds of ash and darkness, a parting. As clouds separated, a foot descended. Bereft of skin and oozing streams of blood, that bony foot stepped as if appearing from the clouds, down, *down.*

Impossible.

Though her oneiromantic dreams had never revealed aught past her death, still, the moment held within it the tinge of prescient fulfilment. For Aeshma had shown her this would come, sooner or later, as inevitable as the changing of the tides. A rain of blood washed over the obsidian plain before that foot crashed down. The demon's weight splintered stone and sent tremors shooting through the field, driving several ghuls to their knees. Even Enodia slipped, catching herself with one skeletal hand. Razor edges gouged the bones in her palm, but she barely noticed.

She had seen this all before, in visions sent to torment her mind since the day she had dared to rely upon demonomancy and invoke the

Old One, this hateful spawn of a Primordial. A shrivelled abdomen. A flayed chest. The demon stood hundreds of feet tall, dragging behind it that awful mace that, like the demon itself, wept continuous tears of blood.

"Run!" Enodia shrieked, at last finding her voice.

Above it all, atop this gargantuan abomination, was that perverse skull, all jutting horns behind which bloomed that incandescent light she knew only too well from her nightmares. The demon hefted the mace, and blood poured from it in a sanguine shower.

A single sweep took a too-slow ghul and the ghost vanished, pulverised by the blow.

Enodia was already scrambling, running toward the sound of crashing blades. The river! The river must have a crossing, a pass through which the Old One could not fit.

The abomination's plodding steps turned the ground tremulous, sending wave-like ripples through the obsidian field. Again and again, Enodia stumbled, twice pitching onto the heaving landscape. Razor-edged shards sliced her hands and further tattered the shroud wrapt around her desiccated form. Then, half crawling, half running, she was up again.

A desperate scramble. Cyclopean dread welled. The darkness swelled too deep for Aeshma's shadow to loom over her, but still, she felt the demon's presence, towering and unstoppable.

Shrieks and splatters sounded behind her as Aeshma tore through her small army of ghuls like a vicious child hurling aside his toys. But the clangour of the Gjöll River grew louder, and soon she saw the mist rising from it. Though obscured by brume and darkness, the glint of a golden roof in the distance caught her eye, and Enodia dashed for it.

"Keuthos!" she shouted, hoping her friend was still here. Somewhere. She dared not spare a glance over her shoulder, dared not look back and see the closing form of the horror that had come for her soul at last.

Golden thatch roofed a massive bridge spanning the river of knives, the bridge's peak rising nigh to sixty feet in the air. The ground heaved again. Massive footfalls growing closer. Relying on every drop of Pneuma she could muster, Enodia raced toward the shelter offered by the structure. Her feet slapped upon the wooden planks, not slowing for an instant. Massive windows created a lattice of pale light streaming down from the astral sky outside and as she raced past each beam, Enodia's dread quickened, imagining Aeshma's skinless hand dipping through a window to snatch her.

Then the bridge shuddered, sending her spilling to the ground. On her knees, she turned and beheld the absolute horror coming for her. Aeshma had dropped to hands and knees and was crawling along the space of the bridge. The osseous maze of its misshapen head was all she could see: that lurid, incandescent gleam sprouting from between its myriad horns. Flayed limbs dragged the demon toward her, and for a moment that stretched far too long, Enodia could only gawp. She had never imagined it would pursue her across the bridge and into the Rimefells.

Aeshma's mind-wracking cry was something between hiss and groan as the demon squeezed in after her.

COME, PYRRHA ... REPAY THAT WHICH WAS PROMISED ...

The words echoed through her skull and yet served to draw her from her stupor. She gained her feet and burst into another run, trying to block out the sound of the shrieking, enraged demon behind her.

Ahead, a wailing wind beckoned her forward. The mist grew thicker, swirling as if possessed of awful life and will. It formed up in foul invitation, calling her inward. It brushed over her necrotic flesh like a silken curtain, having far too much substance. Then she burst out from the bridge onto a frozen shore filled with twisted, leafless trees bent as though in agony.

This was it.

This was the Rimefells. She had passed into the Spirit Realm.

A hand fell upon her shoulder and Hekate hissed, spinning, claws raised to tear into whatever accosted her. But it was Keuthos, the wraith's shroud billowing in the icy winds of this place.

"We cannot linger here ..."

Oh, that went without saying. Enodia cast a fearful glance back at the golden bridge. Would Aeshma crawl the full distance to reach her? Could the Old One cross into this Realm? She did not want to wait to find out and had little hope any of the ghuls they had brought with them had survived its wrath. "Where do we find the Winter Court?"

Keuthos turned, looking back to the river. "Skirt the banks ... Pass

through this Corpsewood ... The city lies upon the peninsula beyond ...
nestled betwixt the nether river and the Moon Sea ...”

"Then let us make haste.”

MOUNTAINS, vast beyond imagining, rose in the distance, their peaks
creeping out even over the omnipresent mists that saturated the Rimefells. A trackless glacier stood between Enodia and those peaks, and
though her path lay in the opposite direction, deeper through the
Corpsewood, still, the expanse of ice called to her. The sense of timeless
depths beckoned, promising secrets buried beneath frozen eternities.
Though Enodia could not explain the sensation, still she felt eldritch
beings slumbered below, holding close forgotten lore.

But Keuthos led her away, past the rotting husks of trees that seemed
more Etheric than real, flickering and ephemeral, though they never
quite vanished entirely. The trees were bent and twisted and bound with
chains. Looking closely, Enodia perceived glimpses of faces within the
trunks and wondered whether the chains served to tether the trees to the
land or the dead within those trees. Or perhaps the better questions
was *why*?

The answer she kept coming back to was as simple as it was bitter:
she wandered through the larder of an eldritch god. This forest served as
a storehouse against the ceaseless hunger that must pervade the
creeping eons. As a wraith, Enodia knew that hunger all too well. It was a
hollow ache in the memory of her gut. An unabating craving worming
through the fraying remnants of her mind, demanding she sate herself
upon soul after soul, in futile effort to fill a bottomless void within.

Hissing, she even contemplated pausing here to gorge upon the feast
on display. Would the dark god know someone had plundered its stores?
With Aeshma perhaps still in pursuit, the last thing Enodia needed was
to find further abominations hunting her. Instead, with a frustrated
groan, she followed Keuthos.

8

———

KIRKE

1 Dark Age

Kirke had wanted Odysseus as a lover. She had not, in fact, expected to fall *in love* with him, though she supposed she ought to have seen it coming. She was forever hurling her heart out into the darkness in hopes someone would catch it, no matter how many men or women had fumbled it in the past. Maybe this time would be different, she told herself. That, and tried not to think of how she hoped to steal the man from his wife. What business was it of Kirke's if Odysseus betrayed his wife?

Seasons, most oft, passed with the rhythm of a languid dance, ambling by her in a moil of meaningless days. Now, though, her days raced forth like frenzied horses, and the season flew by before she'd had the least chance to notice it. The first crisp breeze of autumn rustled her hair, seeming to bear with it a forewarning of doom.

Kirke considered then, instead of harvesting her crop of exotic herbs, destroying them and claiming blight or a late planting or a crazed rabbit had ruined the harvest. She could have made Odysseus wait longer, and perhaps he would have even bought her story. Even if he did not believe it, he would have endured it and tarried here, with her. Such things she mused over but could not bring herself to follow through on.

If she was to have love, it must be real, or the companionship meant naught more than the physical release of it all. She could neither trick him to it nor let him be drawn by circumstances of which he would learn soon enough if he lingered.

So, instead, she reaped her herbs and set to brewing her tinctures. She had, in the interim, given much thought to where the Veil might prove thinnest and he could thus reach the Underworld using her brew. The closest place she could think of was the island of Sarpedon where, long back, Mother had imprisoned the monster they'd made of Medusa. The curse Mother had used had made it impossible for Titans to go anywhere close to the most blighted places on the island, but Odysseus should suffer no such restriction, and Medusa had been dead for centuries now.

With a passionate kiss and an unspoken plea to return to her, she sent Odysseus on his way, and he sailed from Aiaíā. Arms wrapt around herself, she watched his ship sail from her, heart aching at the sight of it slowly vanishing over the horizon.

There were things she had not told him. Things she swore to reveal only if he returned; only if he chose her of his own free will. For she would have him only if he would willingly bind himself to her.

Pandora burst into Kirke's room, naked, xiphos in one hand and swirling ball of flame in the other. The woman others named Nike cast about the chamber in search of danger, perhaps having anticipated the return of Zeus. Unclad and unprepared, still Kirke's grandmother had come to face down the most powerful Titan in the World to protect Kirke. Slowly, seeing no danger—or rather, failing to see the abject horror laced into yet one more thread of the Tapestry— Pandora lowered the sword and allowed the inferno in her palm to dwindle down to a candle.

Watching her, Kirke could not help but admire such valour. That thought, too, sent a fresh spasm of agony wracking her, denying the truth her Sight had revealed. Reflexively, her hand went to her abdomen.

In an instant, Pandora was by her side, kneeling, hand on Kirke's belly, her sword cast aside and forgotten. "Is it the babe? I ... I've been trying to learn to push my Pneuma into another person, but thus far I—"

Kirke caught her hand and held it tight. "It's not the babe ..." Kirke moaned. The pain of her knee returned like a knife sliding beneath her flesh and wedging into bone. "It's ... you."

"Me? What have I done?"

The sound that escaped her was some muddle of laughter and sob, and tears welled in Kirke's eyes. "Everything, I think. Yeah. Um. We're all these uncreated products of our own selves, you know? That, uh ... That probably didn't make sense." Kirke forced a steadying breath. Another. A thousand would not be enough to still the rattling of her nerves now. Not a thousand breaths nor a thousand years. With tremulous fingers, she stroked Pandora's cheek. "It's you. The babe is you, Pandora."

Kirke tumbled from her divan and slammed her knee onto the marble floor hard enough her teeth clanked and she thought she might have chipped bone. Yet the wail that ripped its way out of her throat had naught to do with any injury to her body. Rather, it was a wordless defiance at this final abuse of her mind and soul. The Moirai had wrought a blasphemy so profane it beggared the senses to even try to comprehend the awful circles of it all.

"Why," she tried to scream, but it came out as one more inarticulate cry.

Why? Because history was merciless. Because time was an ouroboros, and the great serpent *was* the awful circle of her life. No, just hers, for cascading imports of the revelation struck home like one hammer blow after another upon the anvil of her sanity.

Pandora burst into Kirke's room, naked, xiphos in one hand and swirling ball of flame in the other. The woman others named Nike cast about the chamber in search of danger, perhaps having anticipated the return of Zeus. Unclad and unprepared, still Kirke's grandmother—her *daughter*—had come to face the most powerful Titan in the World to protect Kirke. Slowly, seeing no danger—or rather, failing to see the abject horror laced into yet one more thread of the Tapestry—Pandora lowered the sword and allowed the inferno in her palm to dwindle down to a candle.

Watching her, Kirke could not help but admire such valour. That thought, too, sent a fresh spasm of agony wracking her, denying the truth her Sight had revealed. Reflexively, her hand went to her abdomen.

In an instant, Pandora was by her side, kneeling, hand on Kirke's belly as well, her sword cast aside and forgotten. "Is it the babe? I ... I've been trying to learn to push my Pneuma into another person, but thus far I—"

Kirke caught her hand and held it tight. "It's not the babe ..." Kirke moaned. The pain of her knee returned like a knife sliding beneath her flesh and wedging into bone. "It's ... you."

"Me? What have I done?"

The sound that escaped her was some muddle of laughter and sob, and tears welled in Kirke's eyes. "Everything, I think. Yeah. Um. We're all these uncreated products of our own selves, you know? That, uh ... That probably didn't make sense." Kirke forced a steadying breath. Another. A thousand would not be enough to still the rattling of her nerves now. Not a thousand breaths nor a thousand years. With tremulous fingers, she stroked Pandora's cheek. "It's you. The *babe* is you, Pandora."

The moment stretched too thin; Pandora stared at her. The sputtering flame in her other hand died, leaving the pair of them in near darkness. Kirke crawled to her table, wincing at each brush of pressure upon her injured knee, and lit an oil lamp.

When she looked back to her grandmother, Pandora sat with her hands folded on her lap, a look of consternation heavy upon her face. Kirke eased closer and the firelight glinted off Pandora's golden, Heliad eyes. Eyes just like Kirke's, though she had the raven hair of her Tethid father.

"It's impossible," Pandora whispered after a moment. "I would have no origin. Nor you, nor Pyrrha, Athene ... all of Athene's descendants ..." Silence settled upon Pandora, and Kirke had not the least idea what to say. Normally, in such times, rambles would have worked their way out of Kirke whether or not she wished to hold her tongue. Now, she couldn't even manage that much. "But why not?" Pandora said after the quiet stretched so far it had begun to feel a physical weight. "I'm like the

Box itself. You were right—we are self-created artefacts of the Tapestry, like scales shed from the ouroboros."

Though Kirke caught Pandora's meaning, she rather wished she hadn't. "Such truths are nettles wedged into the heart. How are we meant to abide this obscenity? Our whole line is a ... circle."

Slowly, Pandora looked to her. "It changes naught. I, um ... As an infant, I was left with Europa, for her to raise me. I was clearly of Heliad blood by my eyes, but no one spoke of the who or how of it, and I thought it mattered little in the end, for my parents had abandoned me. But that's not what happened at all."

"N-no." She could not be saying what it sounded like she was saying. "You are *not* taking my babe anywhere, much less into the past to be raised by *Europa*." To be kidnapped by Zeus and Hekate. Forced into slavery. Raped and abused. All these things Kirke had known her grandmother had endured. But to think of it visited upon her own *daughter* was a thousand times worse. It was intolerable, as was the thought of even a moment of separation. And it happened *because* of Kirke, prompting Hekate to ignite such events, thinking them needful. "This child is mine!" She crawled away from Pandora as if she could escape either Nike or Ananke.

"If I did not, you would not have the child regardless. Because none of us would ever exist. You would consign everyone, thousands of lives, to oblivion."

And Kirke had *seen* Nike there, in Tyros, on the day Zeus came for Europa and Pandora. Nike had stood by and watched as her nightmare played out before her eyes, and Kirke had thought her possessed of a terrible will to allow such.

Kirke groaned, still trying to find further away to crawl from the predator of time that had taken over her grandmother's form. "Maybe oblivion is better than the madness that ensnares those lives."

Pandora shook her head at that. "I don't think so. If you or anyone related to us has ever seized even a moment of joy, has ever wrought the least good in the World, I cannot believe erasure preferable." What, did the sum of Kirke's life amount to more good than ill? Did the sum of *any* of their lives? She doubted it. As if reading the thought from her, Pandora continued, "Even were you to make that choice, what makes you think the resulting timeline would be better than this one?"

Because it could not be more profane, Kirke wanted to snap, but her daughter did not deserve her ire. "How am I to live with this?"

Pandora sighed. "You imagine it easy for me to orchestrate my own torments? You think I *want* to take myself there? Do you imagine, for even the tiniest of moments, I relish the thought of my past?" Pandora swallowed, choking on her words. "But I have to keep hope that, no matter how dire the past or present, still we might create a better future."

"Nyx take you," Kirke spat, and Pandora favoured her with a sad smile.

"I'll linger until the babe is born. Then I will have to go, Kirke. The circle must continue, or *we* won't."

THREE DAYS LATER, on a hazy, drizzle-spattered morning, Odysseus's ship returned. Any joy Kirke might have felt at seeing that—despite having no doubt received his answer from Tiresias—he had come for her evaporated in the knowledge of the bitter truth that lay betwixt them. It was a truth that poisoned her very soul, and she could not burden his by sharing it. Rather, she met him upon the portico of her manse, himation pulled over her hair, peplos flapping about her ankles.

The man looked like he'd come fresh from a battlefield. Not something so obvious as wounds or bloodstains, no, but he was haggard, with dark circles beneath his eyes and a stoop to his step. Kirke imagined passing through the Underworld must do that to a person. Clearly, he needed the comfort of a warm hearth, a hot meal, and a loving companion for the eve. Such was writ so plain upon his face that, in his need, her own will almost broke.

Except inviting him inside now would only make the road before her a thousand times harder. His every smile, every jest, would abrade her resolve with cruel kindness. She could see herself, that very eve, weeping into his shoulder, confiding the truth about their babe. She could see him, in her mind's eye, cursing the Moirai, mayhap even trying to fight against Pandora when she came for the child.

A single night with her now would cost Odysseus a lifetime of pain. Worse, because she could never explain *why* they must allow Pandora to take the babe without revealing the frightful details of timewalking and its import upon the Moirai's Tapestry. To glimpse more than the barest of threads of that design was to court madness and despair; Kirke knew it all too well, and she'd not condemn him or anyone else to such.

"Your wife awaits you and yet you return here?" she asked, proud of how impassive she managed to keep her voice. At least, she thought her tone impassive. If he perceived even a hint of hope, of gladness at his arrival, he would seize upon it as the invitation she could not afford to offer him.

The truth was a dull blade, hacking out her insides one bumbling chop at a time, made all the worse that she could not let him see her in pain.

His face fell at her words. Only for a moment, before his bravado covered it, but she saw the hurt in his eyes, even once his smirk returned. "Oh, I came but to offer thanks and tell you your tonic worked. Ha! Yes, what tales I have to tell of things beheld in the dark beyond life ..."

There it was: an invitation, all but begging her to ask for one more story. And Kirke had no choice but to slap away his hand.

"Yeah ..." Kirke swallowed down her discomfort. "Your son must be, what, ten now? The perfect age for a youth to be enthralled with tales of daring and danger, don't you think?"

The Tethid pressed his mouth into a tight line a moment. "Very true, very true, indeed. Yes, you have the right of it. I think the next I tell of my journey, it ought to be to my son."

"I imagine he'll like that."

Odysseus nodded. "Yes, I think so."

"Well," she said.

"I suppose I best get to him."

"Mmm." She scarce trusted herself to form words on the matter. Would it not be easier to hold him here? It would draw him into her grief, but at least he could offer the comfort of companionship. They could grieve the loss of their child together rather than her passing the Ages here alone, festering in loss and despair. Easier for her ... not for him, though. *Please do the right thing, just this once,* she told herself.

Only when he had vanished beyond the hills did she allow herself to slump against a column and let the wracking shudders tear free.

THE BIRTHING WAS a blur of pain and screaming fervent denials as Pandora stroked her head and whispered horseshit meant to forestall hysteria. And after, after it, when the raven-haired, mushy-faced babe lay cradled in her arms, Kirke held on so tight she almost worried over hurting the child. Lying on a rug by the hearth, she nursed little Pandora, whilst grown Pandora watched, her face an unreadable mask, her golden eyes wild with pain.

"No one has the right to take a babe from her mother," Kirke said, tearing her gaze from the adult Pandora and fixing it on the infant, intent to carve that face into her memory like the most intricately wrought statue. This masterpiece would never suffer the abrasions of weathering or the ravages of time, Kirke swore to herself. It would remain immortal, eternal, a perfect memory, for as long as Kirke walked upon Gaia. Down through the Ages, she would call up the engraving of her daughter's beautiful, perfect visage and know she had done one good thing with her life.

"Not even the daughter herself ..." Pandora's tone turned so wistful Kirke could not be certain whether her words were statement or question. Maybe neither was Pandora. "I ... Time conspired against us all, leaving us to snatch what moments of happiness we might from the tattered fringes of the Tapestry."

For the life of her, Kirke was not certain she could think of too many moments of happiness. Not now. Every joy was polluted by the toxins of a thousand sorrows that must come before or after. Naught remained pure.

When she did not answer, Pandora continued, "I knew time would force me to leave Pyrrha—Hekate—in order to fulfil my promise to save her father, but I tarried unwilling to leave my babe. At least until Kronos came to claim the Box and Prometheus and I agreed I had no choice." Pandora scrubbed at her eyes with the palms of her hands. "I thought, back then, I would save the man I loved and return to my child before she ever realised I had gone." A pained chuckle, thick with self-loathing, tore from her, and she sighed. "Back then, neither Prometheus nor I had as precise control of the Box as I do now. The next time I saw Pyrrha, she was already Hekate. More than two thousand years had passed, and she would never forgive me for having not been there. No matter what I do, no matter how I traverse time trying to save the World, I cannot seem to find a way to fix things with her.

"And, and … and my child and my grandchildren are hundreds of times older than me. You all have oceans more life experience than I do." Tears spilled down her cheeks.

Kirke blinked and found water streaming over her own cheeks as well.

"So, yes, Kirke, I get it. I wanted to be a mother to Pyrrha, wanted to be for her the mother I didn't have, and that chance was stolen from me, and I cannot reclaim it. I *understand* the heart-grinding, soul-shredding agony of this moment for you more than almost anyone else ever could. Like me, and like Prometheus, you have no real choice in the matter." She paused. "There was no reality in which I got to raise Pyrrha. If I had not left her, she would not exist. None of us would. There is no reality in which you get to raise me. If I do not take the babe to Europa, again, we are all gone. You still do not get to keep the babe, and in trying, you unmake thousands of lives."

Kirke's grandmother crawled over to where Kirke reclined and reached her trembling hands for the babe.

"No," Kirke whimpered.

"It shan't grow easier." Pandora's voice shook, her words almost inaudible. Of a sudden, it struck Kirke to wonder if this moment was, in fact, as hard on Pandora herself as it was on Kirke. Here she was, haunted by a lack of a mother, about to deliver herself to the woman she would love in place of a mother, knowing how ill that would end too. Slowly, something else Pandora said settled in on her.

"How old are you?"

Pandora's hands fell to her side, and she shook her head. "With the timewalking, I've rather lost track. I think, perhaps in my mid-thirties now."

And here Kirke was having lived forty-six *centuries* and having so little sympathy for the burdens placed upon the much younger woman beside her. Kirke swallowed. Weeping, she kissed the infant Pandora's brow. "I don't want to do this."

"Nor I."

"I, um … What happens to Odysseus?" She knew she seized upon straws now, hoping to delay even a single breath more. Hoping to forestall the implacable advancement of Ananke.

Pandora frowned, shaking her head, clearly well aware of the ploy Kirke had used. "It won't change anything."

"I ... I care for him." More than she had liked to admit, these past months, growing his child within herself. What if they could be together now, and he never need know about the child they shared betwixt them? There could be another child, in time, even. There could ...

"You cannot save him." Sadness, deep as the trenches of Pontus, laced her voice.

"I can *try*."

Pandora reached out to grasp her hand and squeeze. "Hope." She sighed. "I respect that. We have to have hope." A slight pause as she waged some internal war. "Odysseus dies about nineteen years hence, on a beach in Ithaka."

Though she had known her lover would meet a dire end, hearing it laid out plain still felt like a fresh blade dug into the wound. Eyes closed, she did not try to stop Pandora as she eased the babe from her arms. The child squawked in fury, and Kirke had to clench eyes and jaw both to keep from launching herself at Pandora to save her child.

And then a soft kiss landed on Kirke's brow. "I love you, Mama."

It was the last blow that shattered her, leaving her strewn across the rug like ostraka pulverised by repeated impacts. Wave after wave of lachrymal convulsions seized her, drowned her, tearing her from time and space, and leaving her senseless in the crushing dark of unbearable grief.

9

———————

ARTEMIS

1 Dark Age

nce, on his visit to Ilium, Mithra had spoken to Artemis of the famed gardens of Babilim, hinting she would find them entrancing. The man who would become emperor had not exaggerated. Within the royal sanctum lay the hanging gardens which, at first glance, might seem more a rainforest creeping up over a mountainside than the ziggurat palace of the emperor. Tumbling cataracts spilled over successive terraces, creating a verdant paradise in the heart of the city—though given the sanctum wall, most citizens could only glimpse the vibrant peak and guess at its full grandeur.

Artemis assumed the circuitous route along which Morpheus guided her had been chosen to maximise her view of the gardens, for it looked as though a more direct path would have led to the palace of Etemenanki. But the oneiromancer had instead walked her around the periphery of the hanging gardens, over a bridge that crossed a stream formed by the falls, and past cultivated beds of irises and fragrant blooms of jasmine. The rich, heady scents of tropical flowers saturated the air, masking the urban reek one might expect in the heart of a city.

After giving her enough time to luxuriate in the beauty, Morpheus bid her follow along a stone-paved road to Etemenanki. The ziggurat stretched over two hundred feet high, a wonder of architecture, though to her eye, it paled before the elegant majesty of the gardens. "Did Mithra build all this?" Artemis asked, waving at the green mountain behind her.

Morpheus glanced back in the direction she had waved. "No. Queen Semiramis constructed the gardens in the centuries before the rise of the last dynasty of Nineveh." He smirked as if at some private amusement. "You, out of Kêr-Ys, tend to rather think your continent holds the crown in terms of the complexity of history. As if other lands are not shaped by equally dense, compounding ages."

She nodded in acknowledgment of his point—though she might have countered that all people lay at the centre of their own Worlds, and arrogance was by no means exclusive to Kêr-Ysians—and followed him into the palace. Within the vestibule, a mosaic of cobalt blue and lustrous gold stones caught her eye, and she paused to admire it. The imagery depicted a hooded man and woman seeming to offer people beneath them gifts of papyrus and handfuls of what she took to be seeds.

"The sorcerer Enki and his consort, Damkina," Morpheus supplied, though Artemis had not voiced the question. The names tickled with distant familiarity, but Artemis could not place them. "They first appeared in Phoenikia early in the Golden Age. Some years later, they came here and brought knowledge to the people. Reading, writing, agriculture—all the accoutrements of civilisation so that Man could rise out of the darkness." It was rare for a people to knowingly venerate practitioners of the Art as culture heroes, but it explained how she might have heard the names at some point in her visits to Kumari Kandam. "Come," Morpheus said after a moment more, "the god-king awaits your arrival, and, though his patience appears vast as the sea, I think it best we do not attempt to sound just how deep it runs."

Artemis quirked a half smile at that. Men on thrones tended toward self-importance, didn't they? She expected Morpheus to lead her into a great hall in an attempt to further awe her with the grandeur of Babilim and its burgeoning empire. Instead, the oneiromancer guided her up two flights of winding stairs and onto a landing on the upper level. Over the balustrade she could see into the vestibule where she'd examined the mosaic, though the art itself stood concealed by the overhanging ceiling. Morpheus guided her around to the far side, then through an archway out onto an open-air terrace. After the dimmer interior of the palace, the harsh glare of the Kandamian sun had her blinking.

As she oft did, she allowed a trickle of Pneuma into Tolerance to ward off the afternoon heat. Mithra stood with his hands behind his back, staring over the capital of his empire as though he might know the thoughts and deeds of every citizen. There was a dark-haired boy beside him, tall, though probably not yet in his teens, standing in imitation of the emperor's pose, though the child couldn't help but fidget.

Morpheus swept a bow, though Mithra had not looked in his direction. "My Emperor, I present to you the former Olympian Artemis."

The boy whirled around to face her, eyes wide and openly looking her up and down. The god-king turned too, his languid motion no doubt intended to portray a lack of concern for the time of those beneath him, which Artemis assumed included every other person on the face of Gaia. Though his clothes were finer, the man had otherwise changed little since she had seen him in Ilium, some four decades back.

She felt it as Morpheus's gaze shot to her in silent bid that she too should bow. Which she did not. "Once before you invited me to visit these lands, though you had not claimed rulership at that time."

"Circumstances required a change of dynasty."

Artemis wondered what must have led the man to claim the crown himself, after so carefully arranging a bloodline of Oracles to rule here. How did a seemingly loyal advisor come to usurp the throne he had once served?

The boy by his side shifted from foot to foot, restless, and Mithra took the hint, indicating him with a hand. "This is my son, Prince Marduk."

For the child, Artemis did offer a slight bow. "A pleasure, Marduk." To Mithra she said, "I did not know you were married." Then again, Artemis did not know overmuch at all about the man to whom she now looked for shelter. But idle conversation seemed as good a means as any of forging some connection between herself and the emperor.

The boy's face fell, and he turned away, no longer seeming so fascinated by his Elládosi guest. Mithra frowned, gaze darting to Marduk for an instant before returning to alight on Artemis. "We lost his mother in childbirth."

And Artemis had managed to bumble into a gaffe in her first hour within Etemenanki. "I'm so sorry for your loss." Since young Marduk did not deign to look back, she could think of little else to say.

Mithra's nod of acknowledgment was stiff, almost imperceptible. "You must be road-weary now. The path from Ugart is long." They had stopped at Nineveh for additional supplies, but Artemis had little reason to point it out now. "Morpheus will see you to chambers where you can wash and recover. Perhaps we shall speak again in the evening."

Having gotten used to the deference of everyone save other Olympians over the millennia, Artemis struggled not to glower at the abrupt dismissal. Still, she was the guest here, and the god-king remained well within his rights to expect privacy to console his agitated son. So once more, Artemis trailed behind Morpheus.

THOUGH MITHRA MADE Artemis welcome in his palace, he had not spoken of why he had invited her here or offered her shelter following the sack of Ilium. He did not once mention it in the six months she had lived in Babilim, and thus far, Artemis had decided to bide her time and let Mithra hold the reins of their conversations. She reminded herself, ever and anon, he was king here, and she remained safe from Zeus only at his sufferance. Still, on several occasions, she had bemoaned the myriad crimes of her erstwhile king. All the things Zeus had done. The things he had made her a party to, the woe they had all wrought, scattering suffering across the land like seeds cast into furrows.

Mithra, for his part, seemed well aware of the many deeds of which she spoke. He knew even of how Zeus had murdered Hippolytus and Asklepoius in the final act that severed her last fraying thread of loyalty to her former brethren. He knew, and he hefted a goblet in salute of her loss, of her pain, of her unabating desire for vengeance. Though he did not say such, exactly, she knew that one day she might achieve that end through him.

So, when one night he approached her on the terrace where she stared at the firmament, watching a torrent of shooting stars blaze across the sky and wondering what it might portend, she agreed to accompany him out into the city. He went hooded, his identity concealed from the common folk, at least as much as his Titan height allowed. Artemis too pulled up her cowl and followed as he led her out of the royal sanctum over the bridge spanning the Ufratu River.

In the opposite district lay the priests' sanctum, the Sanctum of Belus, they called it. Artemis had seen the place in passing but thus far had found no reason to enter. Mithra, however, guided her within the sanctum and into one of the nine ziggurats sprouting within its walls.

After a short corridor, they passed into a large central chamber. A deep, wide fire pit cast leaping shadows flowing over the vaulted ceiling and wriggling across the sandstone pillars. At the moment, she saw no other Magi here, so she had to assume either all had gone over to observe the astrological event, or otherwise he had ordered them dispersed in preparation of bringing her here. The god-king paced around the fire pit's periphery, his gaze lingering on its depths just long enough to evoke the memory of another Titan obsessed with flame.

"Are you a pyromancer?"

"No," he said, voice soft but thick with import. "It is not in the undulant pattern of dancing flame we perceive the Ontos, but in Light, of which flame is a conduit. The fire herein is sacred not in itself, but rather for the promise it brings."

"What promise?" She stared at him across the pit. The crackling flames cast an eerie play of light and darkness over his face.

"The Light of Oromasdes. His is the wisdom of Truth, purity of thought, and of Order."

"Who, or what, is Oromasdes?"

"The God behind the World, hidden from sight and yet ever present in the spinning of his eternal Wheel of Fate."

Though she did not grasp his meaning, somehow the weight of his words, the fervour of his belief, proved so heavy it forced her to one knee, to stare into the fire. As if she, too, might see Light there and behold some fragment of the Truth of which he spoke. "You mean this entity is another Elder God?"

"The Hidden God lies as far beyond them as they lie beyond those like you and me, Titans claiming divinity whilst yet walking the Mortal Realm and bound to corporeal forms."

Artemis frowned, a slight tremble running through her. She had not come to Babilim to allow herself to be drawn into the religion of the Magi. Even if Mithra's beliefs proved true, she was not certain she would wish to know. Everything Artemis had seen of the Elder Gods—most through Dionysus, curse him—had proved hateful knowledge she would have unlearnt, were it possible. She did not want to know more, and yet ... She had to know. Teased with answers to questions she knew she ought not to ask, she could not turn away and walk wilfully into ignorance. She had heard it said only the ignorant could hold true contentment for long, but Artemis suspected such only applied to those *also* ignorant of their own ignorance. To know a monster lurked in the dark and pretend otherwise for fear of seeing its shape was not bliss but folly.

"You already know some hint of that which I speak, but still, so much of the Truth lies, as yet, beyond you." He paused. "You must choose whether to ask for the Ontos or turn from it for the comfort inherent in pleasant illusions."

Artemis gnawed upon her lip a moment, warring with the dread curiosity that had gripped her. "I want Zeus's head."

"Zeus ... He is, in the end, but a pawn of the Gnostic Cabal once directed by his father."

Artemis faltered now, struck speechless by the almost impossible thought he had put forth. That someone could lurk *behind* Zeus, manipulating the tyrant's madness for their own ends, seemed to defy reason. Surely, no sane force could or would attach themselves to so execrable a being as Zeus. She and her brother and all the other Olympians had found themselves beneath Zeus, yes, but who would keep the wretch around as a subordinate? "Zeus destroyed his father."

"Yes," Mithra agreed. "And in the wreckage he found the Seeing Pools—the Oracle Mirrors of the Gnostic Cabal. Glimpses of the future and intimations of Truth he could never understand served to further unhinge an already megalomaniacal mind. In desperation to glean answers from those mirrors, the fool erected his palaces above the corrupting influence of the Tartarian Gate. And the longer anyone dwelt upon the mountain, the deeper the tainted currents of that place wormed through your minds. With his thoughts befuddled and his desperation piqued, the Cabal found him a puppet whose strings were all too obvious."

The import of what he had said, of having confirmed that Olympus had twisted their minds—had infected *her* mind like a rot—it stole her breath. Artemis once more found herself staring into the flames, hoping against hope they offered the answers. "How can you know these things?"

"Because the vast expanse of history is a game board in a match played across Ages and Eras, fought betwixt the bitterest of rivals." He waited until she looked up. "One, the Gnostic Cabal, seeks to break the Wheel of Fate, in their misguided desire to free themselves from the weavings of the Moirai. But it is that very Tapestry that holds together history and thus the World. Should they succeed in their aim, the cosmos would unravel along with the weave." Now he strode toward her, the slapping of his sandals upon the ground resounding even over the guttering fire. "Thus another force must stand in opposition, preserving the integrity of the timeline at all costs. Unseen, working in the spaces between moments, the Order strives against the Cabal."

Still on her knees, she looked up to where he paused in front of her. The emperor offered her a hand, and, despite herself, Artemis took it.

"You wish to destroy Zeus? To stop him, to stop the Cabal in their suicidal scheme, I was forced to step up and claim a throne. I must spread my influence across the whole of the Earth and bring it to heel. You and I can root out both the Cabal and their pawn." Hand on her wrist, he pulled her to her feet. "A king needs a general, after all."

He would have her lead his wars of conquest. He would have her build his forces and prepare for in invasion of Elládos. Zeus was, so far as she knew, the single most powerful Titan in the World. Mithra had no intention of making an ill-conceived assault upon him; less so now, after what had befallen Ilium in that war. He meant to bide his time and break Olympus only when all of Gaia closed in around Zeus and his allies.

And Artemis bowed her head. "I accept." For she must be there to witness the fall.

10

PANDORA

20 Dark Age

Pandora had guided Odysseus and his men to Aiaíā and Kirke received them well, though she seemed to hold an immediate mistrust of the Ithakans. On the voyage across the Thalassa, Odysseus had given Pandora some of his tale, at least of how he'd been recruited to the Elládosi siege of Ilium, and how his plan had eventually led to the great city's fall. Perhaps that was what Kirke misliked about him, for she'd clearly been in contact with Artemis, who had made Ilium her home when last Pandora had seen her.

Over copious wine, before Kirke's crackling hearth, Odysseus spent many nights regaling Pandora and Kirke with the rest of his tale. In the end, Pandora had decided she had no right to judge him. He'd been forced into war against his will, and there had fought for his people using the weapon of his intellect. That the result, for his foes, had been tragic, did make Odysseus a villain.

When he'd finished his tale, Odysseus cleared his throat. Pandora, sitting by the hearth, did not look away from its flames. Every time she looked upon his visage, guilt churned her guts and bouts of self-loathing threatened to send her retching. "So then the goddess guided our ship here," Odysseus said, slurring his words, "saying we could be safe here and she knew a sorceress who might help us find our way home."

Kirke held her peace for a time before speaking. Perhaps she wondered what might have prompted Pandora to bring the man here. Perhaps she questioned why Pandora had taken it upon herself to aid the Ithakans in the first place. "Take your rest, King of Ithaka. I'm sure you must be weary from these ordeals."

When the man left, the weight that had pressed down on Pandora grew too much. "He will come to a bad end one day."

"And you want me to help him find his way home before that, yeah? What about the implication of so doing? Have you considered the smallest shift might change the course of his life and thus preserve it?"

Pandora sighed, almost broken by all this. "Yes. Considered it, mulled it over, massaging all the sharp angles of the issue as if it could be shaped into something palatable. You imagine that, were Odysseus to fail to return home, perhaps he would not meet whatever dire fate I have beheld for him. But if he had not met that fate, I would not have known the need to save him from the Laestrygonians, and he'd have died twenty years sooner than the Moirai have decreed for him. Most oft, even a dying beast, one suffering grievous pain, will fight for even one more breath." She forced herself to turn to meet her granddaughter's gaze. "Should I deny him twenty years of life for the chance to say I spat in Ananke's eye?"

Kirke groaned at that. "And when you put it like that, I'm not left with much choice about whether to help him or not. I mean, I could choose to be a selfish bitch, and yeah, maybe I've made that choice once or twice in days gone, but that's the only choice."

Pandora naught but shrug. Indeed, times like these almost made the Unseen Order's claims about the illusions of free will seem like undeniable truth, terrible though they were. But Pandora, she refused to believe that. There had to be hope.

There had to.

So Kirke, using her oneiromancy, sought to uncover why the Ithakans had found themselves unable to return home. Pandora, for her part, wandered the woods around Kirke's manse, aimless. Remaining in Odysseus's presence felt suffocating, her knowledge of his fate an unbearable pressure upon her chest. How did Oracles tolerate living thus? How could Prometheus—oft knowing the bitter ends those around him would come to—keep from going mad every time he looked upon their faces? Even Kirke sometimes dreamt the future, like Pyrrha had. Athene saw it, in the waters.

What burdens those of Prometheus's bloodline bore, for their prescient insights. To know the future, and be unable to change it, must become a crushing weight upon the soul. Too, the Oracle Mirrors had broken the Gnostic Cabal and, it seemed, perhaps had destroyed Zeus as well. Such came the terrible price of prophecy.

So instead, she walked through sun-dappled forest paths, bathed in the streams, and hid from the world, pretending it all might somehow go away. Of course, no such thing unfolded, and in time, Pandora found herself returning to the manse, late at night, after the hearth fires had dwindled down to embers and Kirke and Odysseus must have drifted off to their beds. Or at least she had assumed them gone to separate beds until she heard the echoes of moans coming from Kirke's chamber.

Pandora was uncertain how to feel about any burgeoning relationship between the pair of them. Odysseus had come here with the intent to find a way back to his wife, one Penelope. Pandora thought him rather quick to forget the woman if he found himself in the bed of another days after arriving on this island. But what business was it of hers? Pandora's granddaughter was thousands of years old and could well decide what to do with her heart or her body.

So when she heard a door creak open, Pandora did not look over her shoulder. She saw no need to watch Odysseus slink off to his own room. She did, however, wonder where Prometheus was in this time. Hers was a lonely path, and the past two years she'd spent living with her husband had been the happiest—save perhaps for when Pyrrha was born—times of her life. Maybe she never should have left, never gone hunting for answers about the Unseen Order. She could have lived in Mugedang, as Hina, and been happy. But then, the Eschaton would have crept up upon them all, sooner or later, and her happiness would have drowned along with the world.

History was merciless.

Later, Kirke told her of her plan for Odysseus, absurd though it seemed to Pandora. She was brewing a draught for him, a tonic that would allow him to enter the Underworld. Or at least send his soul there, for a temporary sojourn, where he could consult with the dead Oracle Tiresias, whom Herakles had rescued from harpies long ago. "Is this really the only way to get the man home?" Pandora had protested, for the plan seemed convoluted, even considering the strange, circuitous route she herself had taken through time.

Kirke had chuckled. "Yeah, I've no idea. But the dreams show what the dreams deign to show, and having shown this, I can assure you they'll show no more."

So, the alchemist spent a season growing her herbs and brewing her potion, and Pandora wandered the island, alone more oft than not, as Kirke and Odysseus found comfort in one another's arms. Maybe Pandora could have used the Box, moved on, but she felt a perverse obligation to see Odysseus made it onward. So Pandora lingered here, caught between time, restless as autumn crept in, the Phoenix simmering within her breast, ready to burst forth for need to do *something*. Her foes were out there, spread across the ambit of time, plotting against her.

Maybe she could return to Mu, reunite with Prometheus, and together they might confront the Anunnaki. But, no, he would not pit himself against the Unseen Order, which was why he'd not accompanied her to the Hursag Mountains in the first place. Mahuika, however, would not share his reticence. The Queens of Mu already feared the rising power of the Babilimian Empire. They would not hesitate to move against Babilimian agents with a stronghold upon their continent.

It was, perhaps, not a good plan, but it was *a* plan, and the only one she had at the moment.

"It's you. The *babe* is you, Pandora."

Kirke's words sliced through Pandora like flensing knives, shredding the already tattered vestiges of a soul worn ragged by Ananke. Pandora stood there, naked before her granddaughter, xiphos in one hand and flame in the other. Slowly, the fire in her palm winked out, turned to a puff of smoke like all the final illusions that had allowed Pandora to carry forward, resisting the obscene workings of the Tapestry. A vanishing whiff of smoke, it was all her efforts had ever been, for Mithra had been right all along, and there was no escape from Fate. The ouroboros's coils encircled all that was or ever could be.

Pandora sank to the floor. She didn't remember dropping the sword, but her hands were empty as she folded them in her lap.

The rank absurdity of it all defied all sense of logic. "It's impossible," she whispered. "I would have no origin. Nor you, nor Pyrrha, Athene ... all of Athene's descendants ..." Causal chains, the very force of determinism that ensured the revolutions of the Wheel of Fate, they depended on a sense of order to events. Timewalking—and Oracular insight—meant the future could come *before* the past. But here, now, her very existence had become predicated upon *itself*. "But why not? I'm like the Box itself. You were right—we are self-created artefacts of the Tapestry, like scales shed from the ouroboros."

Was that why they, her bloodline, could use the Box, when it failed to work for Kronos or others? Because Pandora and her kin were a part of it, born from it?

"Such truths are nettles wedged into the heart," Kirke said. "How are we meant to abide this obscenity? Our line is a ... circle."

Pandora forced herself to look up at her granddaughter. Even in the wan light of the oil lamp, the Heliad seemed pale. "It changes naught. I, um ... As an infant, I was left with Europa, for her to raise me. I was clearly of Heliad blood by my eyes, but no one spoke of the who or how of it, and I thought it mattered little in the end, for my parents had abandoned me. But that's not what happened at all."

Kirke recoiled, violently apprehending Pandora's meaning, and Pandora wished, almost more than her own torment, she could ease her granddaughter's. "N-no. You are *not* taking my babe anywhere, much less into the past to be raised by *Europa*." Kirke trembled in rage or terror or, mostlike, both. "This child is mine!" The woman began to crawl away.

"If I did not, you would not have the child regardless. Because none of us would ever exist. You would consign everyone, thousands of lives, to oblivion."

Kirke groaned, still crawling away. "Maybe oblivion is better than the madness that ensnares those lives."

Pandora considered it, just for an instant, then shook her head. "I don't think so. If you or anyone related to us has ever seized even a moment of joy, has ever wrought the least good in the World, I cannot believe erasure preferable." Kirke, however, seemed ready to contemplate giving in and embracing that void. But she did not see clearly what it would imply. "Even were you to make that choice, what makes you think the resulting timeline would be better than this one?"

Kirke's jaw tightened. "How am I to live with this?"

Pandora sighed at that, somewhat at a loss. "Because you imagine it easy for me to orchestrate my own torments? You think I *want* to take myself there? Do you imagine, for even the tiniest of moments, I relish the thought of my past?" Pandora caught herself and choked down a sob. "But I have to keep hope that, no matter how dire the past or present, still we might create a better future."

"Nyx take you," her granddaughter—her mother—snarled.

Pandora could only answer that with a sad smile. "I'll linger until the babe is born. Then I will have to go, Kirke. The circle must continue, or *we* won't."

As the months went by, Pandora remained by Kirke's side, offering what consolation she could. It was the chance she had never gotten to get to know her mother, and the only such chance that Fate might ever allow her. Even in the face of torturous cruelty of the Moirai, Pandora remained determined to claim her own meaning, to define her own life. Oft, that meant propping up a disconsolate Kirke who, at times, fell into pits of melancholy so deep Pandora feared her mother might never drag herself free of them. But always, Pandora was there, striving to serve as a living reminder that they could define their own bonds, and damn the expectations of the World.

When the time came, Pandora had to serve as midwife to her own birth, a role she doubted anyone else in history had ever performed. She stroked Kirke's head, she whispered comforts, and she tried not to weep herself. All these months together, and it was not nigh long enough. She ought to have enjoyed years with her mother. She ought to have run through this house, laughing and playing and always knowing she had warm, welcoming arms to which she could return when darkness settled in. She ought to have had a thousand, thousand memories of the sheltering embrace Kirke could have offered her.

Instead, Kirke now cradled her in her arms for the last time, whilst baby Pandora squalled and pawed with weak, uncoordinated limbs. The woman lay on a rug by the hearth, so fiercely possessive of Pandora that Pandora's soul ached. Pandora sat several feet away, watching them, paralysed with the despair clinging to her now. What would happen if she just left the child with her mother? Trembling, she clenched a fist on her lap. Oh, Gaia, she did not want to go through with this. Surely, the Moirai could not *make* her commit such an atrocity.

"No one has the right to take a babe from her mother," Kirke said, staring at the child.

No, and yet ... "Not even the daughter herself ..." Pandora's heart broke to say such words. She was, for the first and only time in her life, for one moment *only*, a daughter. "I ... Time conspired against us all, leaving us to snatch what moments of happiness we might from the tattered fringes of the Tapestry." Kirke stared at her, her face like crumbling ostraka, ready to shatter at the slightest pressure. "I knew time would force me to leave Pyrrha—Hekate—in order to fulfil my promise to save her father. I knew it, but I tarried, unwilling to leave my own babe. At least until Kronos came to claim the Box and Prometheus and I agreed I had no choice." Tears blurred her vision, and Pandora rubbed them away. "I thought, back then, I would save the man I loved and return to my child before she ever realised I had gone." What a fool she had been, then. A bitter laugh burst from her, becoming a sigh of resignation. "Back then, neither Prometheus nor I had as precise control of the Box as I do now. The next time I saw Pyrrha, she was already Hekate. More than two thousand years had passed, and she would never forgive me for having not been there. No matter what I do, no matter how I traverse time trying to save the World, I cannot seem to find a way to fix things with her. And, and ... and my child and my grandchildren are hundreds of times older than me. You all have oceans more life experience than I do."

She could no longer hold back the tears that came spilling down her face. Kirke, too, had begun weeping, Pandora realised, her mother seeming unable to even form a reply.

"So, yes, Kirke, I get it. I wanted to be a mother to Pyrrha, wanted to be for her the mother I didn't have. That chance was stolen from me and I cannot reclaim it. I *understand* the heart-grinding, soul-shredding agony of this moment for you more than almost anyone else ever could. Like me, and like Prometheus, you have no real choice in the matter." She paused. "There was no reality in which I got to raise Pyrrha. If I had not left her, she would not exist. None of us would. There is no reality in which you get to raise me. If I do not take the babe to Europa, again, we are all gone. You still do not get to keep the babe, and in trying, you unmake thousands of lives."

Pandora crawled over to sit beside her mother, and, though her hands shook, she reached for her infant self.

"No." Kirke's objection was a shuddering murmur.

"It shan't grow easier." Pandora could barely find her voice.

Kirke looked at her a moment, something whirring behind her eyes. "How old are you?"

The question caught her off guard, and Pandora dropped her hands, shaking her head. She didn't see the relevance, nor was it an easy question to answer. "With the timewalking, I've rather lost track. I think, perhaps in my mid-thirties now."

Whatever Kirke thought about that, she continued to sob and kissed the babe's brow. "I don't want to do this," she said, looking not at adult Pandora, but at her infant self.

"Nor I." Gaia, but she wished she saw another way that did not destroy them all.

"I, um ... What happens to Odysseus?"

Pandora frowned and shook her head. Kirke's feeble attempts to play for time would only make all this harder. As if it could *be* any harder. "It won't change anything."

"I just ... I care for him."

Which only made Pandora's heart ache all the more. She had spent the last nine months mired in the awful realisation she had become a kinslayer. She had no father, because she had slain him in a burst of fury. And knowing the why of Kirke's question only served to shatter one more piece of Pandora's already broken heart. "You cannot save him."

"I can *try*."

Oh, dammit. Pandora grasped Kirke's hand and squeezed it. "I respect that. We have to have hope." So should she give her mother a fool's hope? A lie from which she could suck all the juices trying to sustain herself, only to find, in the end, it was a worthless, dried-out husk? But what alternative lay before her? To deny Kirke any hope? "Odysseus dies about nineteen years hence, on a beach in Ithaka, at night."

Kirke closed her eyes, perhaps holding back more tears. It had to be now. She had to do this now, or she never would. She eased the babe from her mother's arms, though Pandora knew she left one of the fragments of her own heart in its place. Tears still dribbling down her own cheek, Pandora planted a kiss upon Kirke's brow. "I love you, Mama."

Kirke collapsed into a sobbing, blubbering heap. For a brief moment, for a drawn-out eternity, Pandora watched her, wanting more than aught in the World to say she had changed her mind. She wanted to push the babe back into Kirke's arms and claim there was another way. But there could never be another way, for the circle was predicated upon itself, and their whole bloodline would collapse if she removed a single thread.

So, having already set the Box, Pandora took several steps back and activated the damned device. Light blurred and collapsed around her.

INTERLUDE: PROMETHEUS

1570 Silver Age

Grief strained and striated the soul, little affected even by the awareness of one's own culpability for pains one suffered. What hollow solace was Prometheus to drive from having lost Pandora, *again*, from the knowledge he had willingly chosen to walk a path of eternal sacrifice? He knew he ought to fortify his heart against the anguish of his life, for he had chosen long back to place the continuance of the World above his own desires. But even if he could truly sever the last vestiges of his own humanity, would that, in the end, serve the people he had striven so hard to protect? Did they need a heartless, soulless phantom to shepherd them, or did he, should he kill his heart, risk leaving Man with an indifferent and callous guide, dangerous as Mitra himself?

Above the rugged shoreline of Atlantis, Prometheus ambled along the cliff's edge, half consciousness of the waves that battered the rocks below. The coastline changed over time, abraded by nature's fury. Even Gaia herself cracked and weathered, and somehow, he was meant to remain sempiternal.

Again she was gone.

This place, this island, it had birthed the Watchers and, through them, the Elder Races. From the seeds of the Tree, it had given rise to Mankind. If any place upon Earth ought to have remained timeless, it should have been Atlantis. But even the names changed, and his friend Atlas, who had claimed this place, even he too was gone, the island now ruled by his daughters. Oh, Prometheus feared for the Pleiades too.

Overhead, an eagle screamed, as if in warning of the damnation he knew was coming. He would have to speak the words soon, though he knew where they led. He would die a torturous death every day, his agony drawn out over years, over *decades*. Not even death could offer him reprieve, for such an escape was denied to him. Knowing that, how could he not muse upon refusing the sacrifice? How could he, if still on some level a Man, not falter on the threshold of such suffering?

Belatedly, he scanned the sky for sign of the bird, but it must have swooped upon prey, for all that lay above was a cloudless blue sky, mocking him with its purity in the face of his impending doom. Most-like, Zeus would turn the harpy upon Prometheus because of his love of birds. Of course, Prometheus's affection for birds had been born from Pandora's. A shuddering sigh burst from him, and he wobbled along the path, swaying as if drunken.

But there was not enough wine in all the breadth of Gaia to drown his fear or his grief at losing Pandora once more. She ought not to have had to endure what she had, and in the years since last he'd laid eyes upon her, his every moment seemed filled with visions of her pained visage. Of the shadows that had deepened beneath her eyes, as her own anguish had worn her so very thin, almost enough to break her.

"You ask too much," he whispered to the Moirai, his words all but swallowed by the wind off the sea. Perhaps they would hear him, perhaps not. Either way, he knew they would remain uncaring, so what did it matter?

His and Aditi's souls seemed cursed to remain forever torn apart, tormented by Fate, and pulled so taut they always seemed ready to snap in twain. And there was no way out, save onward, ever onward.

But if he pushed through, if he remained steadfast even in the face of such torments, maybe he might cling to hope. Hope to see her again. Hope they might claim more moments in time. Hope, even, that when time had played out, Mankind might escape the awful fate Prometheus had foreseen for it.

IN THE HOUR PAST DUSK, the Fire cult had built a tremendous blaze outside Brizo's temple on the edge of Atlantis. The Oracle Brizo was an oneiromancer, but she tolerated the gathering of the Fire cult nearby for her own reasons. Perhaps she felt a kinship to the pyromancers among the cult.

Prometheus had been the first pyromancer, and, over his interminably long life, he had trained many in his Art. In this Era, some of those had taken to worshipping him, their fervour for his teachings only increasing as he denied his own divinity. He would tell them he was but another soul walking across Gaia, no different from them, but still the Fire cults would spring up. Many of the most ardent adherents to these cults had never met him.

He wished he could say it surprised him, but he had seen so many religions rise and fall over the millennia. It oft turned out that those with the least evidence to validate their faith clung to their beliefs with the greatest fervour. They mistook unquestioning adherence to what their forebears had told them for virtue and, as such, refused to listen even when the object of their veneration himself told them they had things wrong.

So he avoided contact with people, their unsought worship—and he had known them to cast offerings of food, animals, or even people in their fires in the hopes of winning his favour—making him queasy. Now, though, he sat among them with a purpose, choking though it was.

He would see her again.

A small solace he might take for such days and years as would soon unfold for him. And for her? For her, it was all about to begin, he suspected. He would see her before his torment began, that much she had already confirmed. He had to cling to that comfort.

He watched incipient images play within the dance of the flames, hinting at things to come. Oft, he could not place events in the timeline and had to live by guesswork or deduction. But he knew what impended now. There was even a grim part of him that almost relished the dread he would stir in Zeus's breast with these words. The King of Olympus had ruined Pandora's life once and would do so again—many times from her perspective. He was a cruel, petty man, who deserved to be brought low. But that would take time, and whatever justice came to him, it would not change the suffering he wrought upon Pandora or Prometheus or any of his other innumerable victims.

"The king shall fall," he spoke, the pitch of his voice only half an affection, for indeed, pyromantic trance crept upon him. The murmurs of the cult fell silent as all recognised the intonations of prophecy. "From lofty heights shall plummet he who would rule all. Through every foe defeated, in the end, cast down by his own child. Vain, to the last."

Prometheus shut his eyes, blocking out the play of more images through his mind. The Fire cult would ensure the prophecy spread. All too soon, word of it would reach Zeus, and then ... One day, he would send for Prometheus and demand an answer.

But the King of Olympus could no more stop the future than Prometheus himself could. Fate was coming for them all.

IN DAYS TO FOLLOW, Prometheus called upon his niece, Kelaino, in her estate in Atlantis. The woman held a symposium, trying to keep the aristoi drunk and pliant and on her side should Zeus turn upon the Pleiades. For the King of Olympus had already begun to grow restless, long before he would have heard Prometheus's new prophecy. They walked along the pools of her estate, beneath the stars, away from the revellers.

"Ward yourself and take precautions," Prometheus warned, "because Zeus no longer trusts you. His paranoia grows ever deeper, feeding upon itself as such things inevitably do, until even the lack of evidence of a conspiracy reaffirms its existence in his mind."

His niece—the daughter of his fallen friend Atlas, really—groaned. "But why now? It's been nigh sixteen centuries since he bound Father and let us rule here."

"He thinks you complicit in the Nectar propagation."

"Neither I nor my sisters have aught to do with that blight."

"Be that as it may, Zeus sees this polis as the focal point of the worst abuse, and thus, in his mind, the source of it. He cannot imagine this happening under your rule without your knowledge or perhaps even your involvement."

"It is without either!" Kelaino blurted. "Surely you can talk to him, make him see reason."

"He will not listen to me," Prometheus said. "You must think to your defence with him. Prepare to offer him proof of your cooperation. Better still if you offer a culprit."

"We offered him Tantalus, nine years ago."

"And the Nectar continued to spread. Someone else is behind it, Kelaino, and if you do not find them soon, the king will hold you to account for their crimes."

With a frustrated sigh, Kelaino drifted from him, and for just a moment, Prometheus watched her go. He wanted to offer her shelter in the Aviary, but the truth was, he would soon no longer be in a position to protect anyone from Zeus, and he feared what the mad tyrant would do to the Pleiades once he was gone. If they would abandon their pride—and their polis—they could flee to Themis and mostlike find safety, but he doubted they could swallow the bitter draught of the long step down from queens to refugees.

He doubled back the way he'd come, walking past the pools and feeling somewhat forlorn. A strange sense of being watched settled over him, and he turned. There, behind a plinth set for a dolphin statue, crouched Pandora, watching him with awe and perhaps a hint of fear. Her regard slammed into him with volcanic force. Pain and relief and hope and terror all warred inside his soul on seeing her face and he struggled to form words.

"Strange," he managed, "how oft a single trait may prove both blessing and curse. Curiosity can serve as both the hallmark of wisdom —and discovery—and as the precipitator of the most painful of falls."

"Some prices are worth a tumble."

"Some," he agreed, with a nod. And now ... Now it was beginning. And his time was almost spent.

PART III

Regardless, it appears there is one—or at least one dominant—breed of spirit native to each of the nine domains within the Spirit Realm. Deep Ones—sometimes known as sirens or mer—hail from the domain of Water, dryads from that of Wood, keres from the domain of Dark, lampads from the Mist, and so on. Those least actively malevolent toward mortals generally appear to be Deep Ones, as indeed, our own patron hails from this reality. Nevertheless, even Dagon should never be mistaken for a true ally. Spirits are mercurial and unfathomable. Let us not forget this.

— First Chronicle of the Circle of Goetic Mysteries

11

ENODIA

730 Bronze Age

*I*n time, they passed beyond the decrepit wood and out, onto the snow-crusted peninsula to the south. Through the mist they stalked, casting furtive glances over their shoulders in fear the demon yet tracked them. Never once did Keuthos suggest separating, though he knew well Aeshma pursued only Enodia and cared naught for him. Enodia found herself pondering—hoping—that, were the situation reversed, she too could have the fortitude to stand beside her friend as vicious agonies stalked ever closer.

Long they walked, lost in the mire of their own dark musings, until at last, they came to the rime-crusted silver edifices of a great city. Like the fingers of a colossal hand, spires rose from a seaside cliff, a fell light seeping out from beneath the layers of ice encasing them. Frigid winds swept in from across the sea, billowing the wraiths' shrouds. Had either of them held life in their bodies, surely that freezing gust would have extinguished it.

"The Moon Sea ..." Keuthos rasped, and Enodia followed his gaze, not toward the silver towers but across the waters. Though the mists of the Rimefells swirled and choked far out beyond the shore, above it all, beyond the sea and over the Gloomwood where dwelt the dryads, hung the orb of the Moon. Enodia had never learnt—even the denizens of this Realm seemed uncertain—whether the moon here was the same one visible in the night sky of the Mortal Realm. Here, it was so much closer, the pocking of its rocky surface plainly visible in some places, where hints of virgin wood and timeless lakes seemed to tease life above.

"It watches us ..." Keuthos said, and Enodia shared the other wraith's impression. Even dead, the thought sent a chill wracking through Enodia. The longer she watched that hovering sphere, the more she felt it pulling her toward it, as if it might snatch up her wretched soul and deposit it upon the moon's distant surface. And too, she was struck by the impression of a fathomless intellect soaring above, something older than time itself.

With an effort of will, Enodia tore her gaze away from the Moon and back toward the Winter Court of the lampads. This was the reason they had come here, and she could ill afford to find distraction in the other domains of the Spirit Realm. Instead, they pressed onward, coming to gardens of ice sculptures that embowered gates leading into towers that, now, up close, she realised stretched hundreds of feet into the air. The greatest of those spires must have pushed close to a thousand feet, she thought, and it boggled the mind to imagine anyone building such a structure.

Enodia cast a wary glance at Keuthos and the other wraith nodded. Together, they passed through the archway and into a hollow hall capped by a vaulted ceiling. Whirling reliefs decorated silver buttresses supporting that vast chamber. From above dangled many-armed iron chandeliers. Metal cages at the end of each arm housed Etheric blue flames, enough to grant hints of light through even the huge vestibule.

The mist grew thinner inside the building, but still it billowed and shifted. Now, it spread out before a procession of lampads who made their slow way down a winding stair that rimmed the tower wall, leading up to a landing above. Each of the pale eidolons carried with them a torch of the same blue flames as housed in the chandeliers.

Without a word, the procession of lampads drifted from the stairs and marched a circle around the two wraiths, the distance between each of them ever constant, though Enodia did not see them so much as glance at one another to maintain it. Each of the spirits was clad in flowing white robes, and though the wind did not reach inside the tower, still those garments rustled and stirred. One of the lampads, a female with jet-black hair spilling from her head in ringlets, raised her gaze to meet Enodia's own. "With prodigious brazenness does one intrude upon the demesne of the Winter Queen uninvited."

Enodia chuckled a raspy, mirthless laugh. "In neither life nor death has anyone accused me of lacking either audacity or will."

The lampad's mouth curled. "The Winter Queen shall decree your fate, whether it be to be welcomed as a guest or cast from atop the spire to plummet into the Moon Sea."

THEY WERE LED round a seemingly endless procession of stairs rimming the interior of the spire. On some levels they passed landings where other lampads had gathered, the groups oft turning their gazes upon the wraiths who had dared intrude into their domain. Other levels were lined with silver-banded doors, leading to interiors housing who-knew how many rooms. Five vast towers here comprised this city, spacious enough to house many thousands of inhabitants. Yet, Enodia saw too few dwellers here to earn the name "city." Perhaps the word was but a holdover from the mortal term, for she began to doubt more than several hundred lampads populated the whole Winter Court. Far fewer denizens than any necropolis in the Roil.

At last they came to the summit. Soaring arches supported a domed ceiling, those arches leading out onto a balcony framing this highest level. Winds stronger and harsher than even those below buffeted them here, gusts become gales. Mists that ought not have reached this high wafted about this floor, churned into swirling eddies by the winds, and yet not blown beyond the terrace. In the very centre of the hall rose a crystalline throne, upon which sat a female, though she faced away, staring out over the Moon Sea. On closer inspection, Enodia saw that the mist billowed out from vents beneath the throne.

Slowly, to the sound of crunching gears, the throne, or rather a circular platform beneath it, turned so the queen could face Enodia and Keuthos. The woman possessed a sharp, Otherworldly beauty, features stern as though carved from ice. After looking over Enodia, the lampad drummed her nails upon the armrests of her throne, a clatter echoing, though it ought not have been audible over the howling winds.

Another figure drifted closer, stepping off the terrace, and passed through the archway until she stood but feet away from the queen. With a suppressed start, Enodia recognised the newcomer, though she'd beheld her on only rare occasions, despite having heard her voice in her head for Ages. "Khione ..." Enodia whispered.

The lampad whom Hekate had long enslaved quirked a vicious smile at Enodia's recognition. "Here come two sorcerers, their souls abraded to shreds with the blasphemy of their temerity." She was speaking to the queen but then turned to face the wraiths. "Do you know what dwellers of the Spirit Realm do to sorcerers, Hekate? Your Art, that obscenity you call the Greater Arcana, it draws upon eldritch power to steal the very will out from the depths of our kind. Through such, you insects would make slaves of gods."

No words Enodia could say to Khione could ever soothe the harm inflicted upon the lampad. Nor had Enodia come here in hopes to make amends. Indeed, the enmity that churned in her gut was, by and large, the only emotion that remained to her now. That loathing that all wraiths felt, it filled the hollow inside her, and so she clung to it like a drowning man holding tight to driftwood. And if that loathing extended to her own self, was she to spare Khione from such enmity?

No.

She turned from her former slave to address the queen. "Queen Milurca, I come to you with an offer the likes of which you will not have heard afore now."

"I am listening, wraith. Tempt me, or we shall see if you have learnt the ability to fly."

Khione flashed her too-white teeth at the queen's words, the lampad seeming certain she would have the chance to claim her vengeance. Enodia pictured it and wondered if she had the strength to overcome the dozen or so lampads on this floor. Perhaps ... Where death enervated most, it had only served to fortify Enodia. With necromantic bindings she forged her army and, using them, grown flush by feasting upon Ages worth of souls.

But then, Enodia had learnt well from her encounter with Hades never to approach such negotiations unless in possession of an irresistible offer.

"In the necropolis of Kek, the ghost king Hades has spent nigh unto twenty-five centuries gathering souls to him. They overflow from his dungeons and work as peons in his city, straining beneath the lashes of his overseers. They fair burst at the seams of that corrupted, foetid city."

The queen waved a dismissive hand. "I care naught for the plight of shades in the Roil. Suffering is their lot, eternal, regardless."

Enodia chortled, the sound foul and tattered. "You think I, a *wraith*, seek magnanimity on behalf of others? Altruism is a vanity best reserved for the living. I ask you not to save blighted souls, but rather I offer you them as a feast fit to last Ages. Imagine ten thousand bound and broken souls marched here to serve themselves up before you and the Winter Court. Oh ... and that would be but the beginning." She let her offer lie there between them, even as the hunger glinted in the queen's eyes. Even as it bloomed in Khione's eyes, threatening to smother the lampad's hate. "Imagine one, possessed of that same eldritch Art which Khione so disdains. Imagine if I could alter the pull of souls toward necropoleis, so that some of them marched here, across the golden-thatched bridge. They would find themselves pulled by strings they would never see, strong as the very fetters of Ananke, ever drawn here. Such would ensure no lampad would ever again dwindle with hunger, sustained upon whatever scraps the Elder Goddess of Mist deigns to dish out to you. Imagine, that, Queen."

Queen Milurca rose from her throne. "If you can do as you say ... you may name your price."

Enodia returned to the Underworld with a small army of lampads in tow. The Mist spirits were, reluctantly, led by Khione, who offered Enodia frequent baleful glares promising vengeance should the chance arise. Still, Enodia doubted Khione would betray her queen's command to aid in the conquest of Kek and defeat of Hades, and the lampads should provide the edge she needed to overcome Hades's defences. Or so Enodia dared hope.

Her entourage had doused their torches to avoid giving away their approach, but still they moved in single file, a long line of pale forms slithering through the shadows. She might have thought her army unseen, and yet still Orpheus came upon them, the bard grim faced as he scurried over ebony sands along the banks of the Styx.

"What is it?" Enodia demanded.

The bard shook his head. "Melinoë is discovered. Hades has bound her in the depths, intent to make an example of her." Enodia hissed in frustration, but before she could make an answer, Orpheus ploughed on. "He is delayed though, preoccupied by the appearance of mortals trekking here."

"As you did?" Orpheus's katabasis had become the stuff of legend around Kek, earning the bard the admiration of all who knew of him. It was part of what made him a boon to the cause. Enodia did not bother to remind anyone she, too, had ventured into the Underworld whilst still alive, long ago.

"Yes, living. And more, the blood of Zeus courses through their veins." Oh. Hades's bitter obsession with his brother was, Enodia thought, his greatest weakness, for it clouded his vision to all other concerns. In truth, Enodia had wrought worse suffering upon Hades than Zeus had, but in the ghost king's mind, it was his brother's treachery that had unmade him. "Hades took Kerberos," Orpheus continued, "and went to confront the intruders."

The full import of his words settled over Enodia and beneath her shroud she allowed herself a malicious grin. The king had left the security of his palace. His rage at Zeus had tied a blindfold across his own eyes, and he marched headlong toward his own execution. "We must move quickly, then." Such an opportunity they could not afford to pass. "Has Hypnos returned from Xibalba?"

Orpheus shook his head. "No, but Inanna has brought the forces of Irkalla and lies ready to besiege Kek, awaiting your command." He hesitated. "I know the men who have come here and called them friend whilst I lived. Ariadne, too, was close to one."

"You wish to save them." Wraith instinct rose, insisting she deny his unspoken plea. She could claim it unwise to risk their forces on behalf of the living. She could say they had no time to reach Orpheus's friends before Kerberos tore them to shreds. She could make any number of truthful excuses. In truth, though, it was *spite*—bitter and fathomless—

that made her seek to deny him. Wraiths dwelt in mires of anguish and sought ever to drag all around down into the bog, to drown them in misery as if it might somehow diminish their own. Maybe realising that was why Enodia fought that instinct. "So be it. Gather those you can and try to aid them if time yet remains for it."

Enodia looked to the gathered lampads. To Khione, the Mist spirit still so thick with loathing she might well have been a wraith herself. "Go with Keuthos to Kek. Join with the soldiers of Irkalla and devour the souls of those loyal to Hades. See that he has nowhere to retreat."

Glowering, the lampad turned to pass along those orders.

"You mean to accompany Orpheus ..." Keuthos rasped. "You cannot face the king without me ..."

"Inanna will not trust the lampads unless you vouch for them. Once it is done, go then, and bring what forces can be spared to join me."

Though her friend clearly misliked her instructions, he whirled to join Khione. "Do not underestimate Hades ..." he cast over his shoulder.

No. She would not make such a mistake again.

12

KIRKE

10 Dark Age

*Y*ears rolled by, grey and wan. Some days, Kirke did not leave the warmth of her blankets. The semi-oblivion sleep offered —when she was not beset by oneiromantic visions—it was the closest Kirke came to relief. Eos came and offered her Ambrosia, and Kirke stored the thing, not caring that she had begun to flit away her immortality. Age would creep in over her flesh. But why should such trouble her?

She had lived long enough as it was.

No, but, in the end, self-preservation won out, and though she had delayed some years, she took the draught. It was a hard thing, that slow suicide which mortals must commit day by day simply by existing.

Sometimes, Kirke amused—tortured, rather—herself by wondering where Pandora was in the timeline, as if such conceptions even made sense. She knew only too well *now* was relative to her perspective, and so Pandora was everywhere and nowhere, and if she ever saw her again, she didn't know which Pandora it would be.

Her mother was gone, her child was gone, and her sisters had, after the disasters of Ilium, abandoned her. So on one of the rare occasions Kirke could muster the will to do more than attend to the most insistent of bodily functions, she made her way down to the village—empty larders so demanded—and called upon Eos. If her aunt was far from her favourite person, she was, in the end, among the last of Kirke's kin who would still deign to speak to her.

Now, though Hyperion's glare stung her eyes, Eos insisted on dragging her out to walk through the gardens. The place reminded her of the home she had shared with Kalypso on Ogygia, so many lifetimes ago. There was a strangeness to the thought, for she had dreamt of Kalypso the past night; of one more person Kirke had once loved and managed to lose, the connection betwixt them cleft by the blade of Kirke's own foolish words and deeds. Kirke was, she supposed, ill-suited for enduring love, just as she had never fit anywhere else in her life. The World and its incomprehensible rhythms had never made sense to her the way it seemed to for others.

An observation that earned her a fierce cluck of Auntie Hen's tongue. Deserved, perhaps. This time.

"I hear that Phoeba has joined the Ninevehan Empire," Eos murmured as they strolled. "It spreads far beyond Phoenikia."

"It's the Babilimian Empire now," Kirke commented offhand. "It's been the Babilimian Empire for decades." Given that Kirke struggled to manage even a passing interest in her own life, she cared about as much for the goings-on in far-off places as she did what happened in a cow's arse. Which was to say, so long as she didn't get shit on directly, the topic was irrelevant and unpleasant.

"You've scarce said a word all afternoon," Eos said, mercifully without a cluck. "I had assumed you only came to resupply your stock of wines."

Well, yeah, there was that. "If it were all I wanted, I would not have come to call on you in your manse. Did you ... did you ever again speak to Father about my banishment?" Kirke wasn't certain why she bothered asking. It wasn't like she had anywhere to go, much less the drive to make the voyage. Despair, she had learnt, was insidious, feeding upon itself until part of her clung to it as though it was the last rock in her life.

Oh ... was that what she sought from her aunt? One more layer of gloom in which she could drape herself?

"Well, yes, but you know my brother is somewhat stubborn."

And there, indeed, gloom lay spread out before her, courtesy of her father. "An elderly mule is 'somewhat stubborn,' Aunt. My father is the crotchety progenitor of all mules. He is the veritable *god* of intractable jackasses. Mere mules bow down at his feet and pay homage to the epicness of his—"

Aww, that earned her a cluck. "*Kirke*. These tantrums do not help your cause."

"Yeah, well, that they cannot make it much worse is also rather the point, I'd say."

"I think you need to ..." Eos looked away at some clamour out in the village. It was a shame, as Kirke was dying to know just what her aunt thought she ought to be doing. Only with that information in hand could Kirke decide on the appropriate orifice in which to tell Eos to shove her advice.

But her aunt flowed out into the village, forcing Kirke to either follow or stand alone in the other woman's too-bright garden like the town fool. The crowd, she soon learnt, had gathered around an arriving Titan who stood head and shoulders above everyone else there save Eos and Kirke herself.

On seeing Athene, Eos folded her arms over her chest. "What does the illustrious daughter of Almighty Zeus wish upon our humble island?" For once, Kirke found Eos's ability to infuse condescension even into the most respectful of words somewhat endearing.

Athene would be hard-pressed to find objection with any *specific* thing Eos had said, and yet, the darkening of Kirke's former sister's face made plain she knew she'd received a barb. Or maybe it was that Athene's gaze had alighted on Kirke, who know wished she had stayed in the damn garden to smell the jasmine ... or whatever. "I need to speak with you."

Eos, frowning, looked back and forth between the two of them, then offered a curt nod. "Well, you can use my sitting room, I suppose. It's past time I go to the market, especially if you happened to come in on a merchant vessel. Some days, I think the traders on Atlantis have all but forgotten Phoenikia, and us with them."

Kirke really ought to have stayed in bed this day. Sure, it wasn't like doing so would have meant Athene wouldn't have come calling on her.

Only, maybe she could have feigned sleep. Aught was better than talking to the woman now, after all these years. After ...

"A woman whose works destroyed the life of my son has no right to name me sister."

Kirke winced at the memory. Still, she waved Athene inside the manse. Unpleasant tasks were best over and done with sooner rather than later. Inside, with an affected sigh, Kirke draped herself over a divan and stared at the smouldering hearth rather than at the woman who had rejected their bond. Kirke would be damned if she was going to be the first to speak now.

Of course, as Athene sat there in grating silence for all too long, she began to suspect her sister hoped Kirke *would* be damned. Oh, damn it. Just as Kirke craned her neck to break the awkwardness herself, Athene finally deigned to open her mouth. "I've come to learn one of my wards has been held prisoner on Ogygia, for years."

"Another fine example of Kroniad parenting, that." Kirke needed wine to deal with her sister but found her languor warred with the desire to wet her throat. Even rising from the divan seemed a momentous effort at present.

Athene's frown deepened and she leant forward, arms upon her knees. "He is held prisoner by the Nymph Kalypso, who, unless I miss my guess, has ensnared him with a lust potion you no doubt taught her to brew."

"Ahh ..." Now Kirke forced herself to sit. "So comes the unspoken accusation that, just as precious Herakles poisoned himself on Nectar and it was thus my fault, once again I am to blame that another of your beloved flock has come to harm from my creations. Never mind that I've not spoken to Kalypso in centuries, nor that, as a grown woman, she might actually be held responsible for her own damn actions. By that train of thought, are you personally responsible for Herakles murdering Laomedon and laying the groundwork for that monstrous war?" It was a low blow because, of course, Artemis, Kirke, and Phaethusa *had* launched the war on purpose, though had Athene known such, Kirke imagined she would already be dead.

Athene rocked back. "Herakles defended himself when guards attacked him. He did not strike first."

Kirke held up a hand. "Yeah? I heard tale they attacked after he bellowed at their king, naming him a liar and a cheat. It is a guard's duty to protect from such belligerence, you know?"

The Kroniad scowled, shaking her head. "You've gall to mention Herakles to me."

"Why? I am done begging your forgiveness!" She lurched to her feet now, trembling with rage that had pent up for so long it felt as though volcanic pyroducts coursed through her rather than veins with blood. Like she must erupt, or the pressure would cave her in on herself. "I didn't give the Nectar to your son, and if he took it, he was a fool for doing so! I'm not going to be held responsible for every second-, third-, and tenth-hand ramification for every act I've ever taken across the span of nigh five thousand years!" She looked about for something to hurl and, finding naught, took an aggressive step toward her sister. "Had you the barest conception of the infinite weave of the Moirai's Tapestry, you would know not one among us will ever have perfect enough knowledge to predict the results of all our choices." Or worse, that choice itself, that free will, was insidious an illusion as the difference between past and future.

Athene endured Kirke's eruption with—she had to grudgingly admit —aplomb worthy of an ascetic. The woman did not rise at Kirke's approach nor shout back. Instead, she offered a sad smile. "Kirke. Your friend, if friend she still is, has ensnared Odysseus with her potions. I came here as soon as I learnt of it to give you the chance to convince her to release him from the spell over his senses."

Wait, what? "D-did you say Odysseus?" The heat flew out of Kirke's temper all at once, leaving her drifting down to earth, unsteady. So the Ithakan never made it back to his wife, after so many years?

"You've heard of him? Yes, he was one of many Elládosi warriors I aided during the war and the last who has not found his way home." Athene paused. "I will see him reach home. I owe those who fought that much at least."

"Took you ten years to care."

Athene scowled. "As a fellow Oracle, you know well enough information comes to us when it wills, not when we would have wished for it." The Kroniad visibly steadied herself. "I don't wish to harm Kalypso, Kirke, though I despise her for holding someone in sexual servitude and stripping them of free will."

"Considering your father's repeated offences ..." The words slipped out, half-formed. Kirke wasn't sure whether she'd have held the accusation back, had she been able, but she didn't really regret it now.

"You think I *like* the things my father has done over his reign?"

"I heard you struck down Apollon and fought Artemis on his behalf. Yeah, another woman you once called sister, wasn't it?"

"How do you know that?"

"What, you think my sister—my actual sister rather than yours, mind—never talked to me? Hard to imagine, right, conversations with your own sisters. Yeah, and on behalf of a tyrannical rapist you raised a blade against her."

"I ..."

"How precious you rate the bonds of sisterhood. A shame they seem but dying candles compared to the blazing need for a father's approbation. Why should that surprise us, though? Is it not a *man's* world?"

Athene paled, her mouth open. Then she wheezed out a shuddering breath. "I'm ... sorry ... I ..."

Had Kirke misheard that? Did mighty Olympian Athene apologise to her? Kirke licked her lips. For so long she'd endured Athene's cold indifference, now she didn't know what to do with this flicker of warmth. Cradle and nurture it? No, she no longer had the strength to kindle such a bond once more. "I'll convince Kalypso to release Odysseus. Do us all a favour and stay out of it from here."

Athene gave her a sharp nod. For a moment, the Kroniad stared at Kirke, maybe hoping for more. Maybe she sought some answer to her fumbling attempt to make amends. If so, Kirke had no more to give her at the moment. So, in the end, Athene left, and Kirke lingered within Eos's manse.

She paced the atrium until jitters—she could not deny the raw mingle of anticipation and dread at the coming altercation—drove her out into the gardens. There she spent some time inspecting the blooms Eos's gardener had cultivated. Or miscultivated, in a few cases. Some flowers would thrive best if shaded during the hottest parts of the afternoon by the house's eaves, whilst others craved every last ray of Hyperion's glory. A few transplanted beds, and Eos would have a more vibrant, healthier crop of flowers.

"Kirke?" Eos asked when she found Kirke preparing one such shifting of the flowers.

Kirke glanced up at her. "Your groundskeeper could have done better in a few cases."

Eos frowned, first folding, then unfolding her arms. "I tend my own gardens."

Kirke kicked herself. Of course Eos did. Because, as with herself, Eos fought against the perennial incursions of boredom and loneliness. Aura was dead, Hesperos off polishing Helios's shiny arse, and no one had seen Eos's husband since long before Kirke came to Aiaíā. Her aunt was locked in her own unwalled, inescapable prison, languishing in the tedium of immortality. And, like Kirke, probably too afraid to surrender that immortality and let death lurch closer.

Insulting Eos's ability at her pastime mostlike would not help Kirke's cause. But then, Kirke had not lingered here to beg. Not anymore. With a huff, Kirke rose from where she crouched in the dirt, brushing the grime off on her peplos. "So. I'm leaving Aiaíā."

"Kirke—"

"I've things which need attending to, but I rather doubt I'll return even when those things are done. It's been over a century now, and I'm through accepting punishments from my father."

Eos clucked her tongue. "Kirke—" she tried again.

"You can smooth things over with Father," Kirke ploughed on, having little interest in her aunt's objections, "or conceal my absence from him as it suits you. As for us, I'd say you ought to send me on my way with your blessings, considering I saved your people from those pirates and my reputation here has kept the island safe ever since. If you cannot offer your blessings, though, at least do not impede me. I wish you no ill, Aunt, but I'll no longer consent to remaining a prisoner, and if you seek to hold me against my will ... well, I bet I could turn you into a lynx or a deer or ... you know, some asparagus or something."

Eos's mouth snapped shut. Then a slight huff escaped her aunt. A long moment she looked over Kirke before nodding. "There's a ship bound for Tyros departing in the morn. From there you can charter passage wherever it is you are bound."

The better part of Kirke had not expected proud Eos to bend. The woman always seemed to think so much of herself and so little of Kirke.

Instead, Eos offered her aid. Kirke embraced her aunt, almost sad to think she might not look upon her face again after this. It had been a strange century for her; maybe for the both of them. "You're not a prisoner here, either."

A mirthless laugh burst from the woman. "No? My brother gifted me this island on the fringe of his empire to govern, Kirke. But was it truly a gift or rather an assignment to keep his sister safely removed from the politics of the Thalassa world? Sometimes the best we can do is bear indignities like marks of honour and pretend they do not trouble us."

"Yeah, sometimes." Kirke nodded. "And sometimes maybe it's better to force them to drop their pretences of magnanimity and either give us freedom or make plain their tyranny."

Eos hesitated. "He would only claim, whatever sentence he next forced upon me, he did for my own good."

Well, true, and knowing Helios, he'd mostlike believe it himself. "Your alternative is to while away eternity in an empty garden, a willing participant in his charade. The choice is yours."

Really, there wasn't much more to say. Well, maybe one thing. "It's not even a very good garden, Aunt."

It took time, of course, to find passage from Tyros to Atlantis, and more still onward to Marsa, on Ogygia, where merchants travelled these days. Once, the island was famed for the cultivation of exotic herbs and spices, popular in the polis of Atlantis. Kirke and Kalypso had arranged such, largely as a cover for their Nectar production. She supposed that, in the years since giving over that production, Kalypso had allowed the legitimate business to falter as well.

Her small ship weighed anchor at Marsa, and Kirke found it felt very little like a homecoming, despite the years she had lived here. Every building was changed, crushed and rebuilt by the merciless procession of history. Every face belonged to a stranger. The sights and smells and sounds all seemed foreign, even the lay of the land but vaguely familiar.

Long, long ago, this island had been the homeland of Kalypso's grandfather, Atlas, and the woman tended it still. She had received it more as banishment than reward from her mother, a situation that pierced rather close to Kirke's heart. Yet her mother was long dead, all Pleiades dead, and still Kalypso lingered here, a veritable queen of this quiet place.

Kirke walked the path to where she'd once shared a modest home with Kalypso. The woman's great-uncle Prometheus—whom Kirke now knew to be her own grandfather, and no actual relation to Kalypso—had taken Kalypso beneath his wing and trained her as a naturalist. At the time when Kirke had come here to join Kalypso, Kirke had found Prometheus intimidating and strange. Well, of course, he *was* strange, if less intimidating now. Was he there now, in his Aviary once more? Would she have aught to say to him now?

At first, Kirke was not even certain she had the right hill. Everything had changed, and she found herself turning about, wondering what had happened to the estate. Queasiness bubbled in her gut as she climbed the slope. Only when she almost tripped over a half-buried stone did she know for certain she had the right place. She knelt, running her fingers over the moss-covered protrusion. This had been part of the wall that had rimmed Kalypso's estate. Had time worn the rest away? Had towns-folk come to claim the stones to build their own homes after the Nymph had abandoned this place?

An unexpected ache lanced through her breast, to see her erstwhile home demolished, even though she'd never thought to return to it. Why should she care it was gone?

The once lush gardens she and Kalypso had tended with such care had become an overgrown forest of vegetation. Kirke rose to drift closer, wistful and feeling grieved even if she could not explain the reason for it. This place, no longer redolent with the scents of herbs and roots, now rather smelled of flowers and loam. Plants burst from the foundations where the manse had stood, she saw from up here, though many of these stones were gone as well.

Pigeons and pheasants voiced their annoyance at her intrusion into their haven, but still, Kirke found herself pulling aside vines and over-growth. She wasn't certain what she hoped to find. A memory? Proof this had once been her home and that something besides herself had survived the passing of the Ages?

But, though the hilltop burst with life, her life here was dead, and these plants had burgeoned out of its rotting corpse. Huffing, she pressed on, circling around until she could see the Aviary. *That*, at least, still stood, so perhaps Prometheus still visited it on occasion. Or at least he had paid someone to tend it.

From this angle, Kirke spied another manse, larger, on a more distant hill, though before the mountain where Prometheus had built his Aviary. So Kalypso had built herself a new home. How long after Kirke had left here had the woman fled this place? Was it too thick with memories for her, too? Yeah, Kirke could understand that only too well.

She scrambled down the back side of this hill and made her way to the next. On drawing nigh, though, she slowed. One thought had run through her mind, over and over, on the sail from Phoenikia to Atlantis, and grown louder once she stood on the boat to Ogygia. She could not bring herself to see Odysseus. Part of her still wanted him back ... but who was she to deny him his long-awaited reunion with his wife? Kirke had driven him from her side for his benefit years back. To seek to reclaim him now would be selfish. To lay eyes upon him without touching him would be masochistic.

She wanted to reach for him, so bad it felt a physical ache in her chest. Every time the justifications arose in her mind—*what better claim did his wife have? If he loved her so much, he would not have chosen Kirke for a time!*—she shouted them down with a fierceness that left her fatigued and despairing.

In the end, Kalypso spied her lingering upon the hill's lower slope. With a slow, steady gait and unreadable visage, the Atlantid descended the slope to meet her, leaving Kirke wondering why Kalypso had not forced her to make the climb. By the time the other woman reached her, Kirke had imagined a single answer. Kalypso had heard from Odysseus that he had dwelt with and loved Kirke, and she too wanted no contact between the former lovers. How strange, in fact, to imagine that Kirke had loved both this woman and the man she had ensnared, and that now they shared the warmth and companionship she had lost from the both of them.

"It's been a long time," Kalypso said. Though Kirke had trouble sussing out the emotions of others, sometimes a feeling rang so profound even she could not miss it. Sometimes, even the simplest of words could be laced with such pain as to beggar the senses.

"Yeah." Kirke swallowed. She wanted to run from this hill, run from this island. Swim back to Atlantis and crawl into an amphora of wine to drown herself. She wanted to throw her arms around Kalypso and beg her forgiveness. To rain kisses on her brow and neck and wonder if aught could ever go back to how things had been. "Yeah." Her voice broke.

"You're here for him."

Not trusting herself to speak, Kirke nodded.

"You can't have him back." No, she could not, more the pity. "You let him go, and now he's *mine*."

Was that what this was? Had she done this to spite Kirke, still nursing wounds dealt more than eight centuries prior? But why not? Some wounds festered, able to heal only after the ill humours were lanced from them, if even then.

Kirke swallowed. "I let him go ... because he was not mine. And certainly he is not yours to hold, either."

Kalypso folded her arms over her chest, petulant and fuming and beautiful. "As decided by whom, Kirke? By you? Are you the arbiter of right and wrong across the Thalassa? If so, I'd like to share a few choice words with the cosmic moron who assigned such a role to *you*."

Well, that drew a wince. "Yeah. That I have made my share of mistakes does not mean I ought not to strive to do better. Or that I cannot spot ill deeds done by others. This ... this is beneath you. You hold a man against his will. You claim sexual liaisons from one who has not freely chosen to give them. There is a *word* for that, Kalypso."

The other woman paled as Kirke's implication struck home. She sputtered some incoherent response, then at last slumped down upon the hillside with an *oof*. With a sigh, Kirke sat beside her.

"You want me to stay with you a while?" she asked. "Is that what you were hoping for?"

"Maybe. I don't know. Not like *this*."

Kirke shrugged. "It's not like that. It's not like aught, save whatever it is like, which is whatever we want it to be, you know? Maybe it's fine, maybe it's even right to just come out and say what you want from life. From people. At least, it makes it easier on people like me, who find reading people harder than translating dusty scrolls written in dead languages."

A tear glinted in Kalypso's eye. "Either way, I'll send the man home. I didn't ... I had not ever considered any similarity in ..." She choked on the words, and Kirke patted her knee in reassurance; the Nymph was clearly ill with the thought of it, now.

"Yeah." Maybe, one day, she could let Kalypso in on some hint of the horrors she herself had done. Maybe she could explain about the Tapestry and the real cruelty of the Moirai, and all of it. But then, she would not do that to her friend any more than she'd been willing to inflict it upon Odysseus. "Is Prometheus up there?" she asked, pointing to the Aviary beyond.

Her friend nodded. "He comes and goes, but he returned from a prolonged visit to Mu not so long ago. He leaves it to me to see his groundskeepers are paid and cared for, so I am, for the most part, appraised of his times away."

Kirke sighed, suddenly uncertain she had been hoping for such an answer. If Prometheus was absent, she was absolved of the obligation of needing to confront him. Now, with him just up there, she had only herself to blame if she never said the things she needed to say. "I've a need to speak with him, maybe for a while. When I return ..."

"You don't want to see Odysseus before that?"

"I've no wish to see him at all. I told you, he's not for me." And it took the sum of her will to hold herself to such.

THE WAY UP to the Aviary felt longer now. Or perhaps it was that each plodding crunch of her sandals over scree brought her one step closer to a confrontation she dreaded. In truth, Kirke misliked all confrontations. They left her palms clammy, her heart racing, and created ill, fluttery feelings in her gut. That and, once her ire bubbled forth, it tended to explode in a torrent of emotion that led her to say—and do—things she ought not to have. Such left her with lifetimes of regret and too many things she could not take back. Too many people hurt by emotions she wished she could control.

Still, the space between her and her destination closed, too long and yet not long enough. Then she found herself easing open the great door to the tower and slipping inside. Within, the fountain burbled, over-flowing with birds splashing about and chattering. Some of them squawked in indignation at her approach, but Kirke ignored them, instead looking up, through the maze of poles creating a network of perches above. Beautiful and vibrant, yeah, but the whole design had always struck her as a lot of effort if all one wanted was to bathe in bird shit.

Kirke took the winding staircase rimming the interior wall, following the path to the next landing. There, beside the edge of the sand for the rock garden, sat Prometheus, nose-deep in a musty tome. "Kirke." He set the book aside and rose to greet her, drawing her into an awkward embrace. At first she tensed, but she couldn't turn away familial warmth when offered, so she eased into his hug and held him back a moment.

Of course, letting him soothe her raw nerves would not make what she had to say easier, so she pulled away and took several steps back. "Did you know? About Pandora, did you know?"

His crystal blue eyes caught the fading daylight as it streamed in through wide windows, seeming to flash with passions otherwise concealed. "I know a great many things about her. That I love her more than aught else in the ambit of the World. That in her soul, I see a companion through the Ages I would, given choice, clutch close and never allow even a moment's separation."

"Yeah, and that's magnificent and all, but I mean to say ... do you know ..." She cleared her throat. "Did you know she was my daughter?"

For a moment, he stared, eyes widening hair by hair, the inviolable facade of composure he always wore cracking. "No." He shook his head. "That's not possible." He was shaking his head, and Kirke had the distinct impression he was trying to convince himself rather than her. "Not even the *Moirai* would dare such profane ..."

There was a comfort, however slight, in learning he had not realised the scope of perversity woven into their family tree. Family circle, rather. "So, yeah. That lover you were just expounding on, that's your great-granddaughter." She knew, of course, even as the words left her lips, she ought not to have said it. He had more intellect and insight than anyone she'd ever met, so he'd have made the connection the moment he knew Pandora as Kirke's daughter. But then, some vile part of her delighted in discomfiting people who seemed too much in control of their emotions. Like, if she couldn't manage such a feat, how dare they pull it off?

Prometheus shut his eyes at her words. His hand flailed in the air, ever so slightly, as if seeking purchase to steady himself with. On finding none, he instead clenched a fist by his side. When he opened his eyes again, that infuriating calm had settled over him once more. "Kirke, I find myself somewhat weary of a sudden. So forgive me for asking if you have some purpose in coming here. If you wish only to visit, I'd offer you a room to refresh yourself first, and perhaps we can talk over supper."

"Supper." Kirke snorted. "Yeah, I climbed all the way up here because I was hungry. Sure. I mean, also because I kind of needed to lambast someone for the cruel spirals of Fate, and you, I'm thinking, seem to know more about them than anyone. So, fair enough, you didn't know about the ultimate indignity."

"Prescience is never perfect."

"Yeah, yeah, I know. No Oracle sees everything, and they never see something they can change. I get it. Only, did you *try*?"

Prometheus barked out a bitter laugh. "More than you can know. Everything I have ever done has been a last desperate attempt to ..." He visibly steadied himself. Whatever it was she'd almost drawn out of him, he seemed to fear speaking it aloud, as if in so doing he might risk unravelling his plans. Which meant ... he *had* plans to escape these chains of Ananke that so bound them all? But if so, if his strategy had stretched out across the Ages, it existed on a scale so far beyond fathoming as to become almost imperceptible. To her ... and to his foes.

"And Mother? I mean, I get why Pandora couldn't raise her. She had meant to, but the chance was stolen from her in what, for her, was but an instant. But *you*... Mother grew up under your care in Thebes, right?"

"She did."

"So why didn't you stop her from, oh, I don't know, *damning* herself, for one thing? Yeah, I think that's a good place to start. I mean, kind of big deal, letting one's soul get abraded, holding congress with foul entities from beyond the Veil, all that. Did it not seem an issue to you? Kinda seems one to me."

He hid it well, this time, but she spied the slight narrowing of his eyes. "Because you, having now had a child of your own, found it easy to change the course of her destiny, I take it?" Kirke bit her lip to keep from screaming at him. He would throw that at her? His vicious blow was made a thousand times worse by the truth of it, undeniable and soul crushing as it was. "Do you imagine I did not strive, in every way I could, to steer Pyrrha away from the Art? That I did not warn, as firmly as I dared, that if she—"

"As firmly as you dared!" Kirke shrieked, no longer able to hold back her fury. "What, you wagged a finger at her and said, 'Oh, darling, it's better if you don't damn yourself with sorcery. Unless you really want to, of course.' When a recalcitrant child refuses to listen to her parents, you *make* her listen!"

He endured her tirade without visible reaction, in the end only reaching over to brush her elbow with his fingertips. "You mean, I ought to have turned her home into a prison, watching her every move day and night, even as she crossed the cusp of adulthood?"

It took her a moment to realise what he had just said. Kalypso's mother had turned her daughter's home into a prison, and it had sparked a rebellion and turned her bitter. Kirke's father had done the same, with much the same result.

"Logic and compassion are the strongest tools we have to change minds, but even they cannot always sway a will stubbornly set toward a course. Nor can they break the currents of destiny that seize upon a soul and carry it where they will it. Ever and anon I sought to find a way to save Pyrrha, in ways you cannot even imagine. In the end, though, you cannot save someone from ... *themselves*."

His strange emphasis on the word had her ill at ease, as if she were missing some essential piece of her mother's story. One, she supposed, she was never likely to have laid out before her.

"Do not be so quick to judge circumstances which you yourself have not lived," he said. "My mistakes over the span of Eras compound upon themselves, forming mountains that cast inescapable shadows over my every step. But as for Pyrrha ... I have spent every century since she turned to the Art wondering what I could have done differently. In the palace of my memories, I have played out a thousand, thousand scenarios, yes, including the violent and tyrannous actions you suggested. I traced the lines of Fate as best I could, and still I found no way free of the crushing grip of Ananke ..."

She had the sense he almost said more. Almost could have said, *not in this*, though she wondered if she imagined it.

"So what, you mean it is impossible to change Fate?"

"If we were to try it, as you say, we would need to do so with the utmost care and deliberateness."

"You refuse to extinguish hope."

"Extinguish? It is ever my role to tend to flames, Kirke. Your mother, my precious child, she has her own plans, and though I have my doubts that she can succeed, a part of me dares to believe ... And as for Pandora, your daughter and my beloved, true hope is *her* domain."

All the fury seemed to melt from her at that, as well as her strength. "Then wherever ... whenever she is, whatever she is doing, we've no choice but to let our hopes ride on her shoulders."

"Hers, always," he agreed, "and some few others."

"Who?" she demanded.

But her grandfather offered only a wry smile in response.

13

———

PANDORA

1545 Silver Age

*I*t was hard to breathe. Waves of pain kept shooting through her chest, as though some vise constricted around her heart. Walking through Tyros, her infant self cradled in her arms, Pandora's eye had taken on an aggressive twitch that made it hard to focus on the path ahead. Trembles ran through her limbs, so fierce she was afraid she would hurt the babe with her convulsions.

The path to Agenor's palace on the Hill of Epaphus might have run under a mile, but it seemed now to stretch a hundred leagues. Or perhaps but a few steps, for all too soon, she was announcing herself as Nike and being ushered inside by frantic door guards trembling in the presence of a Titan. Halls she had run through as a child now seemed so foreign, as if remembered only in dreams. For years, she had longed to return to Phoenikia and hoped to reclaim the home she had been stolen from.

When she had, at last, given over that as a possibility and embraced her life on Atlantis, such as it was, she had thought never to see this place again. But even then, in the depths of her despair, she could never have imagined such circumstances as would have her once more treading down these marmoreal halls, the instrument of her own torment.

And the irony was not lost on her that, though she had always thought herself Phoenikian, she, in fact, had never been from here. Her father was Ithakan, her mother Helian, and her bloodline beyond a confused mess she could never explain. That she was the great-granddaughter of her own husband, she tried not to dwell on.

The tingle of distant memories tickled her mind, and Pandora meandered the halls, watched by nervous servants and courtiers, none of whom dared ask about the business of a Titan. Even when she spied her uncle Phoenix watching, she pretended not to notice. She had loved this man so much Prometheus had named the firebird he created for Pandora after him. Now, Pandora was afraid, if she so much as looked him in the eye, she would burst into a fresh bout of lachrymal hysterics, throw her arms around a man who didn't know her, and blubber on about how much she missed him. He, who would *die* protecting her and his sister Europa. No, Pandora could not face him, least of all unprepared, nor his brothers Kadmus or Kilix, though she spied them, as well.

Too, she would not have chosen to meet Europa, if any choice lay before her. None did, of course. None ever did. Eidetic memory or not, Pandora's recollections of her time as a five-year-old were somewhat hazy, and it took her time to find Europa's chamber. When she was certain she had it, she rapped on the door.

A woman—a middle-aged servant she had seen but could not place —opened the door and her eyes widened. "M-mistress!" she fair hissed over her shoulder. Belatedly, the servant swept a bow before Pandora. "My lady."

Pandora patted her shoulder in reassurance to show she'd taken no offence, then, as the woman made way, stepped around her. "I need to speak to the princess alone." Such was, almost certainly, a violation of more than one rule placed upon the woman, and the servant hesitated.

At least until Europa herself stepped around some curtains into her sitting room and offered a nod of reassurance. "I'll be fine." Seeing Europa turned Pandora's knees weak. That smiling, gentle face of the girl who had been as close to a mother as Pandora had ever known. Those kind eyes, the lips that never remonstrated, save for the worst of Pandora's tempers. A tide of memories came flooding back in, enough to have her swaying in place, afraid of drowning in the deluge. Memory, it weighed more than the greatest stones of mountain peaks and ran deeper than the depths of the sea.

After a respectful bob of her head, Europa invited her to sit and mumbled other pleasantries Pandora scarce heard. Next she knew, she found herself perched on a divan, her infant self stirring in her arms. She hoped the babe would sleep through this. She had taken Kirke's milk and must be exhausted from the birth …

Europa leant forward a hair. "If I may ask, whom do I have the honour of entertaining in my chambers?"

Pandora licked her lips, struggling to find her voice. "Nike."

Europa's eyes widened a hair. She had plainly heard of her, perhaps from stories of the Titanomachy, as the Gigantomachy would not unfold for another fifty years yet. "Well, Goddess, be welcome in my home. To what do I owe this honour?"

"I have …" Hades's take the Moirai! How could she do this? Was it too late for her to return to Kirke? Oh, but it had always been too late for any of them. "I have a favour … to ask."

The princess's eyes darted to the babe, then back to Nike's face. "Your child?"

Pandora couldn't begin to answer that question. Maybe it was better if everyone thought Pandora was Nike's bastard. "The child's name is Pandora. And I … need someone to raise her."

Europa nodded, hiding her emotions well, though Pandora knew they must be roiling behind her eyes. Unlike their male counterparts, female Titans could not openly acknowledge their bastards without facing messy complications, shame, and ridicule. Such disparities grated, even if they had naught to do with the truth of the day. Regardless, Europa no doubt judged the situation thus. For a short time—Pandora knew it was short, though it seemed to stretch on, each breath more difficult than the last—Europa sat there, mulling it over. For a Titan lady to ask an aristos woman to raise her child was not unheard of. But to choose an unwed princess, that would raise no few eyebrows. Europa might face rumours the bastard was her own, too, though her father would silence such as best he could, no doubt.

Finally, the princess rose, reaching for the babe. "Well, Pandora, it would be my deepest pleasure to welcome you into my home. It's a beautiful name you have, isn't it? Oooo," she called, as the babe awoke and stared up at her. Pandora expected the infant to burst into wailing, but the child looked up at Europa as though she already saw her mother there.

And thus Kirke's stint at motherhood was sliced in twain.

Pandora had to clench her hands at her sides to keep them from trembling. Her breaths came out in ragged shudders, and though she tried to conceal her condition from Europa, Pandora was uncertain whether she succeeded. It took all she had, all she was, to keep herself from cracking in that moment. She could not fathom how the Moirai had conceived of such wretched tortures as had befallen her and all her line.

As would still befall Europa, and Pandora could not stop it. She could not spare the woman who had raised her for the first five years of her life. She couldn't change a thing about all this. Instead, she lurched forward and wrapt her arms around the princess, who stiffened, clearly at a loss at having a goddess embrace her. Pandora didn't care about decorum. As she at last pulled away, still struggling to keep from weeping, she stroked one hand along infant Pandora's brow. Then she looked to Europa. "You will never know how much all you do has meant to me. Never, except that I try to tell you now." The hand upon Pandora's brow she moved to Europa's cheek. "For what you will do for this child, I will love you, however many the days of my life should prove."

"I ..."

Pandora rose to her feet before she could allow herself to falter, or to say more, or otherwise jeopardise the timeline. This could not be borne. But one more thing weighed on her. "Europa," she said, struggling to keep her voice. "Life is moments. Only moments, stolen from the greater weave of Ananke as best we can. So each moment you have, each precious, quiet instant heading toward memory, treasure it."

The princess stared at her, eyes wide and mouth agape, struck speechless.

Thus, with a final nod to Europa, Pandora fled the girl's chambers, at last allowing tears to flow once more. Having left yet another piece of her heart behind in that room, Pandora wondered how much of her would still be left before the end of all of this.

As she rushed from the palace, she nigh collided with Kadmus, though the prince gracefully danced out of her way, staring at her with open-mouthed awe in the process. No, she could not speak to him. She could not speak to anyone now, and perhaps the best she could hope for was to escape Epaphus Hill and use the Box to run from Tyros. There was no place for her here, in this time.

So frantic was she, she did not spot the man lingering outside the palace until he caught her elbow. Pandora yelped, and flames burst into one of her palms before she recognised Prometheus, staring into his vibrant eyes. For a moment more, she struggled for words, her mouth flapping like a beached fish. Then she collapsed against his chest and let him hold her as the tide of her grief drew her into its depths.

❧

THEY SAT BY THE SEA, Prometheus stroking the back of her head as she leant against his shoulder, wishing the lapping waves could wash away all cruelties of Ananke. Her husband had a cottage—or a shack, perhaps, as she had little mood to be generous at the moment—outside the city of Tyros. The place offered shelter against the rain, though, with an outdoor cooking fire shadowed by an extended eave of the roof. It gave her a place to sleep, and soon, Pandora knew, exhaustion would claim her. Soon, but not yet, because even rising to reach the bed took more momentum than she could as yet muster.

In the throes of true despair, even the reprieve of slumber seemed an intrusion, and one sought only to linger in the perpetual twilight of one's misery. She wanted to exist neither in this world nor the world of dreams. Rather, she wanted, by force of will alone, to make everything other than how it was.

"I'm so tired," she mumbled into Prometheus's shoulder. "Fate ... It washes me away from myself, layer by layer, until all that remains is a raw, bleeding nerve." A shuddering breath tore from her, and he held her closer, not speaking. Maybe there was naught for him to say, given no words could bulwark her against the ravages of Ananke. "Tell me how all this ends."

He blew out a sigh. "I cannot lie to you, nor can I give you a truth that would satisfy you, save that, nigh as I can tell, you draw close to an ending of these jaunts across the timeline." He hesitated. "I can see how it has so worn you down, and I cannot stand the thought of your suffering, not even knowing ..."

"Knowing what?" She pulled away, scooting on the sand until she gazed into his eyes.

They caught the light of the late afternoon sun and turned lucent. He kept his face placid, but his eyes, those held pain. "Suffering is part and parcel of the World, Pandora. The Wheel of Fate is the crucible of souls, tempering us through endless revolutions. Life is suffering."

Oh, but they had enjoyed two beautiful years together, on a beach not so unlike this one, in a house *quite* unlike this. She longed to tell him of their wedding, but he had not known of it beforehand, nor could she see how telling him of events a thousand years in his future would much ease those years he must live through to reach that time. "There comes a time for us," she said instead, "in which we steal some measure of peace from the fabric of time and the pull of the World."

An earnest smile dawned upon his face, and he leant forward to lay a hand upon her knee. "And so we must take comfort in knowing, life is not *only* suffering. How is it, even now, after the interminable expanse of my years, you still manage to give me, of all people, flickers of hope, Pandora?"

She shrugged. "It's a gift, I suppose."

A single chuckle escaped him. "Yes, you are." He held her gaze then, seeming to peer into her soul, as he sometimes did. When had that piercing intensity ceased to leave her trembling? When had it stopped leaving her feeling naked and helpless and started to make her feel, instead, seen? "What stops you, then, from claiming more time for us, out of this place, here and now?"

"I mean, your home could use a few upgrades. Expansions. I mean, maybe tear the whole thing down and start over, to be safe."

"Do it. Together we can craft something more to our liking."

Yes, she thought, that would do. Let her have her chances, scattered though they might be across the sea of time, still they would remain *hers*.

14

——————

ARTEMIS

15 Dark Age

*A*fter fifteen years spent across Lydia and Helion, Artemis was at last returning to Babilim. Convincing the rulers of Phoeba to join Mithra's empire had not proved too difficult, though for certain some resented Artemis's resumed influence after having abandoned the polis in the wake of the fall of Ilium. Arranging her father to pledge loyalty to Babilim, that was a whole other level of accomplishment. Even once he agreed to the alliance in principle, Helios had vacillated between covert support as he had provided to Ilium and open declaration of his shifting loyalties away from Olympus. He feared losing what he still had. More, he objected to trading one "foreign overlord" for another.

"This is not the first time you have stood before me and begged me to shift my allegiance," he had pointed out. Thrice pointed out, in fact. His argument dug deep, for he spoke the truth: Artemis had gotten him to break with the Ouranid League in the first place.

Even to her own ears, her protestations that Mithra was different to Zeus sounded hollow, as though she deluded herself. In the end, she had worn away the last of his objections by appealing to his pride and self-preservation. Helios loathed Zeus as much as most of the Olympian's subject kings did, and Zeus had affronted the Heliad genos oft enough, after all. Helios wanted retribution, and too, he saw the rise of Mithra much as he'd seen the rise of Zeus. The winds had begun to change, Artemis had told him.

So, after years of teetering on the edge, Helion had joined the Babilimian Empire. Though she had fought only minor skirmishes on the borders, Artemis felt she returned home the victorious general, having added two more provinces to the empire with very little loss of life.

Phaethusa she had found within her father's court, the woman having made her way there after the fall of Ilium, and seeing her again had sent a flush of relief through Artemis. She'd thrown her arms around her half-sister and wept. "I am not so easy to slay," Phaethusa had teased as if so many immortals had not died on those accursed shores. She had asked after Kirke but learnt that their common sister had broken her exile on Aiaíā, and no one knew where she had gone. Artemis had to assume her sister would reveal herself when and if she chose, though she resolved to try to seek her out if time ever permitted.

Now, Phaethusa by her side, Artemis returned to Babilim. After passing through the outer and inner walls, Artemis amused herself by guessing which buildings were new constructions. There were differences, here and there, but she found herself hard pressed to name them all. Men expected places to remain locked in the frame of their memories and oft grew shocked or wistful on seeing time had continued its relentless march without them. Titans, those who had lived for centuries or millennia, tended toward a more accepting approach to such things. Nigh every time she returned to a place after an absence of years, she found it changed in ways great or small. It became a game to test her memory of just how. But then, like other Titans, she found the sea of her memories turned murky by the compounding of too many years. It was always a struggle to keep details straight.

When she presented herself at Etemenanki, she was greeted by an honour guard of Immortals, those elite troops who formed both the imperial guard and the greatest unit of the Babilimian army. They earned their name because Mithra provided each of them fractional doses of Ambrosia to enhance their Pneuma, and thus their health and prowess. The Immortals escorted her, not straight to Mithra but to their commander. A dark-haired, broad-shouldered Titan man of impressive physique. His bare arms were sun darkened and bore a crisscross of lighter scar tissue.

"Welcome home, General," the man said, his regard scraping over Phaethusa before settling back on Artemis.

There was something, not so much in his words as his tone, that had her taking a second look at him. Then she started. "*Marduk*?"

The Commander flashed his teeth in a too-pleased grin at her recognition. Time's march was relentless indeed, and Mithra's son was no longer an eleven-year-old boy. "My father sends his congratulations on your successes."

"Where is he?"

Marduk's face darkened. "He takes counsel with his assassin."

Artemis had heard Mithra employed a particular agent called Nemesis, the most elite assassin of the Unseen Order. She had never had occasion to meet the woman, but everyone feared her. Even, it seemed, the Immortals. Or, if it was not fear the assassin engendered in Marduk, at the very least she created a profound disquiet.

"In the meantime," Marduk said, "you and I are to begin making plans for the expansion of the empire."

"Into Elládos."

Marduk folded his arms. "Not yet." He looked to the Heliad lingering behind Artemis. "This is ...?"

"My sister, Phaethusa. A stalwart ally, I assure you."

Marduk nodded and motioned for a servant. "Find chambers for the general's sister, near to her own if possible."

Phaethusa nodded in thanks and followed the servant. Marduk then turned back to Artemis. "Come, we can talk in private chambers."

After leading her to a sitting room decorated with rich tapestries and silks from beyond the eastern borders of the empire, Marduk waved for her to sit. Artemis reclined on a cluster of plush pillows hurled about the fringes of the room. Slaves brought in plates of dates and goblets of wine, which she accepted. A small brazier sat in the centre of the chamber, and beside this, Marduk himself sat.

Artemis did not wait for him to speak. "Your father does not think us strong enough to move on Elládos even now?"

"You know why. Zeus and Olympus wield awful powers. Impregnable Ilium fell, and Zeus did not need to even unleash his fearful lightning."

"I was there," she all but growled. Prince or not, she did not appreciate the reminder of such memories.

"Since then," Marduk continued, pretending not to notice her ire, "Phrygia remains in chaos. The many kings once subject to Priam vie for control, but none have the strength to solidify their lands. Even as the kings of Ell\u00e1dos stake their claims across Phlegra."

Because with Ares dead, of course Zeus would allow his sycophantic worshippers to carve up his son's holdings amongst themselves. "You mean to say, if we do not claim Phrygia soon, the Ellad\u00f3si will cross the strait and establish permanent holdings."

"We must hold all the eastern lands. We cannot allow Zeus to expand his empire. First we hem him in on as many fronts as possible. Only then will we strike at Olympus."

Artemis gnawed on her lip. "You mean to push past Phrygia. Into Kolchis."

"And Kimmeria beyond there."

Artemis groaned at that. "Themiskyra will not bow before foreign powers, least of all to a male." And Themis had forgiven Artemis for her terrible crime against Koios. Artemis could not betray the woman again. Not *again*.

"Nevertheless, my father has instructed us to annex all the lands south of Arimaspia, and that includes those of the Amazons." Marduk looked at her, sympathy plain on his face. "He told me you had friends among them. Perhaps you can sway them?"

She snorted. "Doubtful ..."

Marduk sighed and set down the date he'd plucked up. "Then ... I think you will need to decide whether your fondness for the Amazons outweighs our loathing of the Olympians. The emperor will not be gainsaid."

She rubbed her brow, not wishing to dwell on such a thing. "For now, let us attend to Phrygia. A great many leagues lie between there and Kimmeria."

Years passed and Artemis and Marduk had brought Phrygia and Kolchis into the Babilimian Empire. In Kolchis, she had found herself with little wish to strive against her half-brother Aeëtes. But, after they had besieged the city for some time, the Magi had come, and something had happened betwixt Morpheus and the king of Kolchis. She did not know just what, and all Morpheus would say on the matter was that Aeëtes and he shared a common mentor, of old.

And now she and the army lingered on the fringes of Kimmeria, watching the clouds of dust thrown up by the Themiskyran cavalry. The women patrolled the border, waiting for the day when Artemis would order her army to cross and thus mark the beginning of an invasion. It was a step she found herself loathe to take, though she knew sooner or later she must do so.

Such had long been the plan, though they had met with some delays when naval battles had pitted them against the growing might of the Muian Empire. The Queens of Mu had arisen and, calling up Art even the Magi did not comprehend, built an empire to challenge Kumari Kandam out of Mugedang. With their magical dances and their strange tattoo arts, their forces had clashed with the Babilimian navy time and again. Their strange magic infused Muian warriors with power to challenge even Titans in hand-to-hand combat, and Mithra lost far more ships than anyone wanted to admit.

After the Muians sacked Asur, Mithra recalled Artemis and set her in charge of the navy. Having spent most of her time in forests and hills, Artemis had not expected to take to the sea as another home, but she soon found an intuitive grasp of naval tactics, and they began to win more battles than they lost. After decades of struggle, Kumari Kandam and Mu reached a tenuous peace that, Artemis assumed, neither side expected to last long. But the armistice gave Artemis the chance to pursue another aim Marduk had set himself on.

Whilst Mithra had not assigned her hunt for the Gnostic Cabal, Marduk had taken it as his mission to identify those who thwarted his father's plans and risked the unmaking of the very World. Artemis could have left him to it, and gone sooner to Themiskyra, but after year upon year of working close by Marduk's side, she had to admit she had developed a grudging fondness for the man. More than fondness, perhaps. They had spent a thousand eves watching the stars, sipping Babilimian mey wine, and arguing points of philosophy, though once Artemis would have thought such topics banal. But she found herself drawn into debates about the justifiable use of power and whether, in expanding the empire by the sword, they became little better than the tyrants upon Olympus.

"Good intentions make for righteous deeds," Marduk argued. Artemis suspected he quoted Magi doctrine. "Zeus holds himself king in order to varnish his ego. My father conquers a World to ensure peace."

"Peace through war?" she had asked, though she'd known what he meant.

"Not the same. Those behind Zeus, should they succeed, risk the annihilation of the cosmos. Their delusions have become their religion, and a dangerous one."

Artemis chewed on that a moment. "And ours? Our religion?"

"Is Truth."

"They would say the same."

"Yes, but we are right, and they are wrong."

Artemis snorted. "Sure. Good to know." She remembered picking up a rock that night and skipping it across the river. "So ... we have to conquer to preserve the World. Such an end justifies any means, yes?"

Marduk spread his hands. "How could it not?"

Such went their many discussions. Sometimes they trained together, each espousing the virtues of different weapons. Marduk conceded the usefulness of a bow, but mostly he favoured a sword or an oversized mace that allowed him to bring his prodigious strength to bear. Artemis preferred a knife for common use, or a spear in cases where she wanted to keep distance between herself and her foes. The mace seemed so inelegant that she had to scoff at his use. "Why, for someone with such an uncanny talent with the sword, would you ever deign to heft so graceless a weapon?"

To that, Marduk had shrugged. "Because even a Titan who had managed to toughen his skin to iron-like hardness would be crushed, driven to the ground, his organs battered. Against certain foes, sometimes brute force has its place."

And one night, while wrestling, when his hand lingered overlong upon her thigh, she found she had pinned him and not released him. Half-naked and drenched in each other's sweat, their gazes had locked.

Artemis was, now, years later, uncertain whether she had kissed him or he her. All she could say was that it proved to be more than physical release between friends.

So when he went to hunt for the Cabal, she so misliked the thought of parting from him that she accompanied him. They travelled far and wide, seeking what sign they could, and, when they stumbled upon Cabalist agents, putting an end to them. On a few occasions, Nemesis would show up—a woman clad in golden panoply, her face concealed beneath a helm—and they would exchange information with the assassin.

The Cabal had infiltrated Atlantis, Kemet, Illyris, even far Hindush, the southernmost province of the empire. But it was in Yueshang, now a province of the Muian Empire and thus hostile territory, in which they had learnt Themis herself had been, or perhaps still was, a member of the Gnostic Cabal.

Such news had left Artemis sullen and disconsolate, for it meant she could no longer delay the conquest of Kimmeria. So here they sat on the border, and she wondered if Themis would deign to show herself.

Marduk sat by the brazier, in her tent, watching her, and Artemis pretended not to notice. She tried to focus her attention on the reports of her lieutenants, bringing intel from their spies. No Kimmerian had as yet crossed the Kolchian border. Neither side seemed eager to begin the inevitable conflict by violating territory. Artemis imagined, if Themis did not come soon, one hot-headed Amazon or another would grow tired of seeing an army of males on the edge of her lands and take a shot at some hapless dathaba. Maybe the unit would lose a few men. Those deaths would ignite a fire beneath her Babilimian forces.

The shield-bearers would race forward, creating a wall from behind which a hail of arrows would rain over the Themiskyran cavalry, darkening the sky. They all knew it was coming, and part of her wanted to just order the charge and have done. But she could not so easily cast aside the years of friendship she'd shared with Themis; she could not bring herself to strike the first blow.

"I begin to think she will not come to you," Marduk said when the last of Artemis's subordinates had left.

Sighing, she settled down on a mat across from him. "She has to know we will invade if she does not."

"Send an emissary to demand the usual tribute of earth and water. There is no need to draw this out. Either they pledge loyalty, or they fall like the others."

They had been over and over this. "With Phaethusa warding against Mu, I have no female emissary to send, save myself, and they pump any male they see full of arrows long before words are exchanged. I could go …"

Marduk waved that away because that too was well-trodden ground. "An imperial general cannot march, alone, into hostile territory and place herself at risk. Even if everything worked out, my father would never tolerate such irresponsible behaviour from one of his highest officers."

He was right, of course. Which did little to make the thought of unprovoked invasion more palatable.

ATHENE

399 Dark Age

Waiting for the battle was, Athene found, the hardest part of any engagement. Her stomach danced in wild frenzies and refused to still, though she had accepted a swig of Korinthian wine Themistokles had offered her. They stood on the island of Salamis, side by side, waiting for the doom that lurched ever closer.

In the night, they had seen the skyline of distant Athenai blazing and she knew Themistokles had been right. Ships had gotten around them and razed their home, and the knowledge of her companion's foresight had done little to abate the queasy feeling they had shared. Indeed, she had seen a single tear roll down the general's cheek. He had not bothered to mop it, and Athene had not seen any reason to speak of it. She shared his grief for a place that had once been her home, as well. A place that her son and his heirs had helped build.

She could not shake the sense that Artemis had burned her city to punish Athene. And maybe, part of Athene had deserved it. She had failed to stop the breaking of Olympus, and now Olympians were tearing each other apart.

Despite her attempt to focus on the battle, and the tactics they would soon need, Hera's words swirled in Athene's mind. Those words, and *Artemis's*. Hera had changed sometime after Athene's return from her exile, that she could not deny. Was it possible ... What if Artemis had the right of it, and Hera was no longer Hera? The woman had somehow shifted from a thorn in the side of Zeus—and everyone else who had ever met her—to her father's most trusted advisor. This, from a man who seemed to doubt women had brains at all, much less they might know how to use them. And now Father took Hera's counsel, and she kept from fighting at Ilium or even in the defence of his own homeland, in its hour of greatest peril.

Was it because of this Nemesis assassin? Was that what Hera so feared that she would risk losing her kingdom rather than expose the king to such a threat? Athene could use the glamour to disguise herself as other people, though she'd never tried to mimic a specific person. Was it possible someone had done so with the very Queen of Olympus? Replaced her?

Such perilous, treacherous thoughts only served to exacerbate the churning in her gut.

For the moment, Athene needed to commit all her mind, all her will, to this one battle. But when it was done ... When it was, she and Hera would need to have a rather severe discussion. And the woman had best have some answers.

With dawn's first flame upon the sky, the silhouettes of triremes appeared on the horizon. Raven dark, a murder of crows clogging the Strait and closing in upon the last tiny island that stood between death and Ellados.

More and more ships joined that fleet, and Athene's heart clenched. Cold sweat beaded upon the back of her neck and dribbled between her shoulder blades, leaving her armour clammy.

If they failed, her homeland would burn. Even as, across the Strait, Athenai still smouldered. The people of her city—of her own namesake —they had needed her, and she had failed them. Athene clutched the pommel of her sword, drawing a pale comfort from its solidity. This day, she would give not another foot of ground.

This day, the seas would run red with Babilimian blood before she let more of Ellados burn. Artemis would pay for each ancient, glorious edifice she'd seen torn down. And she would pay for the aristoi—fools though they had proved—that she had no doubt slain in their homes. So much had passed betwixt her and Artemis, and it seemed impossible to imagine aught save vengeance could remain left now. And still, a part of her stood there, shaking her head, asking herself, *how did it come to this?*

From the shoreline, upon a small ridge so she could get a better view, Athene watched as the naval battle began. There were limits to what she or Themistokles could do at this point. They had relayed what orders they could, and now, for the most part, it fell to the individual captains to execute those orders. So she watched, ready to give the order to light the signal fire that would signify the need to fall back, but only if they must.

Ships rammed one another, turning hulls to kindling and the seas to chaos. Hails of flaming arrows rained over vessels on both sides, burning beacons of death. Even on shore, the scent of charnel and pain reached her. Her grip tightened upon her sword hilt, but there was no foe to strike down. Her enemies were multitude and committing herself to fighting any single ship would avail the war effort little in the end.

Themistokles pointed to something opposite the battle, and Athene spun, fearing the Babilimians had slipped around their lines and landed troops on the far shore of Salamis. But it was, rather, Hera's pegasus dropping down again. Athene's eyes widened now. By coming here after battle was joined, Hera had all but confirmed Athene's worst suspicions of her, for her real stepmother would have fled at the first sign of personal danger. Hera would risk her own hide only as an absolute last resort.

"I have someone I need to speak with," she said to Themistokles.

Whatever he might have said in answer, the Athenian general jerked, an arrow shaft abruptly protruding from his chest. For a single heartbeat, Athene's gaze locked upon Artemis—soaring in the distance, for the woman had launched the shot in the midst of a flying leap—and then her vision of her former friend was obscured. Themistokles dropped in a heap, dead at her feet.

Athene clenched her fists, wanting to scream. At Artemis, at Hera, at the whole benighted world. The general had been a good man and a great leader. She knew she was shaking her head, as though she might wilfully deny this turn of Fate. As if she could demand Ananke reconsider.

Growling, Athene raced toward Hera. She shoved the woman aside from the pegasus.

"Nemesis—" Hera began.

"You I shall attend to later!" Athene snapped, swinging her leg over the mount and kicking it into motion. The pegasus broke into a gallop, and, after several steps, its wings sent them climbing skyward. Upward, the animal streaked, soon cresting above the battle. Athene missed Nephos, but her own favoured mount had no doubt returned to Olympus. She had not wanted to risk the animal in the battle to come. Now, Artemis had left her little choice.

Athene saw the other Titan bounding between burning ships like some springing frog. The woman's preternatural agility meant she waded among Elládosi like a whirlwind of death. None of them could stand against her. No, but Athene would. When Artemis was tangled in the lines of a sinking ship, precariously balanced, Athene drew a javelin from her back. She had only one, but she would make it count.

Taking aim, she flung it at Artemis, infusing it with Potency enough to pierce Pneuma-hardened flesh. But Artemis released her grip before the javelin struck. The woman slid down the ship's canted hull but caught herself in the rigging.

There would be no escape for Artemis. Whatever sisterhood had once blossomed betwixt her and Athene had now good and truly withered, and all that was left was the mouldering stench of decay clogging her nostrils. Athene needed this done, and now. She leapt from the pegasus's back and landed upon the angled mast. With a spear, she lunged for Artemis. The other woman twisted around, beneath the mast, and—impossibly—managed to flip around it and land beside Athene.

Athene whirled, swinging her spear like a scythe to cut down the other Titan. Artemis toppled backward rather than take the blow. The Phoebid kicked her legs, and the two of them landed in a heap, then tumbled off the mast. Artemis might be faster, but Athene was certain she had greater Potency. They scrambled for pankration holds, even as they skidded down toward the sea, then Athene punched at Artemis's face. The woman twisted aside, and Athene's blow shattered the deck. Her fist snared the broken planks, jerking the both of them to a stop.

From nowhere, Artemis's fist collided with Athene's helm. The metal dented, impacting into Athene's jaw. Again and again Artemis rained blows on her until Athene lost her handhold, and again they were slid-ing, skidding toward the deep. Artemis slipped away from her, flying up with her accursed Pneumatikoi of Lightness. The woman vanished into the chaos, and Athene had to think of herself.

She whistled for the pegasus and, when the animal came into sight before Athene would have dropped into the ocean, she sprang. Without Lightness, it was more a matter of a Potency-infused wild leap, but it served to catch hold of her mount. For a moment, she dangled, clutching the animal with desperate fingers, kicking legs in the air with no purchase. Potency gave her the strength to pull herself upward and, slowly, onto the beast's back.

The damn helm obscured her vision, dented as it was, so Athene yanked it off and let it plummet into the sea. She scanned the waves. It was too much to hope for that Artemis might have perished in those dark waters.

No, this day could not end until one of them had slain the other, of that Athene was now certain. Circling with her pegasus, she kept seeking her foe until, at last, she spied the woman, climbing onto a Phoenikian trireme. She banked to bring the ship beneath her and pulled her second javelin. She flung, but Artemis dodged once more, too damn fast. Athene had lost her spear, but her xiphos would still serve to make an end of her foe.

Artemis had begun drawing a bead with her bow. Athene banked the pegasus at the last moment, ensuring the shot flew wide. Except Artemis had not aimed for her at all, had accounted for the manoeuvre. The arrow slammed into the pegasus's neck. It bucked once, sending Athene pitching over its withers. Next she knew, she was plummeting, wind stripping her screams. She had just enough presence of mind to flood Pneuma into Steadfastness the instant before she slammed, back-first, into the deck.

The impact knocked all sense from her, the whole World hazing to black and spots of whirling white. Groaning, she tried to rise, but even with the Pneumatikoi, the fall had nigh broken her. Artemis leapt atop her. On pure instinct, Athene seized her, going for a pankration lock. Then something struck her head. In her daze, Artemis flipped her around. Cold metal clamped upon her wrists.

All at once, the sluice gates of her Pneuma slammed shut. All strength fled from her and, with it, consciousness.

ATHENE AWOKE CHAINED amid oarsmen on a Phoenikian trireme bound for, she assumed, Kumari Kandam. No one spoke to her, and she saw little point in addressing any of the invaders, assuming they even spoke her language. This was ... It had to be prelude to the visions of Babilim that had haunted her for centuries, like half-remembered dreams always in the back of her mind, suddenly drawn to the forefront.

Once—only once—Artemis deigned to descend into the lower decks and stand before her, though the woman had just stood there glaring. Did she dare to judge Athene, when she was the one who had brought war and death to the land she had once claimed as her own? Artemis's assertion she was Lydian was hollow justification after the fact, for the woman had spent millennia living in and ruling over Elládos, only to turn her back upon those who had worshipped her.

"Look at what you have become," Athene said when it became clear Artemis had no intention to do more than rain haughty disdain down on her. "A lackey to a foreign power, rendering murder among those who worshipped you."

Now the woman scoffed. "Spare me the hypocrisy, Athene. You have slain your portion and more over the centuries and wrought suffering aplenty among the innocent and guilty alike. Now you fight and kill in the name of a *madman* who clings to power with a death grip, strangling the very land you claim to protect." Artemis snatched Athene's hair and yanked, pulling her half off the bench until Athene could feel the woman's breath against her face. "The god-king commands you be given the chance to repent, which is the sole reason I've not yet killed you for what you did to Apollon."

So self-righteous. Athene allowed herself a grim smile. "Tell me of the Unseen Order that tugs your strings even as you profess your actions as your own."

Artemis staggered back, releasing Athene. "H-how do you ...?" Her words seemed to have at last struck home, for Artemis stumbled away, speechless, and did not return.

It was Marduk, apparently the commander of the Immortals and son of the god-king, who escorted Athene into the halls of his father. It had proved a long route from Ugart to Babilim, and by the time they reached the royal sanctum, Athene was not only blood and sweat stained, but covered in trail dust and river mud. She was filthy, reeking, and bone weary.

In such a shameful state was she brought before the god-king who sought to claim rule of all Gaia. The Immortals themselves escorted her forward, and she made no effort to resist. The orichalcum chains would have rendered it pointless, even had she not long back seen this day would come.

The stench of opulence saturated the air of Babilim and nowhere more so than in the heart of this palace, with its great vaulted ceilings depicting strange conceptions of heavenly courts and its gold-plated trim framing the frescoed walls.

Athene took it all in as the guards dragged her by the elbows, the tips of her sandals just brushing the mirror-polished tiles of the floor. No colonnade ran the length of this hall, giving the chamber a vast, cavernous aspect. Lines of braziers rimmed the path to Mithra's throne upon the dais, their flickering light failing to banish the gloom that flitted about the hall.

A dozen Immortals stood in the wings behind the throne, hands on the hilts of their akinakai. Along with them, a hundred of his guards rimmed the periphery, ready to surge over her with the slightest motion from their king.

The King of Kings reclined at ease, his face concealed in shadow, while firelight reflected off the emeralds encrusted into his sandals.

Her captors carried her within a dozen feet of the dais, then drove her to her knees before the Babilimian monarch with such force the impact sent lances of lightning surging through her legs. Instinctively, she reached for Tolerance, but the orichalcum fetters blocked any access to her Pneuma. Of course, if the chains hadn't bound her wrists, she could have torn through these guards in a whirlwind. Maybe she could have even fought the Immortals, though perhaps not so many of them.

"The great goddess Athene," Mithra said, face still concealed. "Come to us at last, even as Elládos falls around you."

Athene stared defiance at the self-proclaimed king of the world. "My father will not ransom me."

Now, Mithra leant forward, offering her a hint of his features, from his trim black beard to his intense eyes. "But it is not your father I am interested in, Goddess." With ponderous import, the man rose, giving the sensation of a river changing its course. "No, I have had you brought here for something far more momentous than Zeus's petty struggles. I have summoned you forth from the foreign lands in order to bestow upon you a gift. The greatest of all gifts, in fact, Athene. I am going to give to you ... Truth."

She wanted to laugh in his face. She wanted to dismiss his pompous claim for the self-serving arrogance of all Men who claimed divine insight as justification for following the courses that suited them. It was the great deception of the powerful, convincing those they trampled that a deity willed it thus. For the love of a god, for the fragile hope of pleasing someone that might have their interests at heart, Men would welcome the heel upon their throats of those who so plainly did not.

Such things flitted through her mind. Yet she could not deny a tremble that shot through her at the certainty with which he spoke. Fanatics oft deluded themselves most of all, she knew. And yet ... "What Truth?" she could not stop herself from asking.

Mithra paced over until he stood before her. With a finger beneath her chin, he lifted her gaze to meet his own. "That our lives exist not in isolation but as cogs within a mechanism that ensures the continuation of the cosmos. That we are, all of us, a part of the ever-turning Wheels."

His words rang like blows against the foundations of her World. She could not understand their full meaning, and yet they tantalised with momentous import. Somehow, in the depths of her soul, she knew that once he finished speaking, naught would ever prove the same for her again.

INTERLUDE: ODYSSEUS

1 Dark Age

With Nike's guidance, we landed upon the island Aiaíā and encountered the sorceress Kirke. And here, my son, my story becomes yet more difficult, for I've no wish to lie to you. But the truth ... the truth is that, though I missed your mother and longed for home, for a time, I fell hard for this Nymph.

Perhaps she ... perhaps she used some draught to befuddle my senses and leave me entranced by her. Yes, yes, such must be the case. Well, in any event, I get ahead of myself. Kirke, she had the magic of dreams, and using such, she sought after answers for why I could not return to Ithaka.

"The siren, Thetis," she said, "holds you to account for the death of her son, Achilles. Her magic haunts you."

I would have called the siren's ire unjust, for even as I had found Achilles in hiding—dressed as a girl!—and forced him to the war, so too had I been forced to it. But no one ever said grief would be bound by chains of logic, and a mother's grief least of all. All of us would come to bad ends, I thought then, for none who sailed for Trojan shores would ever be pure again.

"Do you know of the sage Tiresias?" Kirke asked, her words drawn out as dripping treacle.

"I know he died sometime around when the Epigoni sacked Thebes." It was some ten years before the Ilian War began, though it had naught to do with me. "Are you saying the ghost of a dead Oracle haunts me?"

"No," she said. "No, rather, my dream revealed that Tiresias alone holds the answers to the route you must take to return home."

"Uh ... all right. Guess I'll just ask him, then."

"You must," Kirke agreed.

"I think, perhaps, 'dead' means something different where you hail from."

The witch looked up at the night sky as though it held secret answers for her. "I am most known as a witch for my alchemical experiments."

"Yeah, me too," I said, for I had no idea how to respond to any of this.

She rolled her eyes. "I can brew a draught that would allow you to pass into the Underworld, as a kind of temporary shade. You could then question the fallen seer."

My stomach fell and I struggled to keep my voice even. "I rather mislike any plan that involves visiting the Underworld."

And yet, the sorceress had set my path before me. Still, when she told me it would take a season to brew the draught, and I could remain her guest in the meantime, I did not take it amiss. That ... that must have been when she drugged me, yes, and brought me to her bed. I can think of no other explanation for the muddle of my senses.

And so, for a time, I remained on Aiaíā.

AUTUMN CAME and Kirke harvested the herbs she needed to craft her frightful tonic. When it was ready, she told us to make sail for the island of Sarpedon, off the coast of Phoenikia. It was a blighted place, she said, where the Underworld drew close to the Mortal Realm. That, the witch promised, meant it would best serve my needs.

When I sailed for that place, it was with dread as my helmsman and terror my quartermaster. Fear, even beyond what the Laestrygonians had engendered, bloomed in me, not least because the next part of the voyage I must make alone. But if I was to see my men home, I could not demur.

So, to Sarpedon we went.

❧

THERE IS A LEGEND, a dark tale passed among sailors, of a forbidden island along the Phoenikian coast. Every so oft, you may chance to meet a man of the Sea Peoples, or so those who claim knowledge of the island say, and if you befriend one, they might speak of lands more ancient than our own. Of waters deeper, teeming with secrets unknown.

This island, legend claims, was once home to the most blasphemous of rituals. Tinged by madness, insane cultists committed acts so vile Gaia herself remains forever bruised by their impressions.

If such a place ever existed, I imagine it would have felt like Sarpedon. Though the isle lay not so far off the coast of Phoenikia, no local was willing to venture there; of a certain, *they* felt the place tainted. The rest of my crew refused to come ashore, making signs of warding or whispering prayers to Athene for protection. Alone, therefore, with a lamb in my arms, I waded the shallows and trudged along the beach. Perhaps it was my nerves. Hearing the dread the island inspired in the Phoenikians, seeing it unman my own war-hardened crew, it took a toll upon my resolve, I admit. So, yes, it could have been nerves that set the hairs on the back of my neck on end as I ventured inland. The chill that beset me despite the tropic heat might have originated within my heart. That sick sense of being watched, it might have been a product of my mind. Who can say such things?

And the sheep I had brought for sacrifice? As soon as my feet touched upon the sand, the animal began to bleat, a pathetic sound. If a sheep could have moaned, I imagine it would have sounded much like the noise that beast made then.

Kirke had told me to head into the jungle, so I went, casting furtive glances about me, certain some viper or great cat would strike at me from the brush every instant. None did. In fact, I saw no animals at all, save clouds of biting insects that followed unnatural arcs around the forest as if caught in tidal eddies. When a current brought the swarm close to me, some of the vicious things would break away and hunt for my flesh. Yet, I found I could escape them by rushing away a dozen feet or so, and only those with proboscises already supping my blood lingered on me or the sheep.

I pushed through the eerie, too-still woods until I came to a stream. Beyond this stream, there was a rocky rise, one where I could await nightfall without sitting amid roots and brush. Just because I had seen no snakes or other predators didn't mean I wanted to spend hours tempting them. As Kirke had been clear I must not take the tonic before dusk—the liminal time, she called it—I was left with too much time alone with my thoughts. To break the silence, I tried talking to the lamb, but, besides the morbidity of conversing with my sacrifice, I found the sound of my own voice only made the island seem all the more unnatural.

As the eventide swept in, strange noises began to fill the jungle. Not animal-like so much as the impression of a snapping twig, or a bush pushed aside, or a rustle of leaves despite a lack of breeze. My skin crawled, and I cast about myself, seeking a source for the strange sensations. The lamb whimpered, curled up in a ball against the rocks as if it thought to burrow into Gaia's bosom and escape whatever foulness crept around Sarpedon.

Nearby, a moan rumbled from a fir tree, and I could have sworn something within it moved. I spun to look, but everything was still. I blinked and realised the tree wept sap, as though wounded. Or ... almost, it looked less viscous, more blood-like. I blinked again, and the perverse vision was gone, the tree unmarred once more.

Yes, I too now murmured a prayer to Athene. I remember wondering if she could even hear prayers uttered from so distant, so foul a place as I had wandered into. If any god could have heard me then, it felt more like Hades, though the dark King of the Dead answered no pleas.

Instinct demanded I rise, make a mad dash through the woods in the fading, purple light, and swim for my ship. Surely our travails upon the sea could not prove worse than this ... obscene mockery of life. But had I done so, I would never have returned home to you or your mother. Dry mouthed and trembling, I broke the stopper on the phial Kirke had given me. Before I could lose the last of my nerve, I threw back the tonic, gagging on its cloying, honeyed taste and wondering what bitterness the witch had sought to disguise with such flavour.

I saw no immediate change in my surroundings. I cannot say what I had expected in imagining I would see the Underworld. Perhaps I thought of fields of shadow, the fiery flows of Phlegethon, or the sun-dappled fields of Elysium. Perhaps any vivid tale of bardic imagination. Instead, I beheld only the ever-deepening dark of a jungle on a moonless night. The sense of foreboding that already nigh strangled me grew deeper still, a creeping malevolence, worming its way toward me.

In the distance, grunts and moans of people in pain. Flickers teased at the edge of my vision, intimations of human forms, gone again as soon I turned to look.

Dammit, I had come too far to back down now, whatever foul dread polluted this place. There was a wetness in my eyes, and to this day, I cannot say whether tears welled out of my fear or sorrow at what I must do and some unnameable emotion that threatened to choke me. I seized the lamb, jerked my knife free and, with a single swift stroke, cut its throat. Then, as the witch had instructed, I flung the dying animal into the dirt and let its blood seep through the earth, down, down to where the shades of the dead might lap at the energies of life.

"Tiresias, I call to you! Tiresias, accept this offering and taste warmth."

The ground turned porous, the corpse beginning to sink, even as rifts around it opened. Grey, desiccated limbs yanked wan bodies up from the earth, the shades weeping laments even as they crawled free from their prison. Even as they flung themselves upon the corpse and gorged themselves like ravenous beasts.

With a growing horror, I recognised among the dead no few fallen friends. Men who had died in the Ilian War, others slain at Ismarus or by the Laestrygonians. Men dead under *my* command, drawn here now, by me, perhaps to hold me to account.

"Tiresias!"

But it was not the fallen Oracle who rose from feasting upon the lamb but a woman, blood caking her chin and dribbling down her age-ravaged neck. "M-mother?" I bleated, my cries every bit as pathetic as the lamb's had been.

The shade of Antiklea gagged, tilting her head back to swallow more blood with a wet, slurping sound. I blinked away more tears now and, despite myself, began to reach for her, though Kirke had warned me to touch naught and no one. "Mother ... How have you fallen?"

"Grief ..." Her word was but a whisper, a susurration thrumming in the night. "You did not ... return ..." Any answer I might have made caught in my throat, choked me. "Laertes too ... withers in grief ... alone, in rags ... Penelope pines ... and suitors clamour for ... her hand ..."

Yes. That was the first I had heard of the plight that beset my wife and son after my long absence, and I knew, at that moment, I must needs make all possible haste home. Not only for my sake or that of my weary men, but for my family, who needed me.

"Tiresias!" I bellowed, no longer caring what else might hear my cries. No, for I could not bear to linger in this hateful place a moment longer. "Oracle Tiresias, I beseech you, come to me!"

"What ...?" a harsh, if somewhat feminine voice demanded of me. I turned to see an ancient man, his back stooped, though he glared at me with fierce, hollow eyes. Or rather, perhaps not a *he*, for as the figure turned, I perceived a hint of breasts through the tatters of the figure's robe. "Why call for me ... Son of Laertes? Why disturb ... my sleep?"

The Oracle swept bony fingers through the bloody soil and touched them to blue, decaying lips. A shudder ran through the shade, as if wracked by some perverse combination of pleasure and pain. A too-long tongue darted over those cracked lips before retreating back behind blackened teeth. "So ... You hope, perhaps, for a happy future?" A dark chortle burbled forth from that foul mouth, and I struggled to keep from recoiling. "Yes ... you shall return home ... but only after your travails weary you beyond endurance. Only after death haunts your every step for year after year until you long for its frigid embrace."

"How do I make it home, Oracle?" I demanded. "I have spilled blood for you, now I bid you speak."

"As if you were a necromancer to command the dead ... Shed your own blood, then."

Grim faced, I drew my sword and slit a thin line along my palm. As crimson droplets oozed from the wound, I flung them at the shade. That overlong tongue shot out like that of a chameleon, snapping drops from the air. An evil shudder ran through Tiresias, the image sending chills down my spine.

"Speak," I bid him once more.

"The curse of Thetis is bound to the siren's lifeblood. If you cannot convince her to revoke it, you must slay the host body tethering her ill wishes to this Realm."

I blanched at such an idea. "You'd have me swim down to Pontus and, what, slay a princess deity beneath the sea?" Even could I have done such a thing, I imagined the murder of a Nereid would not much endear me to her father, Nereus.

"The princess has fled to the far reaches, the Sirenum Scopuli, off the coast of Mnemosynia."

Rassenia! Such was a land of legend, and few mortal sailors I met ever claimed to have made such a voyage. Fewer still ever did so.

"I give you one further admonition if you would reach home—touch not the sacred cattle of Helios. Woe betide you if you think to repeat your grandfather's theft there." With that, the Oracle shade descended back in the earth as though walking downstairs.

Others came, too, and I saw the shade of our great leader, Agamemnon, and he too—after supping on blood—regaled me with his woes. For on his homecoming, his own wife, Klytemnestra, along with her lover, had slain him for the murder of their daughter Iphigenia. I could not help but see the hand of justice, there, and I found little pity for the man. Still, he warned me … claimed I could not trust your mother, for she too must have found comfort in the arms of another after so many years. Thus he bid me, on reaching Ithaka, to land in secret and observe the woman, and extracted from me an oath to do so.

The parade of the dead continued, and I saw many others who had fought beside me in the war. But the words of Tiresias sat like a lump in my gut, and I found myself desperate for the release I hoped dawn would bring.

When at last Hyperion's light pierced the canopy, I fled, back to my ship, desperate to be gone from that haunted place.

WITH ANSWERS IN HAND, we returned to Aiaía. I suppose I wanted to offer my thanks to Kirke, to tell her the tonic had done its work. I did not linger long with the witch, this time, and soon we made sail. We knew

Thetis's curse would not allow to draw nigh to the Ionian Sea, so instead we skirted the northern coast of Atlantis. No one in the polis claimed to have visited Rassenia, but I heard tale the demigod king of Aeolia, one Aiolos, had made the journey. Legend claimed he had mastered the winds themselves, and such would carry him wherever he wished.

So, to the tiny island off the coast of Atlantis we sailed, hope burgeoning in our chests. None among us had taken it well to learn we must sail past all known lands and challenge sirens, but it meant, at least, there was a chance.

And a chance would have to do.

"I AM OLD NOW," the king of Aeolia told me as we walked along the great bronze wall that encircled much of his island kingdom. The Tethid's hair had turned to snow, and lines creased his face, though, to my eye, I thought strength still lurked in his limbs. "You know, I was a grandfather already in the days of your great heroes, Elládosi. I was there when Perseus sailed against Ketus and saved my granddaughter Andromeda from the monster."

As it was the second time the king mentioned it, I feared his memory had begun to fail him. Given that he spoke of events nigh onto two centuries prior, I imagine he must have lived a full life indeed. Aiolos's hair flipped in the breeze, a fierce mane roiling about the demigod, evoking glories of days long gone. I did not know how the man had lived so long, but his twilight had stolen something precious from him, and the thought of it moved me to melancholy.

The king led me back to his palace then, and after feasting myself and my men, he gave to me a satchel. Within this bag lay a dried gourd with a cork stuck in it. When I moved to check its contents, the demigod slapped my hand. "Within this calabash lie the four winds, Odysseus. Unleash the right wind—not too much, of course—and it shall ferry you where you need sail."

"To Ithaka?"

The king frowned and shook his head. "I would not tempt the curse of a siren, friend. But the east wind can carry across the Thalassa to the

Rassenian coast, and thence you can make for the Sirenum Scopuli beyond Thrinakia."

I recalled, in my youth, my grandfather Autolykus once saying that, to reach Thrinakia, he had to thread the waters between Skylla and Kharubdis. When I asked Aiolos this, the old king nodded sadly. "Perilous waters, and the rise of Skylla cut off most trade out of Mnemosynia, in days long back. Draw too close to Skylla and she will snap sailors from your ship to sate her foul hungers. But the ceaseless maelstrom of Kharubdis is even more unforgiving. I wish I could offer to help you make the voyage, but I have no more adventures left in me." The old demigod snorted, then. "Well, perhaps one last, dark adventure, to a place from which none return."

Remembering the many haunted shades I'd beheld, I nodded, cold and uncomfortable.

"I shall never forget your kindness," I said to him, but the king of Aeolia waved away my thanks.

"My children, my grandchildren ... *their* children are gone now. Should you return, I look forward to a tale of your adventures to entertain me in my long nights, as I wait to join them."

AIOLOS'S WINDS hurled us toward Rassenia at a pace that had the mast straining. After some hours of this, fearing the mast might indeed crack, I eased off the winds, uncertain how many leagues we had passed thus. Days later, we came to the maelstrom of Kharubdis, and I could see why the demigod had warned it would prove worse than any monster. We knew the danger, then, of skirting too close to the Rassenian shore and drawing the eyes of Skylla.

We knew she lurked, either up in the cave-riddled cliffs above the waves or perhaps below, in sunken depths just offshore. But even so knowing, we had no alternative save to risk her wrath.

I ... hesitate to even speak of what unfolded next, though.

The waters around my ship became aerated, bubbles popping all around us. The crew, at the oars, shouted in alarm as if it had not been far too late to turn back. I peered over the gunwale, expecting to see some cyclopean horror rising everywhere I looked. Even that fear could not have prepared me for the enormity that surged upward.

A pair of draconic heads, eyes lit with fell gleam, lurched from the waves on either side of my ship. The creature followed, a colossal torso attached to those sea serpents, as if they were her legs. The abomination had the upper body of a fifty-feet tall woman, with matted, kelp-strewn hair hanging over pendulous breasts, and a shark-like maw that wept blood. Worst of all, though, were the hounds.

Great, howling, slavering beast heads jutted from where her nethers ought to have been. Shrieking, a sound fit to split the heavens, Skylla snatched up my men, Antilochus among them. I gaped in utter horror as Skylla rammed the man into one of her crotch-hounds, bile rising in my throat at the sound of his bones crunching in those horrid jaws.

"Ship oars!" I bellowed, though I did not wait to give the crew the chance before I unleashed the calabash of the winds. At that moment, I cared naught where it flung us, nor if it split my very ship in twain, so long as we escaped the sea monster preying upon us.

A gale ripped from the gourd as I uncorked it, sending me staggering back against a bulkhead. Our sail flew so taut the seams looked apt to burst, and I heard the mast groan once more. But the ship, she *flew*, shot as though from a mighty bow. Skylla bellowed in indignation. A serpent head tore a chunk from the stern, whilst those terrible hands snatched up more and more sailors.

I tried shouting for the helmsman to set our course, but I've no idea if he heard me. Either way, oars snapped and splintered against the monster as we burst away. The current steered us perilously close to the maelstrom, but our speed had us riding so high we skirted the edge and broke free. I looked behind, as best I could while pressed to the bulkhead, and saw no sign of Skylla. Perhaps the creature had slunk off to her benthic abode but I feared she might pursue, so I dared not ease off the winds.

Not even as yards snapped and lines burst, sweeping over the deck like lashes. One hapless man was flung overboard, though from the hit the line gave him, I doubt he lived long enough to hit the waters, much less drown.

Someone shouted at me, but I could not make out his words. The hull scraped over something—the tip of a reef I assume. The next instant, we ran aground, the impact sending me hurtling forward. I crashed into something, and darkness took me.

I AWAKENED to find the crew had brought me ashore and were busy corralling a herd of golden cattle. Panic seized my bowels, and I lurched to my feet, trying to protest. The ground surged up to meet me before I'd made it three steps, vicious and unforgiving of my need to stop my men. As I rose once more, I realised already they were roasting great hunks of beef over a bonfire.

"No, you fools!" I shrieked. "Those are the cattle of Helios!"

Eurylochos, who stood tending the food, turned to me with a sneer. "The Titan is a world away, and we, here now, are *starving*. We lost the better part of our supplies to that attack, and you've no right to deny us plunder where we can take it." My brother-in-law held silent a moment, then spoke again with a cooler voice. "Either join us for the feast or go sleep off that concussion. But do not press, Odysseus. Already the crew grumble that, had you not forced Achilles into war, none of us would be here now."

How quick they were to forget the horrors of the war itself. How they had worshipped Achilles then, how they had prayed, time and again, for the valiant demigod to save them. Ten years they looked to him as their hero, sought always to send him first into the breach. But now he was dead, and they needed someone to blame for their woes.

Despairing, and recalling Tiresias's warning, I wandered from them, dizzy though I was, and made my unsteady way along the beach to inspect the wreck of my ship.

Thus, some hours later, did the Heliad find me. Dried blood marred her khiton, her face, her knuckles, and the blade of her xiphos. "It is not a good day to be a cattle thief," the woman fair snarled, "nor, in truth, to come fresh from the plundering of Ilium."

"Phaethusa ..." I breathed, recalling the name my grandfather had mentioned in his tales of this place. I swallowed, my heart heavy. In the storm of her wrath, I knew my men had perished; such was writ plain upon her visage. My mind whirred for any chance I might find to save myself. If she knew I was the grandson of Autolykus, given his theft of her cattle, I would mostlike only redouble her wrath. "I did not taste the flesh," I stammered. "I bid them not do it ..."

The Heliad stared at me before sheathing her sword. "I am weary of bloodshed, anyway." A pause. "You are far from home, Elládosi."

"I ... I must find Thetis on the Sirenum Scopuli. I must convince her to break the curse she has laid upon me."

A moment, the woman watched me. She snorted, shaking her head. "What a long way you have come to die, then. The siren rocks lay just across this island, beyond a small strait. But if you draw nigh, their song will lure you to your death. They will drown you, mortal, and mostlike feast upon your corpse."

"Be that as it may ... my only chance to return home lies in her forgiveness ... or her death."

Without answering, the Heliad moved to the seaside and knelt, washing her face. She rose, dripping, and shook her head. "Something in your aspect evokes pity. I suppose I know what it's like to lose so many you care for." She hesitated. "Lampetia and I have something of an accord with the sirens. I can call for them. If you can resist their song, perhaps they will hear your pleas. If not ... at least you will have a proper ending to your unhappy tale. It's more than some receive."

With my ears plugged with wax, I waited in a small rowboat, beside the shore, as Phaethusa shouted to a pair of sirens lounging upon distant rocks. They were beautiful, yes, in an Otherworldly way. Nymph-like in their seductive beauty, naked and alluring, yet even from the distance, I could see an opalescent tinge to their eyes.

After an exchange, I saw one of their faces darken, and she bared a mouthful of shark-like teeth a moment before her lips curled back into a cruel smile. Phaethusa trudged over to where I waited and laid a hand upon my forearm, offering a nod of reassurance. Only then did I dig out the wax with my fingernails. Even so, I could not bring myself to cast the protection aside. I kept the globs in my palm, though the rational part of me knew, of course, that should the sirens break into song, any desire I had to cut off the sound would evaporate on the first note.

Grandfather had told me tales of that, too, of his voyage on the Argo, and how, save for the magic song of Orpheus, the whole of the ship would have been lost to sirens. Though lesser gods, the women before me were, nevertheless, deities of the sea, and I would live only so long as they held to whatever word they had given Phaethusa.

After shoving the rowboat into the waters, to my surprise, the Heliad climbed in across from me. It had taken two days' walk to cross Thrinakia and reach the Sirenum Scopuli, and in that time I fancied I had regaled Phaethusa with tale of my adventures since leaving Ilium's broken husk. In particular, she seemed interested in my time living with her fellow Heliad, Kirke, and I supposed they might have been related. Perhaps that was why she helped me now, though she kept her own counsel, and assuming you know a woman's mind can lead one well astray.

Such I mused on as I heaved through high, crashing waves, trying not to dwell on the probability I rowed toward my death.

"What will you say to her?" Phaethusa had asked me the day prior as we trekked the miles along the coast.

"Perhaps I will point out I can hardly be held to account for the results of actions I myself was forced to take."

The Heliad had cast her glance my way, brow raised. "You think to assuage a mother's grief with logic? There is no logic in the anguish of loss, and you cannot pierce those pains with it."

She was right, I had no doubt, but still, I dared to hope I might find the words to cut through the labyrinth of her grief and see reason. Only, if I was to do so, the appeal would come from some place other than pure logic.

I managed to get the boat close up to the rocks, though the waves threatened to hurl us against them and crack the hull. With one hand, Phaethusa caught the edge and held the boat in place, and I admit, I gawped at her strength. I recovered quickly, though, and scrambled from my vessel up onto the Sirenum Scopuli, my sandals slipping time and again upon the wave-slicked surface. The islands were tiny, and I could have walked the circumference of one in a matter of minutes.

I assumed the one who had given me the hateful look to be Thetis and I approached, before falling to my knees in obeisance. "Goddess." I lowered my head to the rocks a moment, before looking up to see her watching me with those pearly eyes. She sat on the rock above me, hands resting on her knees, making not the least effort at modesty. Considering her visage spoke of drowning and eating me, I found little sensual in the moment, nor was it difficult to keep my gaze on her face.

"Goddess," I repeated. "I come to you in supplication, to beg your mercy."

Thetis sneered. A sound escaped her lips, something between a hiss and a snarl. "The sea doles what mercy it wills."

I had to stop myself from objecting that she had taken it upon herself to *direct* the seas against me. "Indeed, Goddess. We live in a mercurial World, I know. Where men delight in enforcing their wills upon others, as if the deny the base indifference of the cosmos to their own plights. Men ... they ... we oft seek to dominate women to balm our own egos. The tale is well known, how you were forced to wed Peleus." Here, I plumbed dangerous waters, I knew, and her face darkened further. "Even so, he gave you a son you loved."

Thetis leaned forward, fingers curling like claws. "Would you lecture me on my own history, mortal?"

"No! I ... Goddess, rather I mean to say ..." I am not easily flustered nor stricken of my wily tongue, a fact in which I take no small pride, I admit. But to look upon the Nereid's face, to feel her loathing wash over me thus, I found it almost impossible to speak. "I have a son as well. When he was newborn, King Agamemnon came to me and compelled me to sail with him to war, though I tried to escape. I feigned madness, ploughing my fields night and day, unable to sail off to war. Agamemnon had his ally, Palamedes, place my infant son in my path. To spare my boy Telemachus, I had no choice but to sail for Phrygia, under the command of Agamemnon. There was a man who delighted in placing his will above others, other kings most of all.

"When he commanded me to find the famed son of Peleus, I could not risk my son by disobeying that command any more than I could refuse any command he gave in the war. I ..." I allowed tears to stream down my face, allowed my voice to break. Most men train themselves, as boys, not to weep, and train themselves so well it becomes hard for them to do so even when tears would prove cathartic. I found it a useful skill, the ability to summon them up in the midst of an impassioned story. It did not hurt that I feared for my life and, too, feared I might never again lay eyes upon you or your mother. "I did not think any man could ever overcome Achilles," I protested. "Indeed, he was my friend." A stretch of the truth seemed useful at that moment. "I would never have imagined he could fall. But it was the Olympian, Artemis, who struck him down. Could I have saved him, I would have done so in a heartbeat." Which was true enough, for Achilles warded the lives of every Elládosi on those foreign shores.

"This man, my friend, my brother, he was stolen from me as well!" I dared edge closer until I could clasp her knees. "Now, I can only hope he has reached lands of sunlit Elysian fields. For myself, I am done with wars and strive to return to the son I never wished to leave in the first place. I … I beseech you, revoke your curse and allow me to be done with all of this."

The siren glanced to Phaethusa. Then her shoulders slumped. "Get gone from this place," she said to me, then. "I release you from the curse upon your soul, King of Ithaka."

I mumbled a thousand gratitudes while backing away on my hands and knees. Only after I had rowed us back and Phaethusa and I had begun the long trek back toward the far shore did the Heliad speak.

"I did not think you could convince her."

"A grieving parent does not wish other parents to share her grief."

Phaethusa shrugged. "Did you know sirens have keen noses? They can scent blood far out in the waters, like sharks." She paused a moment. "I think, though, living under the sea, they are not accustomed to smells of the land, and perhaps might not recognise the stench of horseshit even right before them."

I did not know what to say to that and thus decided it a good time to inspect the straps of my sandals and hold my peace.

No Rassenian sailor would risk Skylla or Kharubdis, which meant my route home lay far, far out of the way, heading first to Kemet. There, from Memphis, I caught a ship bound for Atlantis. When a sudden storm swept over us, I began to doubt the sincerity of Thetis's pledge of lifting her curse. Perhaps she did lift it and then had a change of heart. Or perhaps ill fortune simply seized me.

Either way, our merchant vessel was tossed hither and thither until, beneath lightning and thunder, it capsized. Such is the last I remembered, before awakening on a strange shore, to find myself hefted up by a Nymph. The Nymph, by name of Kalypso, took me to her manse upon the island of Ogygia, and there nursed me back to health. I recall telling her, in those days, of my adventures, but I recall little else for a long time after my convalescence.

I think, perhaps, that like Kirke, she was some sort of witch, for she kept me by her side for years more, and I scarce imagined the time was passing. Then one day, of a sudden, she released me, and it was as if a seaward breeze had blown out the fog across my eyes. The Nymph all but shoved me from her manse, bidding me be on the first ship bound for Atlantis, and even gave me drachmae to pay for passage. She refused to speak of what had caused her change of heart, and I, free willed for the first time in so long, dared not linger to investigate.

I reached the polis of Atlantis, thence to Argos, and thence home, at last, my son. So now I come to find Penelope beset by suitors eager to claim her hand and my throne, though the most of them were not even old enough to sail to Ilium with me twenty years back. You tell me she has kept them at bay claiming she will not remarry until she has woven a funereal shroud for my father, Laertes, but that every night her servant undoes her work. Meanwhile these men beggar my house with their years-long feasting ... I laud the cleverness of Penelope's plan, but it has gone on long enough, my son.

So, Telemachus, now I shall go in secret to see these suitors. You will seal them inside, my son, and I shall slay them all for the woes they have visited upon your mother. You and I shall kill every last one of these bastards. For Ithaka is mine, and at long last, I have returned.

PART IV

There are no waves left. The sea of my mind lies becalmed. I drift, listless, and await whatever end may come.
    — *Melpomene, The Muses' Lament*

16

ENODIA

730 Bronze Age

From the distance, with her small army gathered around, Enodia watched as a Man wrestled Kerberos. Impossible though it seemed, the Man held his own against the monstrous three-headed hound.

"It's Herakles," Orpheus said by her side. "Son of Zeus."

It little surprised Enodia to learn Zeus was still spawning bastards. It did surprise more than a little to find out one of them had the power to challenge Kerberos. Even as she led the advancing army to sneak up on Hades—who watched the spectacle, hand to an arrow stuck in his shoulder—the demigod broke one of the hound's necks. Enodia fair gasped when the man ripped out Kerberos's serpent tail at the root and began to beat the hound with it.

"Hades will kill him for this," Orpheus moaned.

No. "Now," Enodia commanded and Phobetor surged forward, leading three score shades against Hades.

Orpheus tried to race after them to join the fray, but Enodia seized his arm, jerking him to a halt. The bard had spellsongs, which made him too valuable to waste in frenzied melee. "Your friend will die of that venom if you do not attend to him."

The other ghost grunted in acknowledgment and Enodia released him. He broke off, not toward Hades but skirting the battlefield to reach this Herakles and whatever other man sat chained to a chair upon the precipice. Ariadne went with him, and Enodia saw no reason to deny the dead girl.

Enodia watched as her ghosts came upon Hades. The king, wounded and outnumbered, seized the first to reach him with a single, massive hand. Hades stood twenty feet high, grown bloated with his ceaseless feast of souls. Now, he raised the hapless ghost to his maw and bit out the shade's throat, sucking upon a soul like juice from the most succulent of fruits.

So she sang. Ancient Kandamian spellsongs wakened even the blighted landscape of the Underworld. Her Supernal words echoed through Etheric air and stirred psychic currents. In response, the ground lashed about Hades's shins, coiling up them like constricting snakes. The giant Lord of the Dead heaved one leg free, but the effort stalled him, and the shades closed in, jabbing with spears and hurling javelins. With his massive bident, Hades impaled one unhappy ghost. A whirl, and he slammed the twenty-five-foot haft into a mass of gathered ghosts.

Enodia sang and the air around Hades's arms turned honey thick, slowing his movements. He perceived his danger now, and yanking his foot free, he leapt away from the gathered throng, toward the River Styx. Perhaps he had summoned a ferryman with a mental call, or perhaps the bound servant sensed his master's peril. Either way, a ferry already drew nigh, and Hades would be aboard before the chasing shades could reach him.

He would not, however, mostlike expect an army of lampads and Irkallan ghost warriors to lay in wait betwixt himself and the bastion of his palace. The thought brought a grim smile and a hungry hiss as she imagined the luscious taste of his soul dribbling down her gullet.

ENODIA MIGHT HAVE NAMED it hubris, Hades venturing out from the safety of his palace with naught save the protection of his wretched hound. Perhaps he thought Kerberos invincible. Perhaps he had known Enodia had left the area and thought he'd have time. Mostlike though, it was plain simple rage moiled in arrogance that led him astray after Ages enthroned in Kek.

He might have fought through the lampads and the Irkallans. He might have reached the relative safety offered by the walls of his necropolis and called forth his forces. Had that happened, Enodia imagined he could have held the city for years, as the besieging army grew starved for souls and their morale withered like flowers beneath autumn's approach.

In the end, though, it was neither hubris—at least not in thinking himself warded by Kerberos—nor the encroaching foreign army that undid Hades. Rather, his downfall came in the form of the wife he had abducted, raped, and murdered. Hades never imagined Persephone had the will to avenge herself.

Or maybe that was the very definition of hubris.

Either way, when the gates of Kek burst open and the army flowed forth, it was not to save Hades. Under Persephone's co-opted command —loyalty she'd earned over painstaking centuries—Hades's own forces had the ghost king fettered in orichalcum. In chains, he was brought before Enodia who now sat upon his dark throne. The chair was many times too large for her, making her seem but a child in it, and she hated Hades for that as well.

Then again, Enodia hated everyone and everything, as was inevitable for a wraith. Such was the way of things. The giant before her glared at her, darkness seething within the blasted ruination of his chest. Her Helwraiths had torn the crown from his brow and cast it aside, a hateful icon of a vicious ruler and his fallen era.

The throne sat upon a dais atop onyx stairs, the platform serving to elevate Enodia to Hades's level. Still, Hades, on his knees, did not deign to meet her gaze. Perhaps he knew all too well the fate that must soon close upon him.

About the fringes of the throne room, veiled in curtains of mist encircling their feet, the lampads waited for Enodia to make good on her bargain with their queen. She would, of course. Ten thousand souls she would see sent back with them to the Rimefells and more to come once she had worked her Art. There was no breaking a pact between eidolons.

By her side, Persephone stared daggers at the defeated king. On raiding the dungeons, Persephone had been shocked to discover her mother had been held here, a prisoner for seven centuries. The ghost of the Inumiden Titan had withered unto a husk, her mind cracked by the torments of solitude. Persephone had freed her mother and her daughter, seen to them, and then insisted upon them being here to witness Hades's final end.

"You and I," Enodia said to Hades, "have spent Ages with our fingers wrapt around one another's throats."

The king lifted his gaze at last. "*You* and I? You are but the bitch my brother loosed upon those who drew his ire. Am I to elevate a hound to the same status as its master? I would be no better than a dying soldier blaming the spear that strikes him rather than the hoplite who thrust it."

Enodia allowed herself an exasperated rasp in answer. How would he react, were she to admit his unmaking had been prompted by *Enodia*? Hekate's own future self had orchestrated Zeus's rise and Hades's fall and everything between. That it had been woven by the Moirai into the frightful Tapestry did not abrogate her responsibility for it all. And here this odious buffoon knelt, overthrown by her in death as he had been in life, an event for which she had plotted for centuries alongside Persephone, and still he could not grasp that *females* had bettered him.

Well. Enodia had no desire for any others present to learn of time-walking or its dire implications. That was a secret she trusted to Keuthos alone, of necessity, and one she had no intent to ever reveal. So far as anyone knew—save Kirke, she supposed—Hekate died in the Nyxlands, seven hundred years back, and then became Enodia. Such was the truth history would record, in the dusty records of the dead housed within the necropoleis.

With affected languor, Enodia slipped off of the throne and sashayed her way over toward Hades, making her slow descent from the dais. "How very little you comprehend. Even now, in your final moments, you wander benighted in the darkness, mistaking a play of shadows for the entirety of the World. Be at ease, then. The time for striving, the time for straining the disused muscles in your head has passed."

"Zagreus will come for you, bitch."

Enodia chortled. "You mean Dionysus? Oh, *yes*. I await his appearance with unwavering anticipation. For when I have devoured every drop of puissance in your soul, there will be none who can stand against me."

Even on his knees, Hades towered over her, his face vacillating between haughty sneer and the growing apprehension of his doom. Enodia gave him a moment to ponder it, drinking his deepening dread like the headiest of wines. That fear was more intoxicating than even the Bacchic draughts with which Dionysus had once enslaved her mind. Given the chance, she'd have savoured it longer. But she would not risk dragging this out and allowing aught to come between her and her prey. Not now.

With a snarl, she leapt, seizing his throat with skeletal claws, and bore the king down. Hades crashed upon the throne room floor with a heavy *thud*. Then she sank her teeth into the flesh of his neck and began to slurp, draining not blood but the very soul from within him. On and on she gnawed and gorged herself, driven to greater frenzy by his shrieks. Until even those became whimpers. Until his form became a shadow, ephemeral, and broke apart beneath her, consumed in its entirety.

Rivers of power coursed through her, raging rapids of energy so tumultuous she felt the Pneuma might burst the shell of her body. Hissing and gasping, she leant upon hands and knees. How long had she knelt there, shivering, her form flickering and threatening to collapse?

"Hekate ..." Keuthos rasped at last, coming closer until he could offer her a hand.

Still trembling, she took it, and he pulled her to her feet. "I ..."

She felt them, then, the bonds tethering her to her Hel-wraiths, grow stronger by fusing her power with Hades's own. She felt all the dead gathered in this necropolis, souls pulsing like candles or torches in the darkness, lesser or greater of power. A sea of flickering lights in her mind's eye. Now she looked to Keuthos first, then to the gathered throng of lampads and ghosts watching her. Waiting for her words. "I am no longer Hekate."

"Enodia, then ..." Keuthos acknowledged.

The revenant-wraith who had worked in tireless circles to bring her here. But that was no longer her, either. "No ... I am the very Queen of the Damned, now. I am the incarnation of this Underworld, all of which is beholden to me." And the answer seemed obvious, for it was a name whispered to her long ago, with utmost dread. The dread she must now evoke in any who opposed her. "I am *Hel*."

17

KIRKE

20 Dark Age

Sometimes, for a day or a fortnight, Kirke could manage to forget the fateful day that crept ever closer. Sometimes, she remembered the end Pandora had foretold for Odysseus but recalled too her daughter's warning that Kirke could not change it. Other times, she busied her mind with plan after plan, seeking after a way to avert the course of Ananke, but to do so without unmaking Pandora, Kirke herself, and everyone else she had ever loved. The trouble she faced, of course, lay in the simple truth that Pandora had saved Odysseus and brought him to Kirke after witnessing his death in the days to come. If that death didn't happen, Pandora might not bring him to Aiaíā, Kirke might not dally with him, and Pandora might never be born.

Prometheus had claimed that to challenge Fate, one must pick one's moments with utmost care. So Kirke studied the battlefield of her life with the diligence of a grizzled general and still came away with too many doubts. Ever, there were unknowns. Ever factors she could not predict or control.

Not the least of which was nagging doubt that, mayhap, she neither could nor should try to meddle with the Tapestry that held together the World. Curse the design all she liked, she was a part of it, and plucking its threads could end in disaster or futility. Such reasoning could not help but stir sympathy for her grandfather's plight. Plans spanning the scope of Ages and Eras, yes, but for all his intellect, for all his ability to deduce probabilities and intuit events based on analysis of human nature, he never knew *everything*. And less than everything meant he never knew enough.

Kirke lived with Kalypso, and they tried to pretend things could again be as they had been in days gone. But time and pain and loss—and Kirke's knowledge of the Ontos and the timeline—had created a gulf betwixt her and the other woman. She could bridge the divide only by immersing her friend in the damning knowledge that Kirke now possessed, and tempting though it was to have a companion in her misery, doing so would be a cruelty Kirke resisted time and again.

So Kalypso grew irate more oft, claiming Kirke held back, was not herself. That she had changed from the woman she'd known. "Yeah, I changed," was the only answer Kirke could give.

It wasn't that there was no love left betwixt them, no. It was, rather, that the vessel which should have housed that love was riven with cracks, and no matter how much passion and caring either of them poured inside, it continued to ooze out at the seams.

From time to time, she left to visit Prometheus. Once, atop his Aviary, watching the honey-painted sky give way to the bruise of dusk, she had asked him of such things. "How do you live with a relationship when necessity demands you withhold precious truths from those you love most, even or especially for their own sakes?"

He watched the sunset, rather than her. "Suffering on behalf of another *is* an act of love. If your love runs true and deep, it is not necessary that the other person always know or understand what you've done for them."

"Just as there remains much of the Ontos you have yet to reveal to me?" she'd countered.

"Just as," he agreed.

She supposed it was his way of telling her he loved her.

Another time, she had caught him by surprise and found him

silently weeping on the seaside cliff, watching the waves. To his credit, he did not try to pretend he had not been so overcome.

"You grieve for Mother?" she asked. "She's dead, isn't she?"

Prometheus swallowed, blinking away fresh tears. "My daughter died a long time back. So I grieve for her, yes. And for those of us born to this consumptive World encircled by such predatory forces as Ananke." He was convinced, she thought, that whatever his plan to escape all that was, he would have but one perfect moment for it. If that was so, he must believe every attempt he made before that to alter the shape of the Tapestry would fail. He did not like to reveal the burdens that bowed his shoulders in private times, but Kirke had begun to suss them out.

And in the end, maybe that was why she decided not to become him. Why she decided she had to go to find Odysseus and save him from his impending death. She would find another way to ensure Pandora brought the past Odysseus to Aiaíā when she always had. But this future this Kirke would not accept as carved in stone.

Kalypso took the news that Kirke would depart with sullen disappointment, tromping off into the woods to pout and refusing to bid Kirke farewell. Perhaps she had not thought it necessary, Kirke realised not long after, upon finding all the ships had been sent away a few days back. Kalypso did not have the details of Kirke's plan, but she must have sensed, some way or other, that her lover intended to leave her and arranged to make that impossible.

Which, in the end, left Kirke standing on an empty dock, gnawing on her lip and rather vexed. "Kalypso ..." Kirke shook her head in frustration. How did her friend think this would end now? That Kirke would saunter back to her, forgive her for denying her the chance to choose her own course, and maybe then they'd make love by firelight? How was trying to trap Kirke here thus better than when the woman had compelled Odysseus to remain by her side?

For a time, when they'd plotted against Olympus, Artemis and Phaethusa had brought Kirke excess Ambrosia in the hopes of fortifying her Pneuma. She doubted it would be enough to let her cross the threshold from Nymph to Titan, but it had made her stronger. Strong enough, maybe, to swim the channel separating Ogygia from Atlantis, though doing so and then having to cross the island to get another boat would cost her precious time. But what choice remained?

So, after skirting the isle's edge until she could see Brizo's temple on the opposite shore, she leapt into the waves and swam. It was a shame there was no one there to see her audacity; Kirke would like to imagine Kalypso's face on learning what she had done.

❧

Across Atlantis Kirke had sped; chartering a ship, she'd sailed for Ithaka, though the captain had needed to stop at Neritum to inquire where to find the island. Ithaka, it seemed, was a rather unimportant destination among the Ionian Islands, and the Atlantean captain who agreed to ferry Kirke there had not even heard of it afore she begged passage.

They arrived just before dusk, and Kirke, not waiting for him to weigh anchor, had vaulted the side to swim ashore. Thanks to Kalypso's treachery, Kirke had no idea if she'd even make it in time. Pandora had not been able to give an exact date, only a year, and Kirke half considered throttling Kalypso if she was too late.

Because, somewhere along the way, her resolve to change this one thing had hardened into adamant. Kirke had lost too much over the millennia of her life. Far too much. She didn't know if Odysseus still loved her. Hyperion's blazing arse, she didn't, in fact, know that he'd ever loved her so much as enjoyed her company. But either way, she aimed to find out, and more, aimed to spite Ananke just this once. Let this be the perfectly chosen moment Prometheus had mentioned. At least for her, this must be it.

And then, in the darkness, she beheld the collapsing bubble of time created by the use of the accursed Box. No. No! Kirke raced forward, only starlight to guide her. She spilled over something and vaulted forward, tumbling in the sand, rough grains scratching her face. When she rose, sputtering, she beheld the body, left there by the Moirai in mockery.

Shrieking, she crawled to Odysseus's corpse. Dead, as he had always died, upon the shores of his homeland. All the wind inside her lungs escaped in a single, defeated wheeze. She collapsed upon his chest, a puppet of the Moirai, abused until she broke, then cast aside.

❧

DESPITE KIRKE'S mother being regarded by many as the greatest sorceress the World had ever known, Kirke herself remained a passing fair hand in the greater arcana, barely of the second echelon. In truth, she had not sought to rectify such a shortcoming, for any number of reasons. Sorcery abraded the soul, yes, but some in the Circle of Goetic Mysteries had speculated that sporadic use—dabblers as she heard her kind called—might not risk total damnation if they went long enough between spells. More directly, though, every use of the greater arcana opened oneself up to the risk of possession from the very spirits the sorceress called upon to evoke her will.

Some witches, necromancers, called up their ancestors for advice, but Kirke had no such talent.

It came back to sorcery, then, if she wished to speak to her mother now that, as Prometheus had confirmed, she was dead and beyond the reach of Kirke's oneiromancy. She could only hope that, even if Mother had become a wraith, still she would bear enough trace of familial bond to Kirke to protect her from the ghost's predations. So she had returned to her ship, had the captain bear her to the mainland, and in the midnight-dark wood, drawn her circle.

With a bronze knife, Kirke cut a gash the length of her forearm and then flicked blood about the the circle's periphery. The hair on the back of her neck stood on end, warning that something across the Veil had sniffed out the sacrifice and grown curious. Blood, like water, was limi-nal. More potent, even, for within blood lurked Pneuma, the energy of life and souls, and thus did the dead hunger for it.

After a last flick of her lifeblood, she sat in the middle of the circle, legs folded. She shut her eyes and focused on her breathing. On her will. If such faltered, she could well call an entity far more hostile than her mother's ghost. What she was doing held a great deal of risk, she knew. Possession ... damnation ... or, Nyx, an eidolon must just devour her soul here and now and call itself well sated for the night.

No, such thoughts were intrusions. All distractions she bundled into a ball held tight in her chest, then blew them out with her breath, dust expelled from mind and body.

Only when her whirring thoughts had stilled did she begin her cants. They rose in volume, at least within her own skull, reverberating as Supernal words always seemed to do when spoken by mortals. Sorcerers profaned the natural order. But then, at this point, Kirke had tolerated rather enough of the natural order.

She, like sorceresses before her, had decided the time had come to impose *her* will on the cosmos, rather than beyond to its inimical designs. "Pyrrha ... Hekate ... Answer my plea ... Come to your daughter. Pyrrha ... Hekate ... I await you ... Just beyond the Veil ..."

She blinked to let her eyes shift into the Sight and look into the Penumbra. What little colour that dark forest had held bled away, the change so subtle she might have missed it, had the ultramarine hues not sharpened her view of the wood. Trees bent and twisted into unnatural arcs, seeming contorted in pain. Mirrors of the torment that wracked Kirke's soul.

Ghosts flitted about the fringes of her circle, many crawling on all fours, lapping at her blood offerings like feral dogs. Some of their necks craned at too-sharp angles to peer at her, eyes begging for more of the Pneuma-infused droplets. In the distance, deeper shadows moved within the trees. A dryad, perhaps, though the Wood spirit did not approach, as yet. Perhaps it judged her offering too paltry, or perhaps it intended to ambush the ghosts and devour their souls when they at last tore themselves away from the circle.

Then, a pile of rocks groaned and shifted, pieces tumbling inward like teeth caving into a decaying maw. Kirke wondered if aught had changed in the Mortal Realm. She did not have the chance to consider it long, though, for out of the utter black aperture something else had begun to emerge. A gaunt figure, dragging itself forward with a slapping, skeletal arm. Another arm lurched from the dark, this one decaying but not wholly bereft of flesh.

Empty, wordless dread opened in Kirke's gut. Chills ran up and down her spine. The childish, foolish instinct to shut her eyes and will it all away grew almost overpowering. "M-mama?"

The top of a head appeared, one side matted with threadbare auburn hair, the other an exposed skull. When the entity had pulled itself enough free of its earthy prison, it looked up. The half of her face that still had flesh was, indeed, the face of Hekate.

"Mama ... Nyx's bosom, what happened to you?"

The ghost before her hissed, baring fangs. "Do not ... speak the names of the Elder Gods ..."

Kirke nodded. Knowing her mother was dead was one thing. But beholding the wracking of her soul and the ruination of her flesh ate at Kirke and left her struck speechless. She felt as small and useless as some grub wallowing in the dirt, trying to converse with creatures far beyond its ken.

"Why ... call me ... here ..." Hekate rasped. "I ... sit now ... upon the throne of the Underworld ... I have a great many ... things in motion ... and no time for concerns of the Mortal Realm ..."

Kirke swallowed down her rising panic, promising herself she'd have plenty of time to weep and scream and retch later. "I need the Box back."

For a moment, her rotted, unhappy mother just stared at her. "Why ...?"

"Because I'm going to change the past and make a better future for all of us."

A raspy laugh answered that, the sound like razors drawing random gashes inside Kirke's brain. "You ... cannot ... change the past ... nor the future ..."

"The Box, Mama. *Please.*"

"Then ... I will tell you ... where to find what you seek ... One ought to be free ... to learn such lessons oneself ..."

And she did.

And Kirke knew she would never see or speak to her mother again.

18

ATHENE

399 Dark Age

*M*arduk had not allowed her to sleep for days, such that, when at last they brought her to a bed and shut her in the room, dreams took her the moment her head hit the plush pillows.

Vast, beyond the infinite expanse stretching between stars and blanketing the firmament of Nyx. Vast, beyond the ken of Man or Titan, beyond the fragile apprehensions of mortal souls.

Shrouded in the limitless bounds of night, she walked along a sharp-edged obsidian path that seemed to flow beneath her sandals, as undulant as the sea, uncertain if it wished to hold to any shape. Above, crackles of iridescence offered momentary reprieve against the gloom, though not nigh enough to give any shape to the place in which she trod.

From some indeterminate distance, moans and laments mingled with the sounds of crackling flames and the crash of splitting stones. She walked, heed-

less and powerless to turn back, among an abyss of Khaos. A black gulf opened before her, a churning maelstrom of shadows crackling with dark lightning. It stretched beyond the range of her senses, engendering in her breast the feeling she was no more than an insect trying to comprehend the breadth of Okeanus.

From within the vortex arose a sound, at first unidentifiable, though it began to remind Athene of swishing leather, if pieces of leather might stretch for miles across. There came a snapping, as of pustules popped, and something momentous began to rise from the abyss. Layered, bat-like wings unfolded, stretching, revealing tatters and frayed ends. Those wings! They reached skyward, fit to encircle a world, as if the abomination to which they belonged might well hold Gaia herself in its talons.

Amid the snapping wings now came the hiss of a thousand colossal serpents, saurian heads and backs peeking from the moil of shadows only to vanish into the gloom once more.

Now rose a head, bursting with eyes from which glinted terrible intellect, wreathed in a mane of more serpents. Within the head opened a maw, a ring of teeth as from a nightmarish worm, each tooth writhing of its own accord, as if given will.

Athene stood beneath the entity that would have overshadowed the greatest of mountains, and she knew that, before this dark god, all the works of Man and Titan were but motes of dust. Its fathomless, alien mind brushed across hers, and it knew her, down to her pith.

A chorus of discordant shrieks that ought not have come from a human throat burbled forth from her, her very soul screaming in abject dread at the utter abomination before her. The fringes of her mind frayed, tumbling into a quivering, weeping mess.

She, who had once claimed godhood now looked upon the expanse of true divinity in all its infinite horror.

A hand fell upon her shoulder, and she was jerked back into herself. The monstrosity fell away, and she was staring, instead, into a churning, cosmic fire. Flashes of multi-hued lightning coruscated along a swirling vortex of flame and smoke and ash. Even the ground itself seemed to swirl about the gaping void swallowing reality.

The grip on her shoulder tightened, and she looked to see Mithra there. "None who behold the squamous bulk of Typhon, lurking just beyond the fringes of reality, may ever again know the peace of ignorance. Such comes the price of the Ontos, in the annihilation of one's fragile illusions."

Mithra waved his hand, and before her eyes, she saw a flickering image of the Tree of Life, its enormous branches reaching into the atramentous depths of the sky, its boring roots digging their way through the ground and touching her world, all worlds. Within that Tree was a vortex—the same vortex—ceaselessly revolving, sucking light down into it, and spinning it back out in luminous skeins that ran out, along the roots, and into the Realms.

"I don't understand ..."

"The Wheel of Life draws in and ushers forth a flow of souls, of Light, casting them into shells of matter, of Dark. Few remember the process, and thus we remain trapped within the illusion of discontinuity between our incarnations, though we are one." He paused, allowing her to mull over his words. She had heard theories of reincarnation but never given them much consideration. The dead were drawn into the Underworld and ruled over by Hades. Beyond that, what happened if they left that existence, who could know? "Alongside this Wheel runs the Wheel of History, the flow of Ages, in ever-descending cycles of increasing Khaos as Typhon grows restless, grows ravenous. Until an Era must give way to an Eschaton, and the cycle repeats.

"Taken in conjunction, the two Wheels form the great Wheel of Fate. It is the spinning of this Wheel that the Hidden God uses to sate Typhon and leave the abomination quiescent lest, in waking, it consumes all the cosmos. Should Fate falter, should a single thread of the Moirai come unspooled, Khaos shall erupt, and Mankind would be damned into an eternity of Darkness.

"This is the future the Gnostic Cabal strive for, in their self-destructive, unabating seeking after so-called free will. Their freedom is the freedom of eternal agony for all who have ever lived or ever would have."

Though his hand remained upon her shoulder, Athene crumpled, toppling to her knees.

❦

SHE AWAKENED with tears in her eyes, her heart hammering, fists balled into the linens in which she'd slept. Though her orichalcum fetters remained, preventing her from accessing Potency, she had managed to tear the sheets to ribbons in her convulsive nightmare.

As she blinked, lamplight allowed her vision to focus upon Mithra, who sat by her bedside, legs folded beneath himself. Slowly, he opened his eyes as well. "Some few of us were, in the first days of the Earth, appointed to watch over the flow of souls and ensure the continuance of life itself." He paused. "Even when the price of life's existence should prove one of cyclical apocalypses driving Man to the brink of extinction time and again."

"What ... what do you want of me?" Her voice shook, but she had not the strength left to feel the least shame over it. The vision the man—oneiromancer?—had shown her was one of unfathomable terror. But he could have conjured such from his own mind, if that mind was twisted enough.

"I want you to choose a side, Athene. Preserve Fate, and thus allow the continuation of the cosmos, or choose the veneer of freedom and watch all that is be devoured by Khaos."

"T-that's not much of a choice." If aught among this was, in fact, the Truth he proclaimed.

"No. But to believe, you need something more, I think."

Athene swallowed but did not answer.

"You must hear the words ... from the Moirai themselves. You must go and kneel before the thrones of Fate."

19

ARTEMIS

398 Dark Age

*I*n the morn, an aide woke Artemis to inform her that an emissary had come from Themiskyra. Artemis threw on her wolfskin cloak against the day's early chill, then strode out to find Themis awaiting her, surrounded by Immortals. None of Marduk's men had brandished weapons, but nevertheless, they took a Titan in their midst with the utmost care.

"I know why you've come here, Artemis," Themis said without preamble.

Artemis nodded slowly, trying to smile but knowing it must look feeble to the other woman's eyes. "Join me in my tent so we can have some privacy."

The Titan lady hesitated. It was slight, but Artemis caught it. Did she imagine Artemis would hold her hostage here? But then, Marduk had feared much the same should he send Artemis to Themiskyra.

The next moment, Themis spread her hand, indicating for Artemis to lead the way. She had her aide bring a repast of barley bread and almonds. It was simple fare, but the best soldiers on campaign could expect, and Artemis refused to eat what her soldiers could not. Themis made no comment on the food, though she did accept a few morsels of it.

"So," Artemis said, swallowing a mouthful of barley bread and reaching for some mey wine to wash it down, "you know why I have camped an army on the edge of your lands."

Themis worried an almond around in her mouth before answering. "The Amazons will not ride for Mithra."

Artemis decided to take a long swig of the mey. Though she hated the thought of invading without speaking to Themis, in truth, she did not much relish this conversation either. "I would not think you, of all people, would hold much love for Zeus."

"I have none. That does not mean I am willing to cast away the lives of my people in war with him."

Which brought them back to the greater reason why she was here, *now*. "You mean because he is a pawn of the Gnostic Cabal. You cannot, after all, be expected to destroy your own tool."

The woman's eyes went so wide Artemis half expected them to pop out, while her mouth drew up into a tiny 'O.' It took a moment before Themis visibly composed herself. "I don't know what you think you know ..." she began once she had settled.

"I know that at some point, following the Ambrosial War, Kronos began—or rather revived—the Cabal. I know you, Rhea, and two others were members, back then. Others have joined since, but Nemesis has done rather a fine job of yanking out such weeds, root and stem. I assume she has never come for you because your Oracular gift made it easier for you to conceal yourself from the Unseen Order."

Once more, her friend—if such a term applied anymore—seemed taken aback. Enough so, Themis now took up her own goblet and threw it back in a single pull, though it left her gasping. "Gaia! What Kandamian poisons are you drinking these days, Artemis?" She wiped her mouth with the back of her hand, then grunted. "I left the Cabal when Zeus cast down Kronos. He was, as you say, our founder and thus the mortar that held us together. Rhea was already dead, and after I abandoned Elládos, I turned my back on such pursuits as well. Striven though we had against Ananke, its hold upon all of our threads seems unbreakable. Though you cannot imagine the weight of such knowledge upon an Oracle." She flashed a mirthless grin. "And you? Working with the Unseen Order, now? Does it not render your efforts rather moot, defending a concept meant to be inviolable on its own?"

Once, Artemis had asked a similar question to Mithra, and she repeated his answer. "Perhaps it remains inviolable because of our staunch defence of it, or perhaps we defend it because Ananke already accounts for such, and we too must play our roles."

"What a wonderful justification for your own redundancy."

Artemis glowered now. It wasn't as though the implication had never occurred to her, but she preferred not to dwell on it. If Mithra had the right of it, all the cosmos were at stake. And regardless, the god-king held the key to Zeus's downfall. "The other two founders of the Cabal yet live?"

"Laran was mortal and would have perished millennia ago, demigod or not. Ningal, yes ... I imagine she lives. But you shan't find her."

"Has she fled so far beyond our reach?" Artemis misliked the idea of tracking a foe across unknown lands, but if the Cabal truly threatened all existence, she would have no choice, even if it meant tracking the dark Jungles of Kush or passing into legendary Yindai.

Themis chuckled. "Beyond your reach, mostlike, but far, I doubt it. She tends to secrete herself close to whichever events she hopes to manipulate." The Dangunian Oracle seemed to be enjoying Artemis's growing frustration. Small wonder, Artemis supposed, given she had come with an army. "No, you won't find Ningal, because she dons new faces more quickly than you or I might change our garb."

"Who is Ningal? What face does she wear now?"

"I know not what face she wears." And the woman seemed to relish her ignorance, for it meant Artemis would not get her answers. "Only, if Zeus has become a tool of the Cabal, I imagine she lies at the heart of his unwitting conscription." She paused. "That, and that she was the first-born child of Enki."

One of the very founders of the Anunnaki bloodline. Artemis polished off the last of her wine while thinking over all Themis had said. Finally, frustrated by the situation and disturbed by Themis's revelations, she tossed the goblet aside, taking momentary pleasure from its clamour as it tumbled over the hard-packed ground. "I've no wish to war with you."

"You speak as though I forced you to come here. I have never, in my life, showed you aught save compassion and understanding. You murdered my lover in my bed. You sent me, drenched in his blood, into exile, casting me from the home I had built. You helped Zeus overthrow Kronos, inadvertently destroying our last, best hope to be free of the awful futures some of us have foreseen. And despite it all, I welcomed you into my new home, Artemis. I gave you friendship and shelter. Even, I created a new place, where women could live free of the yoke of male masters, achieving the very aims you long sought in your life. Yet now, after all those years of kindness, you repay me by coming to my door with naked blades and razing torches. With men who—their blood riled into frenzies by the churning tides of war—will come to rape and pillage and burn down all I built." Themis fair spat the last words at Artemis. "You do not get to act thus and then have the temerity to pretend your-self not responsible for your deeds!"

Artemis cringed under the woman's tirade.

Whether or not he had been waiting in earshot or lingering close in case of trouble, Marduk ducked into the tent, hand upon the hilt of his akinakes. Artemis waved him away, but the Immortals' commander refused to leave her tent, loitering on the threshold.

"I am more than capable of protecting myself," she snapped. Which eventually got her lover, shamefaced, to slip back out the way he'd come. With a sigh, she looked back to Themis. "You want me to leave here without your pledge of loyalty ..." The woman had provided somewhat useful information on the Cabal, it was true. "I will do so if you swear a different oath."

"What oath, now?" Themis refused to meet her gaze as if the outburst had taken much out of the normally quiet woman and now she squirmed to escape the whole situation. Artemis knew the feeling.

"That you will, under no circumstances, lend aid to Zeus or Olym-pus. Nor will you in any way hinder the Babilimian Empire in any aggressions it takes against Elládos."

Themis rose. "I told you, I no longer hold a connection to the Gnostic Cabal. As for Zeus, I detest the worm down to the pith of my soul. You want an oath, old friend? I *swear* neither I nor anyone under my command will have any part in your war. By all means, let the men of

Babilim and Elládos bleed each other dry." The Dangunian woman strode closer. "Satisfied?"

Though Themis had given her what she'd asked for, Artemis could not help feeling she'd been slapped. "Yes."

"Then we're done. I've a city to oversee, and you have a world to set aflame."

When Themis stormed from her tent, Artemis wondered if she would ever see the woman again.

"It was not your decision whether to spare Kimmeria or not," Marduk had objected when Artemis had ordered the army back to Phrygia. Even knowing what she had learnt of the Cabal—of Ningal—walking among Olympus and manipulating Zeus, still, he plainly misliked that she had overstepped her authority. "Father will be livid at the usurpation of his authority."

Marduk stopped shy of trying to countermand her order and Artemis insisted she needed to speak with the god-king herself. She saw little to gain from wasting their troops in a pointless war with Themiskyra. True, controlling Kimmeria would give them an overland route into Phlegra, but they could cross the strait by barge, if needs be, or close on Elládos with her navy.

As they sailed for Kumari Kandam, Marduk's ire seemed to melt like sweat washed from his brow. Aboard her flagship, a vast trireme, where she stood by the helm, Marduk approached her. Artemis said naught, though she watched him draw nigh from the corner of her eye and noted the nervous way he clenched and unclenched his hands at his sides. "I ... um ... I was, perhaps, too harsh in my criticisms of your choice."

"That must have been hard to admit," she teased, stepping far enough from the helmsman the two of them would be out of earshot.

He shrugged. "A smidge more uncomfortable than an arrow through one's torso."

"I could put one there, should you wish a fresh comparison to make certain of that claim."

He ventured a faint smile. "Not necessary." His smile broke. "Do you ... recall ... when you came to the palace that first day? I was just a boy."

"Vaguely. It's pushing four hundred years now, and such things grow hazy."

"Not for me."

"Yes, well, give it a few millennia to all muddle together."

"No, I mean ..." Marduk's hands had balled into fists so tight his arms trembled. "I mean, in my adolescent mind that night, after I saw you, I, uh ... I told myself I'd marry you one day, even back then. I looked into your silver eyes and thought you the most amazing woman I had ever met."

Not quite knowing what to say, Artemis turned her gaze to the sea a moment, trying not to grin at a young man's earnestness. "I don't remember what being a youth is like, but I've known a good many children in my life. It all feels so real to them, I think."

"It's still real now, nigh four centuries later."

Well, that left her with little choice save to turn back to face him. "I love you, too."

"That, yes, always. But I mean to say, will you? Be my wife, that is? Will you marry me?"

Artemis had never thought to marry. She could never have imagined binding herself to a man's authority in law, even though she had tied herself to several by her heart. Why, then, would she even consider it now? Why did the earnestness writ across his face make her want to bend in ways she once would have scoffed at the thought of? Was it possible that some love might run so deep as to cut through pride, imposing not weakness but granting the strength to tie oneself in knots without breaking?

It had become hard to swallow. Hard to breathe. As such, speaking felt akin to preparing for a war, and a war she must win, for with each passing heartbreak she could see his veneer of confidence—that mask all men wore—beginning to crack. Her mouth was too dry. "I will," she managed in a breathless wheeze.

Relief and elation washed over his features. Marduk reached over to clutch her fingers in his own. "Then, when the Magi deem it auspicious ..."

"That ..." She stroked his cheek with her free hand, her fingers tangling in his brine-damp beard. "And more. I want to enter into married life with a heart free of the burdens of oaths of vengeance. I want to make a future that involves something other than a race from battlefield to battlefield or the need to assassinate insane Cabalists in dark chambers."

He understood at once. "When Olympus falls."

She nodded. "When Olympus falls." *And let it be soon.*

20

KIRKE

20 Dark Age

$\mathcal{B}$eneath a waxing crescent moon, Kirke climbed the slope above Delphi until she found the place her mother had described. There, with her himation flapping in the chill breeze, she looked about, making certain she was alone. It was past midnight, and few were foolish enough to tread into wild places at such an hour. It was not the time for Men, no, but Kirke was still a sorceress.

Never had she tried addressing a land spirit in more than the most casual of pleas before, and never had she received an overt answer. Kirke found, for the most part, that though tutelary spirits tended to be less malicious than eidolons, they did lean toward a perpetual grumpiness. One that meant they seemed best left alone.

"Spirit of the mountain!" she cried, hands raised, feeling somewhat foolish. "Spirit of the mountain, in the name of the sorceress Hekate, I beseech you. Open your maw and release that which she entombed here long ago."

Naught happened. Kirke looked around. Had she found the correct spot? What if the spirit had moved on in the intervening centuries?

What if it had perished all together and the Box now lay buried under countless tons of rock? Yeah, none of this was helping that feeling of being a fool.

"Spirit of the mountain!" she said once more. "Spirit, I beseech you! I come asking for the Box and ask that you offer it up, as my mother long ago bid you!"

A rumble shot through the ground, and Kirke's footing slipped. She spilled onto her arse, scraping it and no doubt tearing her peplos as she slid several feet downhill. Her foot caught on a ledge, arresting her momentum and keeping her from taking a tumble that looked several dozen feet down. Even Ambrosia-strengthened bones might break from such a fall, and Kirke had no desire to put them to the test.

Before she could rise, the mountain hiccuped. Pieces broke away, collapsing inward. A pine tree tore loose, its trunk toppling mere feet away from Kirke with a deafening crash. She was shrieking, arms over her face, as a rain of pine needles drenched her.

When the chaos finally ended and she crawled out of the sticky mess, a crevasse had opened in the slope as though an enormous axe had hacked into the mountainside. For a moment, Kirke stared at the gorge, wondering about the wisdom of crawling inside a hole in an unstable mountain.

"Ugh ... Except if not this, what's the point in living anyway?" she mumbled.

So resolved, she crawled toward the crevasse. The base of it dropped away, and in the faint moonlight, she couldn't really see how deep. The angle was right for her to slide down, but getting back up, especially in the dark, might not prove possible. She clucked her tongue in frustration. Then realised doing so made her seem far too much like her damn aunt. So she eased one foot onto the incline, then the other.

Her sandals immediately skidded, her balance giving way. Kirke caught herself with hands on either side of the gorge, her feet still flailing and finding no solid purchase. "Damn it. Damn it all! Damn the damn Moirai and damn their Tapestry."

She wanted this. It had to work this time. It had to.

She released her handholds and let her momentum carry her into the darkness. Her feet slid before her and many a time her arms banged against the sides, earning her fresh bruises and scrapes. Then, at last, she reached the base of the crevasse and was sent sprawling into fresh, reeking earth. A moment she lay groaning before she managed to roll over. Looking up, she could see the moon and a hint of stars. After blinking several times, her vision adjusted to the paltry light.

Nearby, exposed but one corner still stuck in the dirt, glinted the strange metal of Pandora's Box. Kirke swallowed, almost unable to believe she had found it. That this had worked. With trembling fingers, she reached for it.

Here, her chance to go back. To find a way to fix the whole of the broken World. One more chance.

One, last, precious hope.

She began setting the Box.

❦

KIRKE NODDED. *"For now, we've more pressing matters at home. I want you to send King Aspadas a dream that his daughter's child will destroy his empire."*

"You want him to murder his own child?"

"No." Kirke shook her head. *"Aspadas has a soft spot for his girl and could never stomach her death. Rather, he'll marry dear Mandana off to King Kabujiya of Kissatu."*

"So he trusts his tribute king to keep in line, yes?" Morpheus quirked a smile, and Kirke could imagine what he was thinking. Kabujiya was the son of Kurus, a staunch ally of Nineveh, whom Aspadas's father had well rewarded for his loyalty. A choice the Ninevehan kings would one day regret.

"Desperation coupled with familial bonds makes for impaired judgment," she agreed. *"And Mithra has foretold that, one day, the issue of Mandana will indeed seize control of the dynasty. In the meantime, have the Magi spread a prophecy that a Babilimian will one day become heir to the Ninevehan dynasty. When the time comes, the fulfilled prophecy will ensure Kurus II has the popular support."*

❦

SHE AWAKENED IN TWILIGHT, a city of jagged spires rising up just beyond where she knelt, the sight like some many-spined behemoth she almost expected to see lurch into motion. Then it did move, for the ground bucked beneath her, cutting short her attempt to rise. A cacophony erupted, Gaia groaning in her violent heaves, spires shattering and raining stones like hail across the darkened city. The tumult sent her tumbling as the land broke apart, and Kirke slammed hard into a rising shelf of earth.

The impact dazed her, left her moaning, not quite certain how much time had passed. She pushed herself up on hands and knees and gaped in absolute terror at what unfolded before her. The sky had splintered, pieces of it tumbling earthward like a cracking dam about to burst. Through the rifts rent in reality writhed intimations of squirming tendrils, like some thousand-armed cephalopodic nightmare, worming its way into the Mortal Realm.

Kirke slapped a hand to her mouth, too stricken to scream. A thought slammed into her, appalling in its clarity, and more so because she could not imagine whence came such an idea. But the dread apprehension remained: what if she beheld not the breaking of reality but the falling away of a facade, like plaster flaking off a crumbling wall, revealing what lay beneath?

Those profane tendrils stretched down, toward the blighted, falling city, giving her a better—more terrible—look at the abomination seeping into her world. The arms seemed to glint with endogenous motes of light just beneath the surface, as if composed of both stars and the infinite darkness that lay between.

Tears spilled from her eyes, welling against her fingers where her hand remained clamped over her mouth. Inarticulate moans escaped her. She sat on her knees, rocking back and forth, feeling the sum of her World shredding, her mind fraying. An inexplicable prurient energy had come over her, and she realised with a disgusted start she had begun rubbing herself. She jerked her hand away. Still weeping, she began to crawl from the city, desperate to get as far from the burgeoning madness as she could.

Was this the Time of Nyx? Was this the dread darkness Ouranos had helped Man and Titan escape to give rise to history? Kirke had imagined going so far back in time she could escape the Tapestry. She had not ... had never imagined that, beyond recorded history, she could stumble into such untrammelled Khaos.

A shadow dropped from the sky and she swallowed a fresh whimper.

For a single heartbeat, she thought one of those tendrils had swooped down to prevent her escape. The next instant, she recognised the form was humanoid and yet could have sworn she had beheld *wings* upon his back. But when he stood, it was just a man, hair and eyes dark. He rushed toward her, hand extended. He shouted in some foreign tongue, the words unknown but his warning plain. Kirke let him take her hand, and he heaved her to her feet, then yanked her into a dead run away from the falling city.

The ground continued to convulse, and she knew, then, it was vain to think they could outrun the dissolution of the very World. Darkness bloomed into being here, awakening with a swiftness that belied aught in nature.

Perhaps the man shared her realisation, for he glanced back, stalling a single instant. Then, before Kirke could decide whether to keep running or surrender to the inevitable, he swept an arm beneath her legs, the other encircling her shoulders. He leapt into the air with a bound most Titans could not have managed, and ebony wings *did* erupt from his back. Great beats of those wings hurled them higher, sending them speeding away from the ruptures of Darkness. Over his shoulder, she saw tendrils reaching for them.

Dread at last eclipsed all sanity, and Kirke had no idea what happened next.

WHEN AT LAST her mind ceased its perverse whorls, releasing her from the vortex of madness that had threatened to drag her into its depths forever, Kirke found she lay in a cave. A small fire sent shadows skittering above the recesses, their presence evoking memories of that awful, soul-consuming Dark she had witnessed.

Whimpering, she curled into a foetal ball and clenched her eyes shut, willing it all to be ended.

Something alighted on her shoulder and she gagged on an abortive scream.

"Be at ease." Though the accent was strange, the words were spoken in Elládosi.

Slowly, Kirke cracked open an eye and dared a peek at whoever spoke to her. It was the same black-haired man who had saved her from the city. Through a rather extreme effort of will, Kirke forced herself to sit. As she did so, her rescuer scooted back, closer to the fire.

"The Eschaton has passed and the time for such dread has receded. Indeed, the Earth rotates once more, and thus resume the cycles of day and night." The man wheezed, perhaps a chuckle. "Some things surprise even me."

"Uh, what?" Kirke's mouth was dry and she could, at this moment, have gone for an entire bath house full of wine. "Um, you know, never mind about that, I've not the presence of mind to care at the moment. Two questions: Who are you, and do you have aught to drink? Wait! Answer the second one first, because that matters most right now."

The man stared at her a moment before pulling a flask from his belt and tossing it to her. Oddly, it seemed made of some metal, almost iron-like, though she couldn't imagine iron would keep wine well. After fiddling with the unusual cork, she took a swig and then sputtered it. "Yeah, I didn't mean water. Sure, it has its uses. Better for swimming in and washing and stuff. But in circumstances such as these ... It's got to be wine."

The stranger offered her a small, sad smile. "If you seek to drink away your demons, you'll have a wait before you. I imagine it'll be some time before the scattered survivors of that apocalypse rediscover the planting of vineyards and fermenting of draughts."

"Um ..." That didn't sound good. In fact, it sounded like some of the worst news Kirke had ever heard. "Apocalypse?"

"As to your original question, while I do not like to reveal my nature, given you saw it already, I suppose there is little point in denying. I am an angel, and my name is Raziel."

Raziel? As in ... "As in the Sefer Raziel her mother had spoken of?" Also, what in Gaia was a damn angel, anyway? It sounded related to the word for messenger.

The man scowled at her. Kirke was certain she had misstepped, only she couldn't say how. After holding her gaze long enough he made her palms sweat, the man grabbed his satchel and withdrew a bound book. Which was indeed the grimoire Mother had once stolen from the Circle of Goetic Mysteries. "Are you with the Forgotten, to know about this?" He shook his head. "No, I rather think you an unintended side-effect of

Gnostic meddling in things which they little understand. They fail to apprehend that even their puerile defiance of Fate serves to reinforce its inviolable nature. And thus, another timewalker."

Kirke may not have grasped much of what Raziel had said, but she knew enough to understand him embroiled in some struggle against Fate. "I'm not with anyone, no. But I sure as Gaia's cavernous arse want a way free from Ananke."

"You think that only because you do not conceive of what you ask. But if you are amenable, I will show you why the true path lies not in defiance of Fate but in its upholding. I offer you ... Truth."

Kirke almost laughed. So this man, this so-called angel, was going to convince her why all the awful weavings of the Moirai's Tapestry were, in fact, a good thing? While she thought that momentously unlikely, given the world had just ended, she had nowhere else to be. "Yeah, sure. Amuse me."

❧

Byblos, it turned out, was one of the few bastions of civilisation to survive the fall of the Time of Nyx. According to Raziel it had been founded by Vorsanos in days long gone. Of course, already, she'd heard people using the name Ouranos for that man. The change shocked Kirke, but Raziel's response had been simple and practical. "It is a new Era, with little place for any who survived the last. Such things are inevitably swept up into the currents of history, fading to legend if even that. We too will need new identities, for Raziel is a name from such bygone days, and Kirke the name of one yet to come."

It sounded odd, at first, to think of abandoning a name she'd used for forty-six centuries. Raziel had countered by asking if her life as Kirke had been all she could have wished for. Once more, damnable simplicity, and suddenly Kirke could not wait to begin her new life. There was a freedom in casting aside all the accoutrements gathered over a lifetime like so many soiled linens. Thus unburdened, she could begin anew, and this time with the knowledge she had gained, and the ability to make better choices.

Kirke had cursed her fate for centuries. Had striven to change it after learning the truth about her daughter and her beloved Odysseus's end.

She had wept and raged, swept away by childish passions, as petulant in defying Ananke as a youth who wailed at the unfairness of the sun setting or the body's need for rest.

"It is the continuous revolution of the Wheels of Life and History that keep spinning the Wheel of Fate. And it is that revolution upon which the very World rests. This Tapestry is but another metaphor for causality, and just as you imagine yanking out a thread might unravel history, consider instead that an upset of the Wheel risks the unmaking of the very cosmos. To deviate from causality is to send all of us, everyone who ever has or ever will live plummeting into the maw of the Darkness. That which you beheld at the fall of Vulgeth is but prelude to the infinite, eternal agonies awaiting every soul in the cosmos. Before such unspeakable torment, the transitory suffering endured by those who fail to understand the needs of Fate amount to naught but dust billowing in the breeze."

Perhaps he was an oneiromancer, for in her dreams, Raziel had revealed to her the unvarnished truth of his words. He spoke the Ontos, and she, having glimpsed even a piece of it, could no longer dare to strive against the chains that had always fettered her. It was no longer a question of unmaking herself or even her entire bloodline. For as Raziel had shown her, even if her consciousness was erased, she would find no escape from this.

"There is no recourse to oblivion," he had said, "for your soul, were it not incarnated in this shell of flesh, would yet remain within the great well of all souls and still be subject to the fate of all souls."

There was no recourse at all. Not for her, not for any in the ambit of the World.

And thus, driven with fresh purpose, they came to Byblos with new names. Raziel named himself Enki, and under that guise he helped Men rediscover sciences nigh lost in the cataclysm. He taught them of harnessing the waters to cultivate fields. And when they were no longer starving, he spread knowledge of reading and writing. Of how to make papyrus. In short, he prevented the extinction of civilisation.

By his side, Kirke, as the witch Damkina, assisted his endeavours.

Still, it was not without due shock that she accompanied him to the nigh-overflowing necropolis in the heart of the city. To visit here was to step into some forgotten dream. Any conscious memory she had of the place had dwindled away like the dregs of an ill-tended fire, yes, but still, her mind had conjured up this place from tales told by others. She had been born here, and still would be, in days yet to come.

"Why have we ventured to this place?" she asked, though a niggling suspicion had begun to grow in her the moment they had passed beyond the necropolis's twisted gates.

The beard he had grown in local fashion half hid his answering smile, and, as always, Damkina was left to wonder how much this man truly knew of the past or future. He seemed an Oracle, for certain; perhaps his insight came through oneiromancy, but sometimes he seemed to know too much even for that. "I have been thinking about disseminating some select portions of the wisdom preserved within Raziel's tome." It was passing strange to her that he could already speak about Raziel as though he had been some entirely separate person from Enki. In time, perhaps Damkina would feel the same way about Kirke. "I have mused long upon it, seeking insight."

She was afraid to ask. And yet she trembled with anticipation, the hairs on her arms rising in expectation. "Why are we here?" She had to hear it spoken aloud after all this time.

"Practitioners of the greater arcana have always been scarce, scattered across the Earth, no more than a few hundred across the world even at their peak. Of these, it seems at most a handful survived the Eschaton. Were we to do naught, perhaps sorcery itself would fade into legend, forgotten."

"Perhaps the Mortal Realm would have been better off."

"That's not what happened." Enki looked pointedly at her. "After all, someone trained you. And so I muse on the arcana that those, in the Time of Nyx, termed goetia. And by my side stands the last known sorceress on Earth." He paused. "At least until we create and train a new order. Until we induct those seeking knowledge into our inner—"

"Circle," she finished. "A Circle of Goetic Mysteries." The anticipated shudder ran down her spine and set her trembling.

Enki offered her a long nod, acknowledging she had come to wisdom at last. "Then let us seek out the worthy."

21

PANDORA

1550 Silver Age

Five years, languid and glorious, dissipated like morning dew beneath the harsh sun of Phoenikia. They had built a small manse a short walk from the sea, far enough from Tyros to draw no eyes nor attract attention. It was a palace to her, carved of fine woods and engraved with reliefs by her own hands, depicting peacocks and eagles and pheasants and a dozen other birds across every exterior wall. Together, they had added colours with paints made from berries and natural dyes found around the countryside. When the exterior was done, they set to furnishing and decorating the interior until it was almost as cosy as the place where she had once lived—and he one day still would—on Mu.

It was, however, to that other home that Pandora kept looking back, an ache in her chest at the thought her fondest times lay behind her, while for him it lay ahead. She wanted to pass through her life at his side, not live this perverse existence of sporadic coexistence, oft moving in opposite directions. She wanted to live and love, and raise another family, though both had agreed it could not be in this time. Not knowing, as she did, more burdens lay ahead of her.

Thus, each night she lay awake, pondering if she ought best to leave and have it all over and done with. But how could she, knowing that some few miles distant, her toddler self ran and played and laughed with untrammelled joy, in moments about to be forever stolen by Zeus? She could neither resolve to interfere—and damn the whole timeline and everyone in it—nor simply walk away. She could not tear herself from this place or time, where one of the greatest pains of her life must soon impend, though she knew waiting for it to happen was a self-mutilation of her soul.

In the end, though, Pandora was not one to accept defeat. She had failed to stop Mithra once, but she would take another chance, and maybe, just maybe, save the future in the process.

"I want to know," she said to Prometheus one eve whilst they walked along the beach, listening to the chirp of crickets and the lap of waves. "I want to be able to use the Flame as a weapon, as you do."

"Did you not, in the Titanomachy, unleash an inferno with volcanic force?" He kept his gaze ahead, not meeting her eyes, but she had the distinct sense he was teasing her.

"I've power enough, true, but not nigh the control you manage for it. Beyond that, I want to master pushing my Pneuma into another to heal them. I should have learnt it long ago, but other things always seemed more pressing."

"You cannot settle here," he observed. "Knowing what lies ahead, you remain restless, this time different somehow than the one in my future where we snatched some time of peace, as you said."

It was different, in so many ways. "Can you teach me?"

"The Art of Fire, yes, though not here. I would venture far up, into the Kunlun Mountains, where none save the wildest of goats and the birds might observe our training or risk being burnt by it." He looked to her now. "But of healing, the best I can offer is a target to practice on, and some advice, for I have heard the process described but have never managed more than a trickle myself."

"Kala could do it using the Phoenix's power. I witnessed it."

Prometheus cast a look back, at their distant, moonlit house, as if reluctant to leave it behind. Not for the first time, Pandora wondered what all this felt like for him. She had asked him, once, to describe his experiences, going through his immortal life and meeting her as he did. "Discomfiting," he had said. "And beautiful. Moments of hope shining through eons of loss and regret."

Now, she too looked back and wondered if it was another home she was leaving behind forever, one which, in days to come, she would long for as she did the one on Mu. She could have called off the training, could have settled here and given him what time was allotted to them without the burdens of the future weighing upon her. But Pandora wanted so much more than this shattered existence, and to claim her heart's desire, she had no choice but to stand, one more time, against Mithra and the Unseen Order. In the Hursag Mountains she had fled from the gathered Anunnaki. Next she encountered her foes, she needed to be able to overcome them.

For she had wearied of forever giving ground to Fate or its emissaries.

❧

WHEN THE WEATHER PERMITTED, they travelled long roads into the mountains and spent months training. Under Prometheus's tutelage, Pandora formed whips and blades of fire into whirling dances of death to bring down her foes. She created discuses of flame that would explode on impact, wiping whole tracts of the mountainside clean of vegetation. Later, as she grew stronger, she would summon intersecting parabolic arcs that could explode outward in a lattice of flame sure to incinerate anyone in a hemisphere around her.

Each night, utterly spent of Pneuma, she would collapse by the fire he had kindled and seek to draw strength back in from the blaze. As she absorbed its energies, it would begin to dwindle, and Prometheus would continuously kindle the flame higher, stoking it whenever he was not out hunting for their supper. For, indeed, she ate each meal as though she had not seen food in a fortnight, and still she remained ravenous, never quite able to replenish the sum of all the energy she expended.

Other days, when she needed reprieve from the destruction, Prometheus would cut his arm or leg, and Pandora would try, under his guidance, over and over, to push even hints of her Pneuma into him. He was directing the flow of his own life force to prevent the healing, she thought, giving her more time. But always, it proved only more time for her to fail.

One afternoon, after a frustrating attempt to seal a wound on his bicep had produced no result, he drew her to her feet and guided her to a wide plateau. From here, a precipitous drop pitched off into a gulley far below. But a break in the mountains gave her a glorious view of the land for miles ahead. Beyond the mountains she could see woodlands, and beyond that, perhaps the hazy hint of a desert. "What's out there?"

Prometheus followed her gaze. "The vast kingdoms of Yindai. And beyond, Dangun, and a world that stretches further still than Men or Titans of the Thalassa realise. Gaia is wide, Pandora." Lazy clouds drifted beneath them and Pandora imagined leaping onto them and flying away. Prometheus took her hand, dragging her from her fancy, and led her from the edge, back to the centre of the plateau. "Yindai is not why I brought you here. You have spoken of your encounters with Kala and with Nemesis, both of whom possessed skills you could not counter because you had not seen their like."

In truth, some of the tactics Nemesis used matched those Artemis had taught her, which made sense as one Nemesis was Athene. But Pandora had resolved not to share that knowledge with this Prometheus, given she had already explained it to his future self. Who knew if it might inadvertently have a negative effect upon his time with Athene, once she went into exile in another forty-something years.

The thought made her grimace. Her concern for the integrity of the timeline made her feel unclean, like somehow the Unseen Order had infected her with their perverse dogma. Yet, given all the events of her life led to the creation of that life, to Odysseus and Kirke becoming her parents, how could she know which threads to safely pluck in the past? No, any break with Fate she would make now, it must come in the future, in the time just before the Deluge, when there was no more time.

"Kala fought with a style not the least like pankration."

Prometheus nodded. "From what little I saw of his techniques long ago, I think it some combination of kalaripayat and perhaps some variant of Yindese wushu."

"Oh, sure. That makes sense," she deadpanned.

"Kalaripayat was a martial art developed in Jambudvipa in a bygone Era. Most of the Watchers learnt the art, yourself included. The memories of it lie quiescent within your soul. While you cannot actively recall your past life, with sufficient training and meditative techniques you may allow your body to remember."

Pandora almost laughed at that. But Prometheus was in earnest and soon set to teaching her forms, moving through motion after motion. Their sessions were slow at first. Only when she had repeated a particular form hundreds of times did he begin to perform them with speed. Still, when he urged her to use them in active combat, she had not expected them to work. Not up until the moment she parried his grasp on one arm and landed a blow upon his chest in counter, without a single thought having formed in her mind.

One formed afterwards, though. "You allowed me to strike you. I saw you fight against the assassins of the Unseen Order. You have an uncanny speed."

He nodded, expressionless. "My purpose is not to defeat you, but to give you the tools you need."

She frowned. "And your other purpose? To preserve Fate and ensure the Eschatons unfold as the Moirai have decreed."

He looked away, toward the setting sun. "It is possible for a man to want more than one thing, even if he cannot have them all, all the time. Even if he cannot truly have any of them. No one goes through life with but a single aim, Pandora."

So went their training, and with it, the years bled by, bringing her ever closer to her moment of despair.

WHEN THE DAY ARRIVED, Pandora knew she could not stop Zeus or Hekate from doing what they must. She knew it, and yet, she could not stop herself from attending Agenor's symposium, letting fancies play through her mind in which she unleashed flaming arcs of death upon the Olympian tyrant, watching him turned to cinders. She could, with the control Prometheus had given her, direct her attacks without harming her daughter or the gathered throng. She could see Zeus immolated, never again to lay hand upon a woman. But such were idle fancies, and she pushed them from her mind. Hekate would not have allowed it, and besides, Pandora would be destroying herself, her daughter, and everyone else close to her.

So, instead, wearing a new, crimson khiton she'd bought in town, she came to Tyros, strolled up to the Hill of Epaphus, and intruded upon the symposium. How was she to do otherwise? It was the perverse urge to peek beneath the dressings of a wound you knew ran deep and examine just how bad it was, though you could do naught for it. It was that self-destructive need to watch the moment as a chirurgeon's blade descended, though a wiser woman would have looked away from the pain.

Thus did she wander the crowd, declining every offer of food or wine, for her stomach had turned bilious and the mere thought of aught touching it had her ready to retch. The Phoenix shrieked within her soul, blazing so close to the surface she felt her skin might catch alight, turn her new khiton to ash, and reveal her to all and sundry as the inferno she was.

Burn, burn, burn.

Oh, how desperately she wished she could give in to the spirit's refrain. She would have unleashed torrents of flame against all those who would harm Europa or her own younger self. She would have become the fiery avenger, descended from some unknown Realm to right wrongs that could not be endured.

Then, because the masochistic need rose in her to unbearable degrees, she sought out Europa, though she took care not to reveal herself to the woman. Rather, she watched her adoptive mother chase her five-year-old self around the hall.

"Pandora, get back here!" The child dashed amid the hall, worming her way between the adults as though they presented a maze for her to solve. Pandora remembered this moment, for it had been burnt into her memory, the last happy instant of her childhood. Europa was chasing the girl, and behind, another woman was laughing. Oh ... Kassiopeia, Phoenix's bride from Byblos. Pandora recalled her kindness, the way her fingers would tickle her nose, ruffle her hair, or pinch her ear.

Another woman stared at the display and Pandora noticed her only because of her height. A Heliad Nymph. Kirke. From the way her mother blanched and fled, this Kirke knew something of what would happen to little Pandora. Which meant, this must have been during the woman's stint as a timewalker, so she would not know Pandora as her own daughter, but perhaps as her grandmother?

Pandora strode around the crowd to intercept Kirke, but the woman was so distraught, she stumbled into her and Pandora caught her by her arms. "You wonder if the unravelling threads of time shall reveal truth or madness."

Kirke gaped, looking at her. "Pandora?" Her mother threw a glance back at the hall where the child played, as if there had been any doubt.

"Because it seems too much to grasp," Pandora said.

"Y-you ..."

Somehow, her mother's confusion, rising despair, and terror served to mute Pandora's own grief. Here was a woman who needed her comfort and reassurance, and so Pandora threw herself into providing it. She guided Kirke out into the courtyard where they could talk, free of prying eyes or curious ears. The moment they moved beneath a cedar, Kirke leant against it as though she might otherwise topple over from the strain.

"Until now, I've not seen you at a loss for words." Pandora had meant it as a jest to lighten the woman's mood, though it had come out more earnest than she'd intended.

"You speak as though you know me."

Oh. So for Kirke, this fell even before their months spent in Themiskyra together. Well, it would be a long road still for her to tread, wouldn't it? "I have and I will." From across the courtyard, Pandora spied Phoenix and Kadmus heading her way, and her heart lurched. An irrational fear that one of them might know her as Pandora sent her pulse racing, though both had seen her as Nike when she'd brought the infant to Europa five years prior. Pandora forced herself to look back to Kirke. "The child was me, as I know you've surmised. I—"

But the princes had come too close, and Pandora snapped her mouth shut lest either one should overhear. The pair each dropped to one knee, Phoenix having spied them first. "Goddesses," he said, the way his voice fell in awe sparking sorrow in Pandora's core. "We did not know you were among us."

Pandora had no idea how to address him now, but Kirke answered for her. "Are not all welcome at this symposium?"

Phoenix bobbed his head in agreement. "Of course they are, my lady."

And Kadmus, he stared at Pandora. Was he seeing Nike? Did he fear what her arrival impended? Did he have some inkling his life would forever change in moments? Or perhaps he was afraid she had come to claim the child she had once left with Europa. Oh, would that she could! Would that she could spare little Pandora a single moment of the anguish ahead of her.

And Kadmus, he had given her a puzzle box this day, one she had cherished all her life, until her flight away from Atlantis. She had loved him, too, of course. And he, she realised now, would have tried to net and catch the moon itself if only to bring a smile to her face.

"Hello, Kadmus," Pandora managed, for she could not bear to let this moment pass, knowing she would never see him again. She heard later he had searched for her, and searched hard, before becoming the king of Thebes. A strange road all of them walked.

"My lady," he replied, bowing his head. Was it fear in his posture? The thought only deepened the ache in her soul.

Pandora wanted to reach out and lay a hand upon his shoulder. She wanted to connect with her uncles in any possible way, but such time was lost to her, and she dare not open those gates, for fear she would never shut them against the tide of emotions that must surge forth. Instead, she grabbed Kirke and dragged her away from the princes.

"He referred to you as a goddess, too," Kirke said.

Pandora grimaced at that, uncertain how to answer. She glanced about to make certain no one, least of all Kadmus or Phoenix, could overhear. "The Tapestry's weaves are complex, sometimes gossamer threads we do not always see."

"Yeah, kind of like that answer." Pandora struggled not to laugh. Her mother had a way with words, sometimes. "This is it, isn't it? This is the moment when Zeus will come for Europa. And ... and you'll be swept up in the chaos?"

Oh, Gaia. "It is." She could scarce manage the answer, for speaking it aloud stole yet another piece of her, and surely so few remained now.

"Can we stop it?"

Pandora almost wept at the question. How many years had she spent pondering it? How many myriad ways had she imagined changing the outcome of this day, in ways great or small? She need not slay Zeus to stop herself from being taken. She could, as Kadmus feared, lay claim to the child herself and abscond with her. Even, she could hide Pandora during the pivotal moment and trust Agenor to raise Europa's adoptive child as his granddaughter. A thousand different tacks she could take, all of them ending with with the annihilation of her bloodline.

Once, in discussing it with Prometheus, he had laid bare the depth of the burden. *"Do you think the endless ripples of your life end with the oblivion of a single genos? Have you forgotten Nike's role in the Titanomachy? In the Gigantomachy? Your presence even shaped the destiny of Vulgeth, in the Time of Nyx. All history collapses in on itself with your removal from the timeline."*

"History must unfold as it always has, or all that has gone would collapse in on itself, Kirke. Some things ..." Pandora choked on a sob, unable to speak for a moment. "Some things we think unbearable must be borne, regardless."

Kirke looked shattered. For a time, they walked in silence through the twilit courtyard, the both of them trying to hold on to any measure of composure. "If we cannot risk changing the past for fear of rippling repercussions," Kirke said at last, "then my presence here serves no purpose."

Within such lay the crux of the question of free will. "To say that, if Fate cannot be changed, we have no purpose in it, seems an oversimplification," Pandora said as they strolled. Her removal from the timeline—or Kirke's, or anyone's—would unmake time. How, then, could they be said to serve no purpose, if *all* hinged upon their choices? "We cannot change what will happen—perhaps not even if we tried—but that does not mean we cannot affect it. Or be affected by it."

Maybe the Unseen Order was right and they could not alter the future, for the simple reason that, like the past, it already existed. What choices Pandora would make, she had *already* made, and she could no more alter those yet to come, from her perspective, than she could change the ones made in days gone. Nevertheless, they remained her choices, and those choices *had* somehow shaped the timeline, bitter though it seemed.

Before Kirke could answer, a tumult arose in the great hall, the chaos becoming a blow between Pandora's shoulder blades. It had begun. And she, despite herself, despite her impotence, *had* to see it. She knew Kirke did not follow as she strode for Agenor's hall, but Pandora could afford no time to tend to her mother now. Not now.

At a dash, Pandora burst into the crowded throne room in time to see Zeus stride in through the main gates, Hekate stumbling along behind him as if something had distraught her. She followed her daughter's gaze until it alighted on Europa. And Pandora. Hekate *knew* what she was about, didn't she? The thought only served to further the turbulent churn of Pandora's gut. It had been a mistake to come here. She had known, long before she took her first step up the path to the Hill of Epaphus, it was a mistake, and yet she had not been able to stall her feet. With every blighted step she took, she knew she would torture herself by witnessing this, and she had been powerless to turn from it.

She felt it as tendrils of smoke seeped between the fingers of her clenched, smouldering fists. Every instinct demanded she rush forward and strike down Zeus. It was self-preservation—even if also self-annihilation—and no one should be expected to bear what she would now witness.

King Agenor lurched to his feet but dropped to his knees before the tyrant lord Zeus. Kadmus and Phoenix had stood beside their father, and now they too fell to their knees, though Pandora could see hints of defiance in their postures.

Hekate swept up beside Zeus, whispering something in his ear. A moment later, his gaze landed upon the princess of Tyros. "I will have the girl, Europa, as my pallake," the King of Olympus announced, his words a declaration of war upon Pandora's soul.

She could not allow this!

Burn, burn, BURN!

The heat in her became a conflagration, seeking any means of egress from beneath her skin.

Agenor fair leapt to his feet. "My lord! Surely you might choose someone else. My daughter is the sole princess of Tyros and destined for—"

"For a good many nights upon her back," Zeus bellowed.

Kadmus rose and strode betwixt Zeus and Europa. "This is not Argos!" At the same time, Phoenix seized an amphora and rushed Zeus.

The details of this memory had become a blur in Pandora's mind, as if a part of her had not wanted to remember every piercing, painful component of so horrid a juncture. Now, it all played out before her in awful panoply, movements mired and more agonising for their slowness, and the knowledge that she could stop it all. In an instant, she could change everything by releasing the reins she now held upon the raging inferno inside her. All she had to do was let go, and the bitter history of her past would turn to ashes alongside the rapist abomination who ruled Olympus.

Zeus turned to Phoenix, and Pandora tasted the clean, pungent currents of a storm. The braziers dimmed an instant before lightning erupted from Zeus's outstretched hand. The flash of it blinded her for a moment, its thunder deafening. When her senses returned, Phoenix had been hurled backward and lay in a smoking pile of burnt, ruined flesh. Kadmus tackled Zeus, and they landed on the floor.

Phoenix was ... dead? Pandora had not recalled this, and small wonder. While Kadmus rained blows on Zeus, Europa and little Pandora tried to flee, only to be seized by Hekate. *Pyrrha, don't!* Pandora wanted to scream at her. Instead, she stood there impotent, smoke coiling about her arms, flames threatening to flare forth.

BURN, BURN, BURN!

Hekate dragged both girls out into the atrium, and as Pandora looked back toward Kadmus, a terrific explosion surged through the palace. It shook the foundations, cracking mortar and calling down cataracts of dust as the vast stones of the ceiling shifted, threatening to collapse and obliterate the throng lingering in the throne room. The blast was as if Pandora had released the burning fury inside herself, but it had come from somewhere outside the hall and she could not imagine what had caused it.

Zeus recovered quickly, seized Kadmus, and hurled him away. The prince flew through the air and smacked into a pillar with a sickening crack.

He's dead too! The thought crashed through Pandora's mind for an instant, before she recalled Kadmus and Kilix would go on to hunt for Europa, and Kadmus would become the first mortal king of Thebes.

But the prince did not stir. Blanching, Pandora pushed her way through the crowd—not hard given all were stricken with some medley of shock and panic and grief—and knelt beside Kadmus's body. His breath was ragged, pained even in his unconsciousness.

Pandora cast a desperate glance up at Agenor, but the man was wailing over the loss of his daughter and seemed deprived of all his senses. She laid her palms on Kadmus's chest. Only twice had she ever succeeded in pushing her Pneuma into Prometheus, and only to help him more quickly recover from minor scrapes. Kadmus would mostlike, given the blows he had taken, suffer from severe internal injuries.

"Please, Uncle Kadmus," Pandora whispered. She allowed her life energy to well in her hands, scorching Pneuma surging beneath her skin like a turbulent, boiling river poised to overflow its bounds. "Please don't die."

He did *not* die. History recorded he lived through this.

With a groan of effort, Pandora directed her Pneuma into her uncle. At first, it refused to leave her hands at all, only growing hotter until she feared she might scald his flesh. Then, at last, in answer to her desperate need, trickles of that heat bled into the prince. He bucked, once, and after a moment, his breathing evened out.

Pandora jerked away from him, hoping no one had seen what she had done, for she could abide no questions this night. Already, it had taken all she had. When she rose, her legs wobbled, perhaps from the expenditure of Pneuma, or perhaps from the loss of so much more of her heart.

Ragged, beset by quivers, she stumbled from the palace, spying Kilix rushing in as she did so.

Soon, he and Kadmus would begin their fateful, futile efforts to return Europa and Pandora home to Tyros. They would fail, of course, but in so doing, they would wander into their own destinies.

The Tapestry was cruel, though Pandora almost admired the profane symmetries woven within it. Every thread so perfectly wrapt through the weft, so elegantly abused to the fullest extent, pulled taut but never quite so far as to snap in twain. Such was her life, stretched thin, nigh to breaking.

But not yet.

She was not broken yet.

EPILOGUE

Asura Era, Bronze Age

The Tree in the Dreaming Lands had offered him simple advice, though the hearing of it had shredded Matarśivan's nerves.

If you would seek the Fates, go back to the beginning.

Only one place could have fit that meaning, and thus he flew back to Kumari Kandam and saw that so much had changed and war once more impended. He would attend to it, perhaps. First, though, he flew on, finally returning to the island of his origin. To the great Tree of Life had that birthed both him and his brethren and Mankind.

Perhaps some among the Adityas would have recognised him and tolerated his presence, but he preferred to remain concealed and thus had flown in under cover of darkness and alighted on the grass before the great Tree.

Here, all things had begun. He had awakened, curled in a mound, fingertips brushing against Aditi's foot where she lay beside him. Now, Matarśivan turned about, wondering at what had changed.

Some of the Adityas had settled upon the nearby mountain, for they had to gather the golden apples to brew their Amrita and maintain their power. Aditi's heirs they were, sired upon her by one or more of the Archons, and she had given them this power. Had the Archons—the Elder Gods as they were sometimes now called—helped give rise to the Adityas and Danavas as new races of gods with the sole intent of prompting war and death?

Of spinning the Wheel of Life?

He could not shake the thought of it.

Matarśivan walked the circumference of the colossal Tree, scanning it for sign of the so-called Fates whilst keeping watch for any Adityas who might have sat in guardianship of this place. Then, there in the trunk he spied a hollow, a rent that bored down among the roots. He could have sworn no such opening existed in their days of youth.

Did the breach hold some import? Did it mean the Tree itself suffered from the preponderance of death that war had visited upon the World?

With a final glance about himself, Matarśivan made for the aperture. It was narrow enough he had to turn sideways and withdraw his wings so as to edge through. The space beyond lay in almost total blackness, only a faint hint of moonlight peeking in from behind him.

It was madness to push on without light, but then, madness had long since become his touchstone. Feeling his way with each hand upon a fibrous wall, he descended a gradual slope inside the hollow. The air vibrated here, becoming a hair too thick. A sensation not unlike passing into the Realms beyond. He had entered a liminal space.

Of a sudden, twin flames sprang into being, lighting braziers in a cavern that lay ahead of him. They flanked a pool of water over which dangled roots from the Tree. Their faint light adumbrated the whole of the chamber, giving a hint of a recess that reached deeper into the land than he'd first imagined. Or rather, a space between worlds. If he pushed on into any of the other darkened tunnels here, he suspected he might reach into the domains of the Spirit Realm or perhaps the nebulous Roil.

His hesitant footfalls echoed through the cavern as he paced closer to the well. Wood rose up around the dark water in a ring. He stared into the surface and, though the flickering braziers should not have cast enough light for a reflection, he saw himself. Hints of flame danced about him, perhaps beckoning him back to Agni, even here. Or maybe it was just the reflection cast by the fire, playing tricks upon an over-wrought mind.

"Fates!" he demanded. "Fates, show yourself!"

"Irony," a woman answered.

He spun and saw three hooded, robed figures he could have sworn had not been present in the cavern when he entered. They circled around the well, and he fell back to make space for them.

The Tree in the Dreaming Lands had spoken true. There really were women who wove Fate …

"He comes to seek pellucid vision," a different woman said.

"He comes to grasp the Ontos."

"It is foreknown."

"He has seen much."

"He is weak. It will break him."

"It would break any of them."

"Maybe not this one."

The exchange went by so quickly between the three of them, Matarśivan had trouble keeping straight who was even speaking.

"You see the future?" he demanded.

"The past."

"The present."

"The future."

"It is a web," they said in unison.

Matarśivan wrung his hands. Was this how mortals felt when Watchers offered answers they were not quite ready to parse? "Did you give me my visions?"

"Flickers."

"Hints."

"Nascent talent."

Whatever he beheld was incomplete and he *could* see more if he but found a way to do so. And he would. Was that, after all, not what he truly owed Aditi? For a time he had fled from the agony of the gaping wound she had left inside of him, raw and bleeding in his chest. But she had died because he needed the Dodecadic Circle to the know the Truth. Which meant he would have it. He would have the whole of the Truth. "Show me."

"An offer."

"A pact of eternal service."

"The Ontos for an oath."

Everything must come with a price. But the last oath he had made still weighed upon his finger, the orichalcum band seeming to constrict with each treasonous thought he allowed to bloom. "What oath?"

"You will serve."

"In perpetuity."

"As avatar of history. The guardian of Ananke."

As if serving as Watcher to Agni had not cost him enough. As if it had not cost him his very World. Ah, but if they could say *why*, say what had happened to her, then it could lend meaning to his pain. And hers, for surely she had been wracked upon the Wheel of Life, and he needed to know if he would see her again. If such was possible.

The moment seemed pregnant with import. His pulse beat in his ears. This was it. If he took this course, naught would ever be the same again, and he knew it so very well. The answer was right in front of him and he could grasp it. Or he could turn from it, retreat back into drug-addled dreaming, and cherish ignorance, meandering down nebulous paths through pyromantic hallucinations.

The Fates had not promised him solace. Only Truth. Confirmation— or denial?—of the awful fear that had ravaged the soul of him for so long and gnawed upon his mind since Aditi's fall. Only Ontos.

He took a step toward the well. "I accept."

Though he didn't see them move, the three now flanked him. Each laid a hand upon his shoulders and shoved him downward until his nose brushed the water's edge. Too close to see aught. Too close to everything, and every instinct raged that he ought to push away and deny. Cyclopean dread welled in his soul, animalistic in its need to escape and preserve its equilibrium. Then they shoved him under and it was too late. Into the murk, and all before him became a dance of shadows beneath the faint light of braziers.

A vision in chiaroscuro, in which all the cosmos played out in aphonic mummery. Before him lay a lucent fountainhead so bright it stung his eyes to look upon it. And beyond, a writhing whirl of the Dark, throbbing with prurient need, thrusting itself upon the unprotected luminance. Then, a World thrown up around the encroaching Dark, a black wall to seal it in and bound the nascent cosmos, denying the Dark access to claim more than it had.

Even while orphaned light—the Prakasa that was souls—withered beneath its depredations.

He stood upon the threshold of a caliginous court. Silhouettes ringed the endless chamber, the sum of them extending beyond their forms, their essences trying to overflow the mortal shells they adopted. And before them, one rising taller, first amid the kings of creation.

A man who was not a Man at all.

A flicker, a shift of shadows, and the court fell away, leaving naught save the dark expanse and the inescapable sense that some squamous bulk slithered about it, winding itself amid the gloom. Or worse, he suddenly feared. Many such bulks, like a writhing nest of serpents, coils drawn upon one another even as it closed ever inward.

Its presence evoked such primal dread his breath and heart stopped, his chest becoming as stone. Even thought refused to form, save the realisation he stood at the centre of existence. His knees gave away, and, blinking, he beheld a great spinning wheel and knew it for a construction of his mind. A visible manifestation of the Wheel of Life that would draw up more and more of the captured Prakasa to serve as a feast for the writhing god at the heart of it all. Though it could not yet reach the luminance beyond the wall, all the Light within the World would slowly serve to gorge the abomination.

Though he could not breathe, still, he felt his gaze forced to look upon the fringes. A dozen—or perhaps a hundred!—black, saurian necks slithered into view, coiling about the Wheel. Within the vault of this space, he looked upward only to see they conjoined into a great amorphous mass from which formed and unformed manifold phalluses and vulvas, half of which bent back to engage in perpetual self-intercourse.

Wings like those of a desiccated bat enshrouded the cavern, wide enough they could have wrapped themselves around the whole of a city. And past those threshing appendages lay a parade of eyes, whatever mass they belonged to concealed within the choking shadows of this place.

The silhouettes he'd seen before now paced about him and he knew them. For he'd lain with them and called them his gods. Called them the

Archons, the rulers of the World. Their forms flickered and for a hairsbreadth something squirmed beneath the surface, like shapes in defiance of all order of fauna. Eldritch contours marred their shapes, gone again so quickly he might have imagined the dread of it.

Before he could be sure, he found himself lurching upward, retching putrid water out and back into the pool, though he had not realised he had swallowed it. A sea of the stuff poured from his lungs until he collapsed on the loam, heaving and gasping for air. Had he more of the precious stuff he'd have screamed himself raw.

Tremors seized his body and left him ravaged, caught in convulsions, even as his mind circled back upon itself, unable to parse his momentary glimpse of the whole of the cosmos. Flickers of the insanity he had beheld kept flitting before his eyes and, almost, he welcomed the utter descent into complete madness he knew stalked him. Just a nudge, and his very self would collapse at the Truth that had opened up before him.

This was the Ontos.

Still panting, he pushed himself up on his elbows and caught his reflection in the now stilled water once more. His eyes ... his eyes had gone from green to vibrant azure, almost like sapphires.

Yet whatever changes the Fates had wrought in him paled before the revelation he had beheld. Such a Truth choked him.

The World itself was but a cage to hold in the eldritch gods of Khaos, and slowly, with each revolution of the Wheel of Life, they made true on their promise to devour all Prakasa. One day, the entity he had seen—Yaldabaoth, the name came to him, borne upon the currents of his glimpse of Truth—would rise and consume the cosmos.

The Ontos was that, from the first moment of time, all Men were damned.

Join the Skalds' Tribe newsletter and get access to exclusive insider information and a selection of free books to kickstart your Matt Larkin library.

https://www.mattlarkinbooks.com/skalds/

ALSO BY MATT LARKIN

Gods of the Ragnarok Era

The Apples of Idunn

The Mists of Niflheim

The Shores of Vanaheim

The High Seat of Asgard

The Well of Mimir

The Radiance of Alfheim

The Shadows of Svartalfheim

The Gates of Hel

The Fires of Muspelheim

Tapestry of Fate

The Gifts of Pandora

The Valor of Perseus

The Inferno of Prometheus

The Madness of Herakles

The Threads of Theseus

The Face of Hekate

The Wrath of Artemis

The Circle of Kirke

Heirs of Mana

Tides of Mana

Flames of Mana

Queens of Mana

For my Juhi and Kiran.

Special thanks to my family and my team that helps bring these projects to life:
Sarah, Regina, Felix, Shawn, and Francesca.

9 781946 686886